The Forest of Silver Leaves

Steven Titus

Cover illustration by Steven Novak
Interior illustration by Eric Titus

Pure of Heart~ People of Old ~ Enter with Risk ~ Far from Home

The Forest of Silver Leaves

Contents

ONE - The Odd Morning Rituals ~ 4

TWO - Imaginings at Woodland Academy ~20

THREE – Ciara ~ 31

FOUR – The Flicker through the Trees ~ 46

FIVE – A Coffer Delivered ~ 71

SIX – The Door in the Floor ~ 92

SEVEN – The Forest of Silver Leaves ~ 111

EIGHT – The Watchers of the Wood ~ 130

NINE - A Guardian's Midnight Tale ~ 142

TEN - Further into the Forest ~ 151

ELEVEN - The All Hallows Festival ~ 171

TWELVE - A Grant Family Secret ~ 190

THIRTEEN - A New Morning to a New Life ~ 210

FOURTEEN - Shadows of the New World ~ 237

FIFTEEN - Tales Become Reality ~ 246

SIXTEEN – The Heart of a Secret ~ 265

SEVENTEEN- A Song for Lady Emma ~ 283

EIGHTEEN – The Veiled Crest ~ 296

For Stephanie, my very own Emma,
For my mother, who loved her son's stories,
And for my Ally, whose honesty makes me stronger.

Chapter One
The Odd Morning Rituals

When no answer came from the bedroom that Monday morning and the blooming scent of lilacs floating on the late summer air came pouring in through the open window, the Grant family had feared that Emma had been taken. Jonathan burst into the room, his eyes darting from the rumpled star pattern cotton sheets to the window frame open enough for a body to slip in and then out. He cupped his muscular hands to his mouth, ready to shout to his son and wife. Then above him a pitter-patter of footsteps thumped into the ceiling. Jonathan's arms fell, his fists balling up. He moseyed over to the window, bent low and forced his head out past the white painted frame.

"Emma? Please tell me you're not on the roof again!"

The night before her first day of the eighth grade at Woodland Academy proved to be a restless one for Emma Adacia Grant. She tossed and turned, her legs tangling in the bed sheets. Her luminous sapphire eyes lit up the bleakness of her bedroom for countless hours. Those tiny fists dug into her sockets, rubbing the area below her eyes that bore a dash of freckles.

Her legs had been twitching, bundles of muscles re-acting to her shaky nerves. The thought of what people would make of her this year was poison in her veins. Minutes passed into hours as she lay down in every sleeping position imaginable. When Emma concentrated on the pitch black, her ears tuned to the hum of the air vents and a serene silence arrived. But still, sleep would not come.

By dawn the birds had gathered on the nearby trees. Their morning symphony of chirps was enough to keep Emma curious, her mind humming away. Falling out of bed ever so carefully, she casted a mindful eye towards the door and moved to the window. An inch at a time she lifted the window with a squeal of gears and groan of aging wood, mindful that a swift opening would have been loud enough to awaken an elephant. "One step at a time" she told herself from the window to the thirty-year-old ash tree, its thick branches stretched out high and long enough for Emma to climb her petite self up to the mahogany colored tile of the roof.

The countryside of her Northern California community was like no other; and Emma had a wealth of plane tickets to prove this. Houses around her were spread apart far enough by ten to twenty acres in this distant rural suburb of Forest Lake. Emma could see the town through the morning haze just past five miles to the south.

Her mind was not on the famine or the sad fact that her family had not traveled that summer for the first time in years. The news headlines were far too much for her mother to look past and admit that these things would pass. The bullets would not stop and the storm clouds would multiply on the coasts, just when there seemed to be a slow defeat to the selfishness of reigning in greed of the world. "Think of how fortunate we are to live away from all that disaster," Jonathan would remind Emma and her brother. But as Emma parked herself down at the apex of the roof, her longing eyes breathed in the western view, away from civilization that was soon to visit their lives.

Emma's heart stirred at the sight of the Moonlight Wood. The whole west, a mere mile from her home, was a patchwork of green shades that pushed the boundaries of color from north to south for endless miles.

Closing her eyes and clasping those tiny hands together, she thought of one day the limits of that land fading away, limits that were held in high esteem not only by the government, but by her family under pain of punishment. "Never go there," they told her. "We might have too soon," her brother would remind them, his tongue becoming sharper by the year. As usual, Emma's parents piercing shushes followed, their eyes not on her brother Bo, but on Emma, to gauge her reaction.

She could hear the breeze rustle the leaves of the Moonlight Wood on that fair morning. With a prayer on her mind, to an image of whatever power dwelled in the deep recesses of space, the forest and her meditated into one. recess

"No teasing this year. Please don't let it happen again." Emma whispered out to the morning breeze. Her options were weighed in that tiny moment. The first elaborate plan, as simple as a hot thermometer on the tongue to raise the mercury, began to hatch in her mind. That soon faded with a memory of the glance she once had of the thinnest medical file on record at the school.

"That'll fly," Emma said in disgust. "When's the last time I went to the doctor?"

"Emma?" Jonathan called out from below. "I can hear you up there! Get down before you cause us to have a heart attack. Do you want Mom to come over here?"

She grit her teeth together at that prospect. Dad had to be smoothed over first. Emma took side steps down to the nearest branch that hung over the tree. Skirting the rules of safety, Emma had no fear in leaping off of the fifteen foot rooftop. She landed flat on her feet in front of her window. Jonathan leaped back, clutching his chest.

"Could you not do that! One morning without that…is that too much to ask?"

"So what? It's not my fault if I can't break a bone."

"Well don't push the envelope. Your mother is lucky I yanked you from that barrel at Niagara Falls last year."

Before Emma could fire back, Jonathan held out her Woodland Academy uniform - a knee length tartan skirt and a white, long-sleeved button down blouse with an optional wool sweater. The crest of two elks around a drawing of the school on her uniform was unavoidable of her grim prognostication for that first day of school.

"You win today, Elky," Emma said, with a sneer. She held out her arms, like a child to be picked up. Jonathan, in one swift movement, yanked Emma from the yard and plopped her down on the carpet littered with Emma's books.

"You have to go to school, sweetie," Jonathan said, a determination in his voice.

"Dad...why do I have to be the only one who goes to a private school? Why doesn't Bo have to go too?"

"Because when he was thirteen he hadn't skipped a grade and then continued to be one of the smartest kids in the school."

Emma couldn't hide the smile from the flattery. "Top five anyway, Dad."

"Do me a favor this year, will ya?" Jonathan said. Emma knew that as he hid his smile, that her father was hearing her mother's stern family directions. "Don't show up the teacher. Trust me. I can tell from the parent/ teacher conferences how frustrated they get with you at times."

Emma gathered up her clothes and threw them over her right arm as she made her way to the shower. "It's not my fault I know what they're going to say before the words come out of their mouth!"

By her wrist, Jonathan tugged Emma back from the hallway. Kneeling down to meet her at eye level, Jonathan placed his hands upon her small shoulders. His gentle, handsome face with lines from lack of sleep creeping in along the cheekbones so reminded her of the man her older brother was growing to become. "Don't think you don't make me proud of your abilities for your age. Just try not be such a show-off."

"But what about…"

He shot up his right forefinger, silencing Emma. "Or try to ask a million questions like you always do…"

"I'm trying to defend myself…"

Jonathan silenced Emma again the only way he knew how, with that forefinger and those focused, unblinking eyes.

Emma sighed and with habit threw her arms around her father's neck, giving him a little extra squeeze to make her frustration known. "I'm not a show-off. No one else speaks half the time. And I know the answers!"

"Fine. Fine," Jonathan said, laughing a little. He gave Emma a playful slap on the back, which made the air escape from her chest.

"So…you're gone this time for how long?" Emma scanned the calendar of pictures from American national parks beside the dresser mirror. There were four red marker slashes within the second to last week of August. "Four days? That sucks! I was going to bake cookies for everyone this week."

"Bake'm this weekend. If I finish my trades ahead of schedule, I'll come home straight to you guys, okay?"

Emma forced out a smile, the retainer that she only wore at night to fix her slightly crooked teeth, still sat on the roof of her mouth.

"Oh and do me a favor…stay out of the garage, the driveway, and the attic for the next hour. Your brother and I are getting things ready for my business today. Understand? Stay out of the garage!"

Dressed in her spotless school uniform, Emma leaned against the flaking, sun-bleached auburn trim of the entrance to the garage. Sans her polished, black buckled shoes, Emma's bare feet rested on the pavement as she balanced a bowl of apple cinnamon oatmeal with a few splashes of milk mixed in. Emma appreciated her father went the extra mile to buy the milk from Weiss Farm, considering they wouldn't find much at the grocery stores with rationing after the summer droughts.

Being confined to her bedroom by the family for that hour before school while Jonathan worked was ritualistic. Still, Emma liked to keep the illusions running by playing the local pop music radio station, all the while her spry feet deliberately slipped out of the bedroom window to walk around the ranch style home to scratch that curious itch.

"Will, you hold the ladder steady?" Jonathan barked, his trembling body not ready to leave the safety of the ladder for the entrance to the attic in the garage ceiling. His oldest child, William Bo, stood at the foot of the ladder

"I am!" Bo yelled back in his late teenage growl, clamping his hands down. "You're the one who's shaking like a leaf up there."

With a heave, Jonathan pulled himself up. Emma could hear the muffled sound of a cardboard box being crushed. "Son of a...who put that there!"

"You did!" Bo said, running his hand through his manicured light brown locks.

"What are you up to?" Emma said, her mouth full of oatmeal.

Still holding the ladder, looking up with craning neck, Bo snapped out of his daydream. "Stay in your place, Em," Bo whispered.

"That's not sexist," Emma said with a scoff. "No thanks."

"You know that's not...ah, forget it!"

She set aside her bowl onto seat of the lawnmower. Her gaze was fixed on a massive oak chest resting along the far wall. The sophisticated heavy padlocks were open, the keys set in the keyhole. Her hands ready to spring and investigate, Emma could not help herself as she gently set aside the lock and opened up the nearest chest. "Look at this! Dad brought some of those blankets again."

The blanket, stitched with a silky semblance of a bird's wing, was not a first time purchase for Jonathan Grant. Emma remembered stealing one for an afternoon last winter. All she had wanted to do was to snuggle up inside this warm as wool blanket, sip some hot cocoa with tiny marshmallows and read volumes of fantastical tales before the crackling embers of the fireplace. The punishment for spilling some of the melted chocolate and the sooty presence of the fire into the fibers of the blanket cost her several days of grounding. She felt even then in that garage, as she had many times before, that the blanket felt as if the fabric was lifting from her shoulders when even the tiniest breeze came by.

Bo covered his mouth as he began to laugh. "Remember D.C?" Bo said, gesturing to the blankets.

Emma repressed her giggles as she threw the cream colored blanket over her head, covering her entire body. She picked up one of the distressed bronze candelabras to bob around like a haunting spirit.

"Ooooo, stay away from this hotel!" Emma said, altering her voice to sound like a spook. "They have bad room service and room 315 is haunted! Beware of the Ides of Room 315...Whoa!" Emma's feet collided with the lawn mower and she fell with a crash, rattling the lawn care tools hooked upon the wall. Emma couldn't help to remove the blanket for a good few seconds for she was giggling so hard, nearly gasping for air. Regaining her visible footing, she saw Bo's hand clasped over his mouth as he laughed, looking as if he might go crazy from holding back.

"What did you knock down?" Jonathan said from deep inside the attic.

"Nothing," Bo said, taking deep breaths as he laughed. "Sounded like a big dumb animal crashing into the wall."

Emma's mouth went wide. Still too amused to be mad, she slapped the blanket like a wet towel in Bo's direction. He caught the precious trade and threw the gentle fabric back into Emma's face.

After a feigned attempt to fold up the blanket, Emma picked up a set of shiny, golden and crystal vials from the open chest. They so reminded her of tiny, twisted flower vases with corks that held back no apparent liquid. She held them up, the light beaming in through the dust ridden, web covered garage window that Adacia complained that Jonathan never cleaned. The polished glint of the vials reminded Emma of the crystals and jewels she had seen in European travels. Each one held a price tag on them that read **Thirty Silver Dollars**.

"Bo, will you come up and help me lower down the next case? This one is going in the shed with everything else." Jonathan called from the recesses of the attic.

"I'm fine down here, Dad."

"Not from where I'm standing. You better get used to the job you're gonna have in a couple years. Get your butt up here!"

Bo shook his head, muttering to himself several times over as he withdrew his cell phone from deep in his pocket. "Just keep thinking that, Dad. Just keep thinking that…" As Bo checked his messages, Emma tilted her head to look at him, sensing what he was looking for.

"That girl never called back, did she?" Emma said.

Bo paused, mid way through his text, his fingers turning red as he pressed into the keypad. "Nope. Never did, even after I was patient enough to be cancelled on three times. Why did I believe her the first time she cancelled on me when she said she found out that she had some life changing information?"

"What? She got knocked up by her ex?"

Bo closed the text pad of the phone against the door of the fridge. "No! Not really." He resorted to climbing the ladder. "Listen, I don't want to talk about Sydney."

"She was a big bowl of crazy, man. Did you hear her laugh?" Emma said, letting out a sound similar to that of a whinnying donkey.

Jonathan's trudging boot steps went cold. Emma froze and covered her mouth, remembering that she was supposed to be on a mission of stealth. "Bo…is Emma down there?" Jonathan called.

"No. That was me," Bo said, sending a glare at Emma.

"What? Are you talking to yourself? Quit dilly-dallying!"

Emma mouthed a quick 'thank you' to Bo. His eyes circled around in the sockets in return, a cold shoulder then present as he made his way up the ladder.

In the millisecond after the screen door beside the garage opened, Emma's heart shot up to her throat. Her mother had to be going out for her morning jog around the block. As quick as her bare feet could fly, Emma dove behind the nearest chest, just large enough to conceal her petite five foot frame.

Through the tiny holes in the wicker, Emma could see Adacia in a black tank top and track pants with her weathered white tennis shoes standing at the entrance to the garage. Her green eyes were fixed on in Emma's position. Staring ahead with her green eyes, right above her gorgeous face and cheek bones, like her daughter, Adacia tied back her brunette hair back with a tie. Emma knew she was done for, ready to be drawn up for a creative new punishment for being somewhere she shouldn't have been.

Instead of emerging, she hunkered down, every silent breath a deliberate one. As Emma did this, she held onto her most prized possession that hung around her neck on a smooth black string. The silver metal star, inlaid with white and blue crystal, which Emma inherited when her Grandmother passed away, seemed to stay polished, never losing its luster nor ever developing a scratch.

"Hide me…hide me…"

"Bo, is it that hard to put away your breakfast?" Adacia said, picking up the bowl from the mower before she dogged the ladder and walked inside the house.

Emma peeked up from the wicker chest. The door to the house was open and no Adacia was to be seen in the dark hallway. Not a fool to linger, Emma shot out from the garage. Out around the front of the house she ran where no one would be looking. With a headfirst heave into the open window, Emma groaned her way back into her bedroom. This time she made sure to wipe away any evidence by using a towel from her laundry basket to wash her dirt flecked feet.

"Get ready to leave in twenty minutes, Emma," Adacia said, knocking on her door. "And turn down that trite pop junk," Adacia said, annoyed. "I taught you better than to listen to that."

Emma turned down the volume on her internet radio station on her laptop, knowing full well she listened to a few top forty songs on that FM station as a guilty pleasure. "Sorry, Mom." She flipped to the pre-set A.M station. A buzz of the radio filled the air waves for a long thirty seconds and then, a rustle of pages followed by a man's voice.

"From NPR Washington this is Peter Clemmens. Small riots continued in much of the south and west over state and FEMA drought relief efforts and water shortages that the President says are spread too thin now in preparation of Hurricane Katherine barreling up the east coast..."

Emma pulled the plug from the wall. "Enough!" she said, pushing her radio aside as if the device itself was to blame.

Emma had one more act of espionage to engage in that morning. From her nightstand drawer, she removed a screwdriver, anchored with duct tape on the underside of the drawer. Tossing aside her pillow, she jumped onto her bed to come face to face with an air vent embedded into the wall. Emma waited a good minute, listening for her father's footsteps on the far side of the house, and for any creeks in the uneven floor that would indicate that Adacia was lingering outside of the bedroom. When she felt the coast was clear, she put her screwdriver to work and removed the air vent panel that had been painted blue to match the color of the room she painted years ago with her father. Standing on her tip-toes, she reached far inside with her right arm into the vent that sent out a wave of cool air.

"Thought I was leaving home with you…there! Gotcha!"

From the vent Emma removed a book, a plastic coating around the binding for protection. She ran her hands over the aged cover, the fibers within embedded with years of dust, read *From Sea to Shining Sea: A Collection of New World Tales.*

With a heave, Emma tossed her leather backpack and Bo's messenger bag into the back seat of the only automobile the family owned - a four-door sedan hybrid. Adacia flicked the key in the ignition. However, she never released straight away, which created a grinding sound so cutting, the awful noise made Emma wince.

Bo pressed the lock on the inside of the house door, closing it behind him. Instead of taking a seat next to Adacia, he ran off to the mailbox at the bottom of their driveway.

"Where are you off to?" Adacia said, her arms up in the air.

Motioning with one finger to wait, Bo stuck his arm into the mailbox. Emma took pride in the fact that she helped her handy father install as her father called the "imported wooden mailbox" into the post a few weeks back. Jonathan Grant never fell short of his fascination of tinkering with antiques, taking apart perfectly good clocks and various pieces of machinery, figuring out how they work. Then, in reverse, he placed every item together, back into their rightful place. Jonathan liked to think that Emma had gained her 'healthy' curiosity from her him. Adacia never failed to mention that Emma's was worse.

Emma looked through the back window of the car to notice that Bo's face was lighting up as he looked down at a white envelope with a blue ribbon and a red wax stamp. Who had sent Bo a letter on a Monday morning was beyond her.

Adacia laid on the horn. Emma only half-jumped out of her seat, feeling Adacia would be losing her patience. "Get-in-the-car! Emma has to get to school."

Bo ran up to leap into the car. "Do you want me to drive, Mom?" Bo asked.

Emma and Bo exchanged their usual nervous glances in this situation. Adacia placed both of her hands upon the wheel and took three deep breaths through pursed lips.

"I think I'm fine today."

"Are you sure, Mom? Maybe Bo wants to show off by pulling up to school in the car," Emma said, leaning in as Bo nodded his head in agreement.

"What are you trying to say? That I can't drive?" Adacia said.

"No, that's crazy," Emma and Bo said in perfect unison.

Adacia narrowed her eyelids at her children, suspicious. "I have my eye on you two."

"Not while you're driving," Bo whispered. That smart remark got him a slap across the shoulder from Adacia.

"Who's the letter from?" Emma said, her voice mingled with sweetness and sarcasm.

"Who said it was a love letter?" Bo fired back.

"You did. What's her name Casa-something...what's that word I read once?"

"See Mom," Bo said, eyes not leaving the letter. "The books have finally pushed out useful sarcasm."

Adacia pulled the car down the driveway and out onto the road. "It's Casanova. Listen Blue Eyes, why don't you leave your brother alone? He is obviously nervous about this."

"Thank you!" Bo said. "See, I'm sick of people thinking I can't handle these things." He tossed Emma a dirty look, to which Emma stuck out her tongue in a perfect reflex to his taunts.

"So how did you meet this girl?" Adacia said. Adacia and Emma formed a chorus of chuckles. Bo turned away to gaze out of his window the whole way to school without so much as a peep.

The Grants' home in Northern California seemed to be at the edge of civilization at times for Bo and Emma. The brown and red trimmed ranch style home was a five to ten minute drive to the nearest town. Only three stoplights were on the road that meandered through prairie and patches of pine and oak trees. On that morning, the car passed by an abandoned housing development. A whole section of country side and forest was stripped away for a small subdivision that was dug out, but never had anything more than a few layers of concrete planted into a desolate, muddy plain. What was a patch of woods was a mere pile of wood chips in the hole of an un-built home. Emma had to turn away for a deep disturbance quaked within her at the devastation of this patch of nature.

The car cut down the road, rounding a hill that took them north before going east once again. Emma pressed her nose to the window. The trees in the wide valley below again showed how unmistakable the fact was that Emma lived close to the Moonlight Wood. The forest held continual fascination for Emma ever since the family moved into their home. As best as her memory could serve, the move to the outskirts of Forest Lake had occurred six or seven years ago. Emma had always struggled to remember many things before the age of five, a problem her parents brushed away as growing older and forgetting her infancy. But Emma was aware with almost every fact she memorized in her school history books, to recalling verbatim what words came out of the mouth of her family that she did not forget things like others did. Her memory was photographic and yet multi-dimensional, like she could see a problem like a puzzle.

When the moon was full, Emma liked dig her feet into the limbs of a honey ash tree alongside the back porch and climb up to crawl her way onto a roof that was beginning to cool from a day's worth of sunshine. There she could see the powerful beams of moonlight at work in the wood on warm summer nights and brisk fall evenings. Emma swore that she could see within the forest patches of glittering silver, like a jewel sparkling in a clear stream. That light came from just beyond the forest edge where thick, tall redwoods seemed to guard like pawns on a chess board. Once, Emma had discovered by using whatever maps she could find in the school or public library that by measuring the edge of the giant forest she estimated it was 1,500 square miles within. And yet on every map, no public or private roads were shown leading in or out of the Moonlight Wood, listed to be under control of the United States government.

When her family tossed what they called her 'conspiracy theories' aside, Emma tuned her ears into cafe and grocery store chatter from the locals in Forest Lake that sprang up about the wood. The legends, no matter how reasonable or downright hokey, all spoke of the bone chilling vibe that ebbed out of the darkness and penetrated into every soul that approached its borders.

From the car window, her telescopic eyes saw what Adacia and Bo could not in a field a few miles away. A tiny figure, dwarfed by the landscape walked along the forest edge. Emma kissed her fingers and touched the glass where the figure appeared.

"Have a good day, Daddie," Emma whispered to herself.

Adacia steered the car along a bend in the road and carried the children due east to Forest Lake, leaving the Moonlight Wood now to Emma's memory.

Chapter Two
Imaginings at Woodland Academy

The school day got off on the wrong foot when Emma tripped over her dress shoes. She attempted to ascend the front steps of Woodland Academy with her head held high and confidence with proper posture. At once, she caught herself from falling by gripping the chipped metal railing. Her body lurched back into the chest of a boy two steps below.

"Oh, I'm sorry!"

"Watch it, you idiot," the boy said.

Emma turned around to come face to face with Pace Angles, the boy with a legion of knuckle-dragging followers. He attempted to rub out a splatter of energy drink from his latest trendy jacket, a tan, artificially weathered windbreaker with a dozen impractical zippers sewn into the front and sleeves.

"Oh…you," Pace said, shaking the aluminum can of *Insulin Explosion* in front of her face. "Crazy Emma. Learn how to walk, you freak."

On a normal day, any random retort would fly out of Emma's mouth. But remembering Bo and her father's advice, Emma learned to land the sucker punch where it counted. Pace's dishwater blond, well-manicured locks, were a perfect target that morning.

"Nice high-lights, pretty boy. Did Mummy and Daddie get sad when they realized they have a little girl in their house?"

Pace mumbled and crinkled the aluminum can in his hand as he stalked off inside.

"Where are you going?" Emma called after him. "Pedicure?"

A handful of the students making their way inside laughed at Emma's joke. A young black girl of Emma's age edged out of her shyness for a split second, moved her eyes up from the ground and flashed an approving smile as she passed her up. Emma smiled back at her, curious as to whom the newbie at the Academy was.

With her self esteem bank full enough to put one foot in front of the other, Emma sauntered inside. "I gotta listen to Bo more often," Emma whispered to herself.

The opening day assembly dragged on for close to an hour. Every second on the clock face ticked off in slow motion. Even the most well-mannered students and by the book teachers had to fight off the boredom and the fear of nodding off with whatever daydream they could float to in their minds. There seemed to be no end to the school administrators covering the laundry list of rules and schedule examinations that they read by from a series of papers in golden binders on the podium that read on the cover – '*Making Woodland's Future for Today.*' Needless to say, by a student snoring in the front row, the student body didn't share those sentiments.

During the endless, inane babble, Emma and her class sat at the end of seven rows of foldable chairs at the back of the hall. Yet again, as Emma scanned the unrecognizable faces of the boys and girls in Ms. Anderson's class, her esteem fell like a stone. She could already hear her mother's voice in her head – "time to meet some new people."

'She has no idea, as usual,' Emma thought. Years had passed since she was a kid, not knowing the pain of being teased for not conforming. She slouched in her chair and looked at the iron beams and foamy fire retardant splattered in-between them on the ceiling. Emma began to daydream about what stories might be in her new book she brought for silent reading.

Her mind drifted to fantasy thoughts of a previous tale in the *From Sea to Shining Sea* series about a Greek brother and sister with magical powers used to defend their land called the Kingdom of Augustus.

A cloud began to form over her eyes, worse than any morning eye goop. In a flash, her vision went black. Sitting up in a panic, Emma's vision returned in a few seconds, accompanied by a shooting pain that went through her sinuses into her brain. Clutching her hands to her temples, a searing migraine headache throbbed in the veins and arteries in her skull. Her eye sockets felt as if someone was pulling on the nerve bundle.

"What's going on!" Emma said, louder than she realized, forcing a few kids to turn around.

Within a few seconds, the pains went away. Her congested sinuses cleared and her blood pressure evened out. Her forefingers massaged those sore temples.

"Ms. Grant, is it?" The twenty-two year old, five-foot nothing, straight out of college Ms Anderson bent down and touched Emma's arm. "Ms. Grant?"

"Emma Adacia Grant. Yes. I'm okay. Just a weird headache."

"Do you want to go to the nurse?"

Not an ounce of ache remained in her body. Taking a deep breath, her sinuses filled without a clog. Her vision cleared up like a fog being blown away by a breeze.

"I'm fine. Nothing's wrong." Emma knew this wasn't the first time she had lied about the odd things her mind and body would do to her. Bo had to be home that evening and not gallivanting around town. She needed to tell him first.

Ms Anderson nodded, looking long at Emma as if she was going to start flopping around on the floor like a fish out of water.

Then, like the murmur of ghosts on their haunt, the rumors began. Emma followed the sounds of whispering in the crowd of students in front of her. About two rows ahead Emma witnessed Pace Angles spread a new batch of lies, under his breath, as he pointed towards Emma. When Pace had spoke in the ears of the 'Detention Crew' of boys and the gossip driven, back-stabbing, high-maintenance and trendy girls around him, they all began to laugh that sickening type of chortle only made to crush a heart. The painful phrases of 'Crazy Emma' and 'Erma Grunty' permeated out from Pace to the crowd like falling dominos. This time Emma had no clever snap back. When Emma, her face flush with emotion, caught Pace's glance, her blood boiled as he winked to complete his payback.

Emma wanted to forgo being diplomatic. Soon she would throw her aluminum folding chair at Pace's pretty-boy face and break what she swore was a surgically altered nose. Emma's hands, wrapped around the base of her seat, were gripped so tight that she did not notice what the other students next to her saw – the aluminum chair bent under her strength.

"Are you okay?" A girl with blond braids next to Emma tapped her on the shoulder. Emma looked like a lion about to spring. "What's wrong with your eyes? They're all red!"

"Ugh, nothing is wrong with my eyes," Emma said, even though she could feel as if heat was radiating from them. Emma then began to consider the dozen or so students staring at her in shock and awe. The anger, close to white-hot, fell away when Emma considered these faces and the girl's question. Emma's fantasies of making Pace cry like a prissy little baby fell away to harsh reality.

"Yeah. I'm fine. Thanks."

Emma took a deep breath, her lungs retreating from hyperventilation. Having experience with such overwhelming feelings that her brain fed her body, Emma knew she couldn't allow the students to dig their knives in any further at the sight of her mouth gasp for air. She closed her eyes, folded her arms and waited for the end of the assembly to come.

"This day already sucks."

Silent reading had come to be the best class period of the day for Emma. She took advantage of the half-hour her class was granted to read from any book. Ms Anderson didn't show much respect for the school board rules on "no newspapers or magazines in the classrooms for the new school year." On a front desk, Ms Anderson would promise to have three newspapers or magazines of world news. Emma liked the fact that Ms Anderson, with all her youth and ambition, promised to take fifteen minutes each morning to "have a discussion" about what the kids read in the media outlets.

The few others that followed Emma's journey into uncharted waters of stories and novels were worthy of balancing out, in her opinion, the smart-mouth morons who to her looked as if they used the time to practice their ABC's in-between bouts of staring into space with drooling mouths.

When Ms Anderson started the digital clock, counting down from thirty minutes, Emma pulled out a prized book from her bag. *From Sea to Shining Sea* was only one in a set of fairy tales in a collection that her Grandfather Nicholas had at times delivered to Emma. Those tales were written with such historical detail within an ancient world of fantasy that Emma felt as if she was sitting in her Social Studies class, pouring over an American or European history she had yet to be enlightened with.

Emma invested her time into the first story entitled *The Scar Faced Mage*.

The world lingered in a curtain of darkness in the years before the dawn of the 24th century. The primal agent of the Shaitain, the Dark Mage Rakshasas, with his blood red gums and teeth that had rumored to send chills down the backs of women and children, had begun his reign of terror by the order of Lord Orion. Only rumors existed of how he obtained his trademark scars on his cheeks, neck and arms. A victim (Timothy Johnson of Avenmore) that spared him said "the mage told me he cut himself every time he killed. He said he wore them with pride." Historian D.K Goodwin of Old Elm University theorized that Rakshasas's "rather violent techniques, sparing no mercy as he tortured Croatoans..."

Croatoan. The word echoed in the recesses of Emma's mind. A gate had opened within. "Croatoan...Cro-a-to-an...Croatoan...where have I heard that before?"

"Emma? Please, keep your thoughts to yourself until discussion time," Ms Anderson said.

When Emma gazed back down to her book, her blood pressure spiked as the ambient noise of the air conditioning through the vent dimmed. Emma's temples sent out a series of pulses. Her punishing headache returned. Though much lighter and manageable than before, the gnawing pain was distracting for then her vision became cloudy. Soft whispers filled the room. Rolling her eyes at having to hear another round of cruel rumors, now penetrating the silence of her classroom, Emma let out a loud "shhhh" when the whispers grew in strength.

"Emma," Ms Anderson said, looking up from her lesson plan on her desk, "No one is talking except for you. Stop disrupting the silent reading."

"Sorry," Emma said. False alarm, she thought, still on her guard as her eyes found their way back to her book. The headache continued to gnaw and bite.

A chill enveloped the air inside the classroom. Emma crossed her arms for warmth. She cupped her hands and breathed her hot air into them. Why the school had dropped the temperature of the air conditioning any lower was beyond her. The chilled halls, which most students called "The Freezer" never bothered Emma. Her body was resistant to wearing multiple layers, unlike the other students who wore hoodies or jackets around the halls. But as the cool air in the room turned frigid, Emma began to wonder why no one else complained. Her own breath was crystallizing in the air into pure vapor.

"This is crazy…why doesn't someone turn on the heat," Emma said. Her jaw fell when she looked up. "Whoa!"

A steady dusting of snow began to fall from the ceiling of the classroom. The spiraling flakes fell onto Emma's face, melting on contact. Then, the white paneled ceiling dissolved into a thick formation of chalky gray clouds that lifted up into the atmosphere.

"Emma, please remain in your seat." Ms Anderson's voice was more distant with every word.

"Do you guys see this?" Emma said, walking into the center of the room.

No response came from the confused faces of the students. Emma closed her hand over her mouth as her fellow classmates, teacher and every item in the classroom from the linoleum tiles to counters with plastic homework bins to desks blew away like grains of sand in a desert sandstorm. From the indecipherable mist of the broken bits of Emma's classroom, there formed a pond set in a classically designed polished stone courtyard long enough to fit three football fields. Complete with bridges over the water and stone buildings of several stories in height surrounding the rectangular plaza, the very image of them filled Emma's mind with cozy cottages and grand gilded halls, wrapped around idyllic nature.

"What is going on?" Emma said to the emptiness. "Where am I? Hello?"

At a steady pace, the snow continued to fall and collect in her hair. The chill in her body faded when she looked down to see that her school uniform had been replaced with jeans and her button up black wool winter jacket.

Emma closed her eyes, tight. "Dream. Wake me up. I need to wake up in my classroom." But Emma could not summon her lucid capabilities. She was drifting in no period of slumber. The chill of the wind pricked at her face, prying her eyes open. "This is real. Hello?"

Then, a shrill scream of a woman filled the air. Emma turned right around, scanning the empty streets. A cloud, too low in the sky to be natural drifted over the city. From the cloud a long, smoke filled arm came down to land behind the row of classically styled buildings down the block. Descending to the ground from the cloud were wisps of vapor, some of them formed into flesh and blood gangly bodies, devoid of all color in their skin. More screams flew up into the city from the landing sight of those creatures. Emma could feel something draw near, just around the corner. Her blood thickened with the most uncomfortable trepidation. The snow continued to fall in the wintery silence.

"Who's there? Do you need help?"

The screams multiplied, coming closer, all a drowning chorus of tortured souls. Some were so loud Emma felt as if they could pierce her eardrums. Deciding that people were injured or worse beyond the stone square, Emma approached the corner – maybe they wouldn't notice as she slipped in and dragged a wounded woman to safety. From around the bend of the rock and stone of the trade goods store to her left, a voice began to cut the air like a squeaking mouse.

Turning the corner, Emma found what looked like a rather large man, hidden under an oversized black cloak, whimpering.

The screaming told her people were in trouble, and that her instincts told her she couldn't idly stand by. Touching her star, tucked beneath her jacket, Emma knew she had to charge forward. The man remained, shivering, dormant, and patient. With a big gulp, she swallowed her fear and pressed the heel to the toe of her shoe into the stone, edging forward.

"Are you okay…"

From under the black cloak, the sallow, soulless face had glowing red eyes, far beyond any light or magic trick. A congested death rattle increased with each heaving breath as the crimson eyes continued to stare down Emma, melting snowflakes that fell within inches of its face.

"What are you? What are you?"

A fell voice filled the air, coming from what Emma noticed was an abnormally sized jaw in the hooded shadow of the translucent-skinned demon.

"I have found the Alastar."

From around the opposite corner, further into the town a droll, hoarse voice responded. "Bring the Alastar to me. We will be most rewarded by our master."

"Help! Help!" Emma had been taken, her joints seizing, her voice box suffocating like a child that had awoken from a nightmare.

The phantom's wormy hand reached out from underneath the cloak. Blood began to drip from underneath the fingertips and fall onto the cobblestones. His rib bones flexed underneath at the prospect of his capture

When Emma began to cower by placing her left arm out, a light appeared underneath Emma's jacket in the most beautiful glow of blue and silver. Remembering her faith in the device, Emma pulled out her jewel to see the light of the star, blotting out the smoky darkness of the phantom that continued to grow like a beacon in a lighthouse.

The light became so intense that the area surrounding Emma became a haze of glowing, foggy white light. The creature cowered, covering his bloody eyes. Hissing a low and long squeak as it bowed low, the phantom retreated back into his fabric shell, scampering away in the haze. Though her ego wished to taunt the retreating creature, her nerves made her whole body shudder with the sight of the demon's blood droplets in the powdered snow. Those drops of crimson floated into the air and faded into the mist.

Then, Emma's ears began to ring with the highest decibel pitch she had ever heard. The ground beneath her shook with a faint earthquake. The clouds above rumbled with an afterthought of thunder. A fell voice, which had no clear origin in the mist, called out.

"The world is changing. You will be here for proof. Find me, little Emma."

And then, without warning the light that shot out from her star jewel went dark. The roar in her ears ended and all became pitch black.

When Emma began to wake, she could feel she wasn't alone. The voice of a young girl carried over the empty space to a small bed of white, sterile linens that Emma laid upon.

"Oh, good. You finally woke up."

Chapter Three
Ciara

A water-stained tile in the ceiling of the nurses' office of Woodland Academy hung above Emma as she blinked awake. She followed the black lace of her necklace down to her star jewel. To her relief, the beloved star, whose light had gone cold, remained in its place below her neck. Emma pushed up off the thin, worn down mattress with a strange ache present in her muscles.

"I guess this is what it feels like to be sick," she muttered to herself. The stale, sterile air filled her lungs as she discovered rows of white linen beds in the dim room.

"How did I get here?"

"I don't know. You here when I came in."

Turning around, Emma noticed a black girl of about twelve, her long legs pushed up against the end of a bed near the darkened corner. The girl leaned over, coming into the florescent light. Emma recalled her familiar face from that morning, sauntering past Emma as she insulted Pace Angles on the front steps.

Emma had to cover her mouth to avoid laughing at the sight of the girl. She had a full tissue stuffed up each nostril. Her nose looked as if the skin around would soon bruise.

"What did you do to your nose?"

The girl rolled her eyes. Emma could tell that she had already worn out her vocal chords by telling the story a dozen times.

"I was trying to play soccer in gym with a bunch of girls that actually talked to me. They were the first ones all day. What is it with these stuck-up brats in this place?"

Emma shrugged, letting out a tiny smirk. She loved this girl's attitude.

"I guess I was trying to show off or something. I kicked the soccer ball against the wall and it bounced back and nailed me in the face at like twenty miles an hour." The girl winced as touched her nose with her forefingers. "I wish I had another ice pack." She held up a water filled, unfrozen pouch to Emma. "I've been waiting for a half hour since school was over to have my mom pick me up."

"The day's over?" Emma said to herself, looking around the room. "How long was I out for?

"Dunno. You were here when I came in at the end of my last period....ouch." The girl touched her nose again.

Hoping out of the bed, Emma made for the nurses supply desk. She opened each drawer, her curious hands finding a first-aid ice pack. Cracking the dry ice inside, Emma rubbed the package with the palms of her hands to get the sub-zero feeling going. Once the pack began to slush up into ice, Emma handed it over.

"Thanks," the girl said. She placed the pack against the bridge of her nose, breathing in the soothing relief. "Oh, that's nice. How'd you know where the ice was?"

"I was in here a lot last year. One time, last February, I fell twenty feet from the bleachers onto my shoulder."

"Ouch! How many bones did you break?"

"None," Emma said. She leaned in, curious. "How many should I have broken?"

The girl removed the ice-pack to lean forward, brush her thin, shoulder length wavy hair out of her face. "A lot. What did you do? Did you get pain pills?"

Letting out a little giggle and modest shrug at the truth of her resilience, Emma hopped onto the bed next to the girl. Emma swung her feet back and forth under the bed – the little kid still at heart.

"Wow. Maybe those kids were right about you? Your name is Emma, right?"

Emma nodded as she looked away. Even in thick cinder block walled separation from the rest of the school the taunting would haunt her wherever she went.

"I'm sorry, Emma. I'm not saying I believed what they said..."

"No, it's cool. Maybe I deserve it," Emma said. "Did they tell you what happened?"

"Some kids were saying you passed out in your classroom. The nurses were saying that you kept twitching when you wouldn't wake up." The girl snapped her fingers, a solution on the tip of her tongue. "Sleep walking. That's it. You probably fell asleep in class and started sleep walking. My mom used to do that at home. She scared me so bad once that I thought I was gonna pee my pants when she ran into me in the middle of the night when I went to use the bathroom."

Emma flashed a smile, sympathetic and kind. Emma considered the truth that the girl could never believe her, like all of the others. She could imagine this girl bolting for the principal's office, screaming 'Crazy Emma. Crazy Emma.' Only one person would listen to her storyteller take on the vision of the phantom in the city square - Bo.

"Yep. I was sleepwalking. I gotta go see a doctor about that." Emma's eyes began to well up, the emotion of the day going south, aware it would haunt another night's sleep. Her fingers found her star jewel and at once it seemed her nerves calmed. "My name is Emma Adacia Grant."

"You always go by your full name?" the girl said, cocking an eyebrow.

"Sounds good when you say it all together. What's your name, soccer star?" Emma said, playfully touching her own nose.

The girl swung her feet around, leaning over to Emma with open arms. "Ciara Williams," she said, embracing the sniffling Emma.

"Oh, friendly," Emma said, receiving the hug. "Cold! That's cold."

Ciara pulled back the ice pack that she imbedded into Emma's neck. "I'm sorry." Ciara re-applied the now solid ice pack to her nose.

"I hope your nose didn't break."

"Me too. I was just starting to like my face."

Emma giggled, remembering the feeling she had every morning when she stared back at her adolescent face growing and changing with her body in the past few years. She noticed Ciara's blue eye shadow. "I like your make-up. My mom doesn't let me wear any."

"Really? Oh, well I don't think you need any. I like your freckles."

"My dad says they make me look 'cute as a button,'" Emma said, shaking her head. "Whatever that means....wait!" Emma turned her head. That keen awareness she felt noticed a familiar prescience stalking in the distance. Voices began to filter into the room. "Do you hear that?"

"Hear what?"

Listening, Emma began to work her way towards the closed door next to the nurse's desk. Raised voices passed through the cracks in the door from an office away.

"I think my Mom is here," Emma said. Opening the door as not to make the hinges squeal, Emma quietly slipped out of the nurses' office.

"Nice to meet you." Ciara said, leaning up to wave.

"You too!" Emma whispered.

With soft feet, she crossed the rows of secretary desks. The computers were all quiet, the lamps dimmed in the hours after school.

Adacia stood just inside the entrance to Principal Drake's office, toe-to-toe in a battle of raised voices with the balding, skinny as a rail, yuppie-looking principal who wore an atrocious combo of a puke green tie and a mustard yellow shirt that when combined looked like the toppings of a Chicago style hot dog.

"You refused treatment for Emma, Mrs. Grant. I'm telling you, to your face, that you should seek out a secluded place to get her examined."

"Good choice of words! My daughter is not diseased so please stop referring to her like she needs to be quarantined," Adacia said. "She is the picture of health." Her hands, turning red with vigor, gripped the headrest of the principal's guest chair.

"All I am saying is that you need to take her to the doctor," the Principal said. "We are not liable for her condition since you refused to have her examined."

Emma ambled up to the door. "You told them to not call the ambulance?"

Principal Drake jumped back in shock, clutching his heart. "Oh, God! These kids are gonna give me a heart attack one day," Drake said. He reached into his drawer, fumbled with the wrapping on an antacid tablet before swallowing it. "Yes. Your mother did, Emma. I guess your condition is a liability for treatment."

Emma flashed a confused look at her mother. Adacia widened her eyes, gesturing with a nod of her head over to the principal.

"Oh, my condition. Mom must have forgotten about my condition," Emma said through her grinding teeth, speaking to Adacia. "She was supposed to put that on my school physical. How stupid of her to forget that."

The principal sifted through a file on his desk with Emma's name and picture on the front. Emma detested her school photograph. Bo joked that the end result of Emma's portrait, her eyes half open in a haze, looked worse than on a driver's license.

"Hmmm. The form seems to show that you didn't make mention of the problems with the nerve endings in her brain, Mrs Grant. That is a serious issue. What if she died?"

"She wouldn't have, trust me," Adacia said.

Principal Drake gazed at Adacia with suspicion. "I can't believe what I'm hearing! Trust you that your daughter can survive traumatic brain trauma and hemorrhaging?"

"You don't know my daughter. Listen…" Adacia paused, turning to look at Emma with a cold, sincere state. "Blue Eyes, could you please step out of the room for a minute?"

Her patience bottomed out, Emma threw her arms up in the air and proceeded to walk out of the room. Only, to further antagonize her mother, she stepped out slower than a geriatric with a walker. Emma could feel her mother's blood pressure rise as Adacia huffed and puffed a few feet away. Taking the door in hand, Emma took a very lady-like curtsy and then slammed the door.

Stepping away, Emma shook her hair with her hands by running her fingers along the chestnut strands, trying to calm down. She stared at a Norman Rockwell painting hung on the wall. She felt a kinship with the sad, desperate looking bunch of Rockwell's Chicago Cubs baseball players around their dugout, being heckled and mocked by the fans.

Turning away, she couldn't ignore the itch that persisted in her mind. The voices of her mother and the principal were still audible in her keen ears. Tip-toeing back to the door, Emma leaned in from against the wall and peered inside with her left eye.

"I am sure we can work something out, Principal," Adacia said. She placed her tender right hand upon the forearm of the Principal, making sure to touch his skin, and rather seductive at that. The principal seemed to lose focus on his surroundings. His face became a haze, empty, dead only save for the eyes of Adacia that caught him. "We are going to forget that Emma had an accident today. It is a shame you shoved her medical record and the school injury report in the shredder."

The principal nodded, and smiled. "I know. I feel like an idiot!"

Adacia held tighter to his hand, her voice soft enough to lure in a siren. "Don't be. You are so good at your job. Don't let those kids bother you with taunts about your clothing."

The principal started laughing. "Little jerks. My Mom loves my mustard ties."

"I'm sure she does. And we forget this happened…" Adacia's tone deepened, her stare making the principal swallow. "Are we clear?"

"Crystal clear." The principal took Emma's accident report in hand, turned on the shredder, and allowed the incident to pass into a lost memory. Adacia let go of the principal's hands. When she did, his body quivered as if he shook himself awake. "Thank you so much for coming in, Mrs Grant. I'm sorry those children picked on Emma."

Adacia produced her car keys from her purse. "Glad you could see things my way."

Emma pulled herself away from the door, her mind packed worse than before with puzzles in a vacuum of answers. "Whoa! What did she do?"

Adacia sauntered out with an air of caution about her. "Let's move before he changes his mind." She took a firm grasp on Emma's wrist and tugged her along.

"Make sure you don't make me forget what just happened," Emma said, mocking her mother by sliding a gentle right hand onto hers.

Adacia released her grasp and held her hands out. Emma wondered by the wide eyed gaze her mother held if fear had crossed her eyes. "Mom? What is it?"

Adacia clutched her keys tight, her unblinking stare at Emma constant for seconds on end. "Nothing. How do I know I wasn't hitting on him?"

"Would you prefer I told Dad that one or that you schmoozed your way into making him forget?"

"Or…" Adacia said, pushing Emma along, her tone rather urgent, "You could go with option three and believe that we're looking out for you! Get in the car already. We have to talk!"

The Grant family sedan meandered through the side streets of Forest Lake. Adacia turned onto the main strip of the town on the edge of the wild. Emma's curiosity helped her press her nose to the glass as the car glided past the candy striped tent over the town's sweet shop, Cupcake Ally.

"You're not sick in the head," Adacia said, breaking the long standing silence since the school.

Emma turned around to face her mother, the desire of a raspberry cupcake vanishing. "Then why did you tell Principal Drake that I have a condition?" Emma said, using her fingers to make air quotes. "And why did he even agree to let this whole thing slide. What did you do in his office?"

"What do you mean?"

"You know what I mean, Mom!" Emma copied the stare of her mother with her pupils wide, her gaze fixed.

The leather upon the steering wheel stretched under Adacia's solid grip. Emma turned to see a race of emotions cross her mother's mind, her eyes darting left and right.

"You're a special girl, Emma. And I don't mean in the foolish way that everyone is told they are 'special' just to raise their self-esteem. Your father and I knew you were unique the moment I became pregnant with you."

Emma dropped her act. "How could you know that? I wasn't even born yet?" Emma said, trying to search her mother's mind.

"Because…" Adacia said, pausing to take a long breath. "Because when Bo was three, I was stricken down with an illness, like cancer. When I recovered, the doctors told me that I was sterile, that I couldn't have any more children. Then a year later, for a reason that no doctor understood, I became pregnant with you. I gave birth to the healthiest baby girl. Considering the logic behind my body's condition, there is no reason you should have been born."

With a gentle turn of the wheel, Adacia moved the car into the nearest diagonal parking space along the Forest Lake strip of Ma and Pa shops. With a turn of the key, the ignition was shut off. Adacia's right leg began to shiver with more than a simple nervous twitch. Emma reached out to her.

"Are you okay, Mom?"

Adacia sniffed and cleared her throat, placing her closed hand to her mouth. "I'm fine. Thank you." Adacia leaned over to look up at her reflection of her emerald eyes in the rear view mirror, blinking out the moistness that had spread to her eyelashes. "At your age we can't be sure of the person we will become. We are all shaped by whatever elements of the earth and circumstances of people who drift in and out of our lives. Many believe that you, Emma, were supposed to be born. Anything outside of that is up to how you evolve. Do you understand what I mean?"

Emma had never heard her mother speak like this. The wisdom of the ages had somehow by osmosis drifted into Adacia's mind. "If I'm special, shouldn't I be able to rise above those elements and things of life, like you said?" Emma threw up her arms again. "I don't even know what the heck I'm saying."

"You do. You want to prove that you're special? Go on then...prove it!"

Emma hesitated to respond, wondering if there was some gladiator type challenge awaiting her. "Prove what? Do I have to kill a bear or something?"

"A bear? No, you goober. And you know what, you're right. Prove what? I've always said that you're too young."

"Too young?" Emma said, her voice becoming incensed. "What are you talking about?"

Adacia sighed, rubbing the back of her neck, looking stumped for words. "Emma, just know I want you to rise above the expectations."

Emma growled. "I feel like I having a conversation with a self-help book. What expectations, Mom?"

"The kinds of things people will expect you to be in the coming years." Adacia un-clicked her seat belt and leaned over to give Emma a soft kiss on the forehead, followed by a gentle touch of Emma's hair with her forefingers. "My mother, your Grandmother, I think only wanted me to be one thing - a leader. When I wasn't exceptional, she couldn't hide her embarrassment of me. I saw it. We fought so much."

"Why? Was she embarrassed?"

Adacia huffed, and nodded, almost to herself. "Let's just say that I will never put that kind of pressure on you." Adacia said, leaving the car. "Come on. Step inside the music shop for a bit."

Adacia closed her door harder than necessary, shaking the car. Emma remained her seatbelt still in place across her body. The thoughts that accompanied her mother's disclosures rushed around her mind like traffic at a busy intersection, all unconnected, all the branches sprouting more questions.

"Come on now, slow poke," Adacia said, opening Emma's door. Emma slipped out of the car and followed her mother down the block to the Forest Lake music shop, *When The Tunes Go Marching In*. The building was easier to spot with streets less crowded that year, with businesses of luxury or frivolous items abandoned. Though her eyes had a fleeting sadness for the out of business paint on the windows, the only thought that dominated Emma's mind as she dodged the cracks in the concrete stretch of uneven sidewalk was the wish within her that Grandma Ellie had lived long enough for Emma to have remembered her.

Emma walked about the store, unable to help herself from gliding her fingers along the strings of the guitars that hung upon the wall. When her mother wasn't looking, she squatted down before the piano. Emma banged out a few notes in proper tune, spazzing as if she was on a blues jam.

"Emma!" Adacia said, her eyes darting about the store, embarrassed.

Reluctant to back off of the piano, Emma hopped over to Adacia.

"You sure you don't want to pick up the piano or flute again, sweetie?" Adacia said, stroking her daughter's hair. "Don't listen to those kids in the school band room. You're better than you realize."

Emma moaned, unmotivated by Adacia's persistence. There was too much on Emma's mind to even think about taking up lessons again. Personally, she thought her flute performances sounded like a goat was dying. Either that or she knew her mangled notes could have killed one.

Jose, the owner of the music shop, emerged from a curtained off back room. He placed a fiddle in an opened case with the yellow repair tag still attached, onto the glass case beside the register.

"Here you are, Adacia. Almost didn't need an adjustment," Jose said. "I've never seen such a finely crafted fiddle such as yours go so long without repairs."

"I've used this model for every performance since I was a teenager," Adacia said, placing her fingers upon the restrung fiddle to pluck the horsehair strings.

"Every performance? Even including the album?" Jose said, leaning forward, raising one of his bushy eyebrows.

"Including that one," Adacia said. Emma caught her mother doing a poor job of privately holding back a proud smile. "Perhaps another album in the years to come. We shall see."

Emma proceeded to lean on the glass case, staring down at a range of harmonicas for sale. When she wasn't pressing down upon the keys of every keyboard or picking at every guitar and mandolin hanging from the wall, Emma loved to watch her mother connect with every crafted angle of the fiddle that Adacia had played since the days before she met Jonathan and started a family. Emma ran her fingertips along her favorite part – a curled carving in the fiddle's wood, inlaid with an everlasting, untarnished gold and silver paint that ran from the top to bottom on either sides of the fiddle like jade ivy on a brick wall.

"Well thank you, Jose. This was a gift from my mother," Adacia said. "You outdid yourself again."

Adacia took her fiddle out of the case with one hand and placed the padded end against her neck. With her other graceful hand she drew the horse hair bow across the new fiddle strings. Jose took care to lower the volume toggle on the radio behind him to silence the Count Basie tune.

Adacia began to play the sweet, folksy Irish music that stole the heart of all who had the privilege of hearing such beauty. The strings sang out a rhythm that made Emma tap her feet to thoughts of far-flung lands where notes held a cultural mystery that no lyrics could accentuate. Adacia played on, her concentration fixed, her fingers on the strings becoming her voice in every note of the explosive Irish reel *The Bucks of Oranmore*.

Emma was so taken by her mother's unflappable skill that she almost didn't notice a familiar face emerging from the lesson rooms at the back of the store.

"Ciara!" Emma yelled loud enough for Adacia to lose her concentration, the bow strings scraping.

Guitar case in hand, Ciara bounded over to Emma with a thirty-something woman following in her wake.

"Hi! You weren't at school today," Ciara said.

"Nope. I had to go to the doctor to get my melon checked out," Emma said, pointing to her head. Adacia winked at Emma, confirming the satisfaction of the cover. Emma did her best to bite her tongue. "Your nose looks a lot better."

Ciara self-consciously touched the slight puffiness that remained.

"See. I told you it looked better." The short, somewhat stout woman with evident crow's feet on her face, tapped Ciara on the shoulder in reassurance. "Hi there. I'm Ciara's mother, Michelle."

"Nice to meet you," Adacia said, shaking Michelle's hand as she held onto her dangling bowstring. Adacia cleared her throat, her eyes staring through Emma. "Waiting."

"Sorry. Nice to meet you too," Emma said, getting the clue.

"Hello there. Just got here in time to pick up Ciara from practice. My job keeps me late sometimes so I just wish we knew some other people in town," Michelle said, proceeding to nudge Ciara with her forearm. "So? Who's this?"

"Oh, sorry. This is Emma," Ciara said, setting down her guitar case to provide full attention to Emma. "She was the girl I told you I'm friends with at school."

"Oh so you were the girl who gave Ciara that ice pack," Michelle said, clapping her hands together. "That was so thoughtful. What a great friend to have!" Ciara nodded in tandem.

There it was – "friend" – the word that cured the ills of Emma's mind that afternoon, better than any spoonful of good medicine.

Chapter Four
The Flicker through the Trees

In the weeks following Emma and Ciara's first encounter the girls had gone no more than a day without having a conversation. There was a shared school lunch table, separate from everyone else who whispered their poisoned gossip in their direction. Those selfish things did not penetrate the bubble that surrounded the girls. When the little world they crafted for themselves was threatened, Emma in her renewed confidence was usually the one to speak up with such sarcastic ferocity against students like Pace Angles, Ciara needed only to stare back, break into a wide smile and wave off their foes. With that faith in Ciara, on a Saturday late in that September, Emma woke up early with a fever of anticipation that her friend was to show up with a backpack full of chewy sweets, cheesy romantic movies and her guitar case for the first sleepover Emma would ever host.

Adacia tugged the scraping legs of the kitchen table along the terra-cotta floor tiles to make way for Ciara. She took a seat on the floor, opened her guitar case, and began tuning those strings to the best of her ability. Emma hopped onto the countertop to lean against the wooden cabinet and prop her feet up against the refrigerator, ready for the show to begin. After taking a seat across from Ciara, Adacia with her bow string in hand, fiddle in the other, gestured to the sheet music and accompanied lyrics of a traditional tune called *Across This Land I Have Roamed*. Adacia slowly led into the song. Ciara followed with guitar, her singing voice mesmerizing Emma with a soulful presence.

Across this land I have roamed
My heart in the past, my feet with the road
The world I had left taught me much
To live with my guard in a land unkind

> But still I could not return
> To the memories of a love overturned
> Across the sea I had found
> The love of my life turned me around

The consummate professional, Adacia continued to glide her bow across the strings, nodding on occasion to Ciara in support. There, Emma could tell her mother's nurturing persona and instincts of a teacher had kicked in. The sheer rhythm and soul in Ciara's voice seemed to pull Emma up from her slouch like an invisible hook and make her clap along.

Ciara began to blush as she looked away. "I'm not that good, Emma."

Emma stopped clapping and folded her arms to look rather uptight, smirking away. "You're totally right! No talent there at all."

"Emma! Nonsense. You have some talent, Ciara," Adacia said as she stopped playing. "I've been trying for years to try and get Emma to play anything - consistently that is," Adacia said, giving Emma a stern glance.

"I like to listen more than play music, Mom," Emma said.

"You play around more than you listen," Adacia said, never missing a beat.

The doorbell chime rang throughout the house. When Adacia sighed Emma knew who had come to the front door.

Jumping off of the counter, Emma sprinted from the kitchen to open the front door with one swift pull. An older man with a few distinct wrinkles and lines on his gentle face and stout hands stood on the wooden porch. He held out a small package wrapped in large emerald leaves, sealed shut with a golden twine.

"Grandpa!" Emma said, jumping into the arms of Nicholas Elwyn. Quick to react, Nicholas embraced his spry Granddaughter.

"Good to see you, little one!" Nicholas said as he was quick to set Emma down, wincing as he straightened his back. "Oh! Maybe not so little anymore. What are you eating? Lead?"

His presence accentuated what she thought was a surprisingly youthful appearance he wore for being a man of seventy-four. His vision had even remained acute, with Emma noticing that he only needed the assistance of thin eyeglasses when he ventured into the great stacks of his readings.

"What's this?" Emma said as she tapped the package that Nicholas held.

"This my little Blue Eyes...is for you."

As soon as Nicholas handed over the present, Emma tore into the packaging. Taking off the smooth leaves Emma discovered an aged hardcover book entitled *The Howl of the Undiscovered*. The cover illustration showed the divine light of a tiny faerie woman emitting from the branch of a tree, almost hidden by pitch black night.

"Cool! Another faerie tale book." Emma flipped through the two-hundred odd pages of various short tales, each with penciled illustrations of magic makers and mythical creatures that stole her heart with the splendor of a magical world. "Thank you, Grandpa!"

Ciara snuck out of the door, her shoulders scrunched in, shy, as she extended her hand. Nicholas shook her hand with a curious glance at Emma's new friend.

"You must be Ciara," Nicholas said, pointing.

"That's me….huh…" After catching a glance, Ciara took Emma's book, staring at the cover in surprise. "I have this book too. I thought my Dad said it was rare."

Nicholas stared at Ciara for a good few seconds, his eyes squinting. "Your father gave you this?" Nicholas said, his palm upon the book. "Are you sure?"

"I'm sure. I've got a copy at home. He gave me one when I saw him a year ago."

"Who's your father? What's his name?" Nicholas said.

"Ummm, detective Grandpa?" Emma waved Nicholas's attention over to her.

"Sorry," Nicholas said, backing off. "Didn't mean to be one."

Ciara handed the book back to Emma and leaned against the wall, looking as if she wished to dissolve into the house shingles. This was the first time Emma had seen Ciara talk about her family outside of her mother. Emma could tell that Ciara was more than just a private person; she trusted almost no one.

"He doesn't live with me and my Mom." Ciara eyes wandered past the porch as she fiddled with the bronze ring on her right middle finger. Emma had realized just then that she'd seen Ciara wear that ring every day, the silver edge surrounding a top that had a half cream colored, half black mixture under two symbols that were beyond the knowledge of Emma's experiences.

Nicholas nodded and knelt down, the attention shifting his Granddaughter. Emma could smell on his brown cotton vest the familiar aromatic odor of chopped wood and autumn leaves.

"You wasted no time spoiling the surprise, Grandpa."

"I spoil you so what's the difference. Where is your mother?"

Emma could feel a soul gathering behind her. With the gesture of her thumb over her shoulder, she signaled Adacia appeared in the doorway. Her presence startled Ciara but not Emma. Being caught with another one of Grandpa's books froze Emma in fear of retribution. Adacia's smile had turned sour.

"What-is-that?" Adacia said pointing an inquisitive finger at the faerie tale collection Emma proceeded to guard by pressing the binding tight to her chest. "Dad! Why do you give those things to her? They'll just fill her head with ridiculous tales. Last time she read one of those, she tried to jump off of the roof onto the trees."

"Like the *Tree Jumpers* story, that was a good one," Emma said, pleased with her previous acrobatic skill, only somewhat aware that she was taking a far too liberal interpretation on the story of forest guards who leap through a knot of long and slender trees like squirrels onto branches.

"Imagination is the promise that good history and literature brings, Adacia," Nicholas said. He stood up, one hand reaching for his lower back, the other out, hands open, inviting her in. "Now, could you at least greet your father before yelling at him?"

Emma could tell that Adacia had feigned an embrace. This was in stark contrast to the strong affection behind Nicholas as he held tight onto his daughter much longer than her loose embrace held onto him.

"We need to talk," Adacia said, gesturing with a nod of her head. "Come inside."

Emma wished to follow but was stopped by Nicholas throwing up his hand as he stood firm, halfway inside the house.

"No. I am sorry but you need to stay outside from a bit, Emma," Nicholas said in his kind voice before he procedurally closed the door in Emma's face. The lock clicked into place.

"What's the big deal about the book?" Ciara said as she leapt from the porch onto the green grass of the long, sloping front lawn.

Emma shrugged, moving away from the door. "Mom always yells at him whenever he gives me one of these books."

Emma liked to think Bo never told their parents about those books because he reveled in defying their authority, even though Bo thought them to be too violent for Emma to read. To play fair, Emma never asked Bo why on some late nights, when she couldn't sleep, she would catch him reading her faerie tales by the light of a wood burning fireplace or a single luminous lamp in a lonesome room where he played self-therapist to his woes.

Emma led Ciara around the house, over the bits of gravel that had separated from the blacktop driveway, and onto the back yard. There they saw Jonathan taking a small wicker chest inside of the shed. Painted brown with a crimson trim, Jonathan's shed needed no nailed down list of demands to follow when entering; Emma was never allowed in there. Knowing this, Emma, with a reflex, looked away for fear that her father thought her curiosity might be growing that day.

"Dad," Emma said. "You should go inside."

Jonathan nodded, almost slamming the doors shut with his palms before he locked them in place with a brass key. Once Emma heard the aged lock click into place, she felt comfortable enough to turn to her father and see him eye to eye.

"Is Grandpa here?" Jonathan said.

"Yeah. They're arguing again over another present he gave me."

Jonathan tilted his head forward, rubbing the back of his neck, looking as if he was mentally preparing himself. "Here comes the peacemaker, putting out the fires." Jonathan made his way past Emma and Ciara to the back door of the house. "Listen. Stay outside for a bit with Ciara." Emma winced as she prepared for her father to treat her like a boy for a few seconds out of each day, that time giving her a hard, encouraging slap on the shoulder. The sting remained for a good half minute.

"Thanks, Dad," Emma said, rolling out the pain in her shoulder.

Soon, the screen door was shut in Jonathan's wake. The seal was made even further by another door and a lock that latched into place, ringing in Emma's ears.

Ciara plopped herself down on the fresh cut grass of the back lawn. Her face was long, solemn, as she sat staring off to the prairie to the west of the house with her legs crossed. Emma stood watching her friend for close to a minute, unsure of how to act.

"Are you okay?" Emma edged closer. She held out her Samaritan hand.

"I think so," Ciara said, shrugging her shoulders. "I thought I was fine to talk about my Dad but I guess I'm not." Ciara fiddled with her ring once again, rotating it around her middle finger.

Emma hated when adults would tell her, 'I know how you feel.' Here, she didn't want to repeat their mistakes. She pulled out her star necklace and sat before Ciara on the lawn. "This was my Grandma's."

"It's beautiful. You wear it every day, right?"

"I really feel alone without having my star on me. I can't explain it." She placed the necklace back around her neck to let the star rest against the collar of her brown t-shirt. "It's all I have, I mean from anyone outside my parents, Grandpa and Bo. They're all gone."

"What happened to her, your Grandma?

"Mom's mother died about a year after I was born. I can't remember anything about her, or anything else before I was like five years old."

"What do you know about her? Was she pretty? Did she play fiddle like your Mom?"

"Mom said she taught her how to play fiddle but I have no idea what she looked like. I've never seen a picture of Grandma Ellie."

Emma then remembered the time she rooted around the attic to search for family relics. Her clandestine search ended when Emma slipped on the wobbly floorboards Jonathan didn't nail down. Her foot went down through the kitchen ceiling. She couldn't help laughing when she covered the dinner Adacia had just then made with bits of drywall, insulation and her tennis shoe, which landed in the middle of a French silk pie with a plop. That failed mission placed Emma in the dog house for over a week.

All Emma found on that investigation or any other for that matter was that Grandma Ellie's belongings were lost in a nursing home fire about the same time she died. Bo later told her that the necklace, Grandma's favorite piece of jewelry, was only saved because he wore it until Emma was old and mature enough to handle the responsibility of owning the star every day of her life.

"So..." Ciara said, looking as if she was trying to piece things together of Emma's broken family tree. "What about your Dad's side with his parents?"

"Dead. He was raised by his brother when his parents died in a car crash. Daddie was only fifteen. His brother, my Uncle Dave, is a total jerk. He kept all of the inheritance for himself. My Dad and him don't talk anymore." Emma then realized that even though she saw pictures or her father's parents and far flung relatives in Chicago, her mother seemed to always have far better crafted stories for her side of the family to make up for the absent visuals. That was enough to stop Emma from asking thousands of questions, all in a tenacious row.

"Listen," Emma said, tapping Ciara on the knee. "Grandpa is such a nice man. He didn't mean to hurt your feelings by asking."

"I know," Ciara said, closing her hand to lock the ring in place. "Mom said I shouldn't wear the ring if I'm gonna get so upset." Ciara grabbed a tuft of grass, tore it from the lawn and began to toss pieces in Emma's direction. Emma followed suit with the grass, tossing some back at Ciara.

"So it's just you and your Mom," Emma said.

"Yep."

"Are your parents divorced?"

"I don't know what they are. I've seen my Dad about four times. The last time was about a year ago in San Francisco." The grass that Ciara held in her clenched hand tore from the dirt below.

Emma wanted to speak and fuel her desire to connect deeper than she had ever before with anyone other her family. Though, knowing her talkative self well, she bit her tongue, forcing her to slam on the breaks.

"Emma, I don't want to talk about my Dad unless...unless I want to. Okay? Just make sure you ask me."

"Sure. You can count on me."

"Thanks. I thought I could," Ciara said, nodding and looking away once again to the west.

"And I'm totally cool to talk about anything about my family."

"Yeah, I thought you would," Ciara said, not wasting time to flash Emma a sarcastic smile.

That would start what would be a ten minute grass and twig throwing fight between the girls, giggling like two idiots, tearing up the manicured yard that sat at the edge of untamed, bountiful nature.

Adacia never took more time to prepare a meal, aside from a few choice holidays, than when Nicholas came to visit. Sitting at the kitchen table, Emma's eyes looked past the banquet of roasted meats, vegetables sautéed in butter and herbs, gooey caramel candies and decadent chocolate desserts on white porcelain plates. To Emma the whole circumstance seemed odd that her mother put forth so much effort into pleasing a man she was so aloof to.

A good hour after the meal, when Emma lay down on the worn carpet of the living room floor in tandem with Nicholas to rub their packed bellies, Bo had arrived with a sour look upon his face. Ciara quick stepped in front of Bo's path in the narrow hallway with her hand held out.

"Hi!" Ciara said, doing a horrible job of hiding a transfixed smile.

"Bo, this is my friend Ciara," Emma said, running up from other room.

"Wow, you're Emma's brother," Ciara said, a certain forced softness to her voice. She never let go of Bo's hand. Her gaze was a dreamy one, never wavering from William Bo Grant's handsome features.

"Hi. Nice to meet you," Bo said, casting an odd look at Emma. "You can let go, you know."

Ciara snapped out of her dream, bashful. "Oh, sorry. Sorry…it's nice to meet you. I'm sorry, I shouldn't have done that."

"It's fine, Ciara" Emma said, tugging her towards the door. "Let's go on that bike ride."

"Sure," Ciara said, giving her body a shudder. "I'll see you outside."

Bo waited until Ciara let the door close behind her until he spoke. "What is up with your friend?"

"You didn't notice? Gosh, no wonder you have so much trouble with girls," Emma said, adding with a giggled delivery. "She thinks you're hot."

"How is that funny?" Bo said, giving his sister a light smack on her shoulder. "That's not funny."

"Oh, never mind," Emma said, her smile fading. "So I'm guessing the date didn't go well."

"I thought we had a lot in common," Bo said, using his hands to demonstrate his frustration. "I don't know...she shied away when I tried to kiss her or even get her number."

"Wow. That good, huh?"

Bo sighed and opened the fridge, plunging his head inside, separating himself from Emma by the stainless steel door. Emma didn't pry any further, feeling Ciara's crush was enough torture for Bo that hour. At that juncture Emma could pull out any break-up phrase from the gallery of rude and foolish girls that Bo had dated in the past and apply one to this girl from his high school history class. Having been forewarned by Bo, and from the lessons Emma learned from all of the bad relationship stories he had assembled like necrotic scars, Emma promised her brother that she would never break-up with a boy by telling him how nice he was or how much he would be better for someone else.

In the garage, Adacia loomed over Emma and Ciara, her arms crossed, her stern eyes focused. Emma could feel her mother's gaze pierce through the back of her head.

"What is it, Mom?" Emma adjusted her bike seat and gears. She didn't want to slip and fall onto broken gravel like she did that past summer. Her mind drifted to that day when she couldn't understand Jonathan thought it a remarkable feat of resilience that she winced just once as he used a tweezers to remove tiny stones from her leg after the crash.

"Do you remember the rules for going out on a bike, don't you?"

Turning around, Emma held out her hand to Adacia, releasing one of her fingers each time she spoke of a new rule. "Always wear your star, don't go into the Moonlight

Wood, stay off of the highway, stay on the shoulder when cars come…and wear a helmet."

"That's lame. You have to wear a helmet?" Ciara said.

"Pretty lame to have bits of highway in your skull, I know girls," Adacia said, with a scoff. "Does your mother not make you wear one?"

Emma and Ciara exchanged an amused look, trying not to chuckle.

"They look kind of dumb. Nobody wears them," Emma said, gesturing to a hot pink bicycle helmet that hung on a nail on the garage wall. "I mean come on, when have I needed one?"

"Alright then, but the first accident Ciara has, she is wearing one," Adacia said, throwing her hands up, looking comfortable with losing an argument for once. Adacia dug into the recycling bin and gathered a thick handful of college mailings and pamphlets, fingering through them in slight disgust. "Good to see Bo promised to comb these over.'"

"You can't force him to go to college," Emma said.

"That boy needs direction," Adacia said. "I don't want to force him to do anything but he has to start making choices on what he wants."

"Doesn't help if you have no idea what you want, Mom," Emma said, shaking her head, regretting that she was pulled into the debate on Bo's future once again. Emma threw her right leg over the bar of her bicycle, hopped onto the seat and began to pedal out onto the uneven blacktop.

"Wait a second!" Adacia shouted. Instead of stopping, Emma made slow loops with her bike, standing on the pedals as she maneuvered like a circus acrobat. "You're not going anywhere without your brother."

"Why can't I just go with Ciara?"

Bo emerged from the house, slamming the garage door shut. The startled Adacia jumped, dropping the college pamphlets onto the cement floor. Bo dislodged his bike from the wall with a considerable amount of effort. "Mom wants me to baby-sit, that's why…get down already!"

"Okay, Grumpy McGee," Emma said, continuing her circles as she looked from Bo to their mother. "If you are, you have to buy Ciara and me ice cream and pizza. It's what the baby sitter does, you know."

Bo mumbled a nasty choice phrase under his breath as he turned away from Emma to mount his bike. Emma liked that Bo knew never to say anything when facing her because more often than not, those tiny whispers found their way to her ears.

As Bo pressed his weight down upon the pedals of the paint-chipped, joint-groaning excuse for a bicycle, Adacia slapped him on the shoulder.

"Ouch! What was that for?"

"Your attitude," Adacia said, crossing her arms once again, satisfied. "Go on. Look after your sister, now."

Emma began to pump the pedals with her small frame. "Come on, Ciara," Emma said as she sailed past out onto the road, the whir of the rubber tires accelerating on the pavement. Just when Emma past fifteen miles per hour as she flew with all the strength in her legs, Ciara and Bo caught up to her, each one appearing on either side.

"Yeah, you're not as fast as you think," Bo said, keeping Emma's ego in check.

They rode the edge of the right lane. Bo lead Emma and Ciara several miles from home down infrequently occupied country roads, flush with yellow fields of switch grass on either side. From time-to-time they passed by clusters of ash trees. Their many fingered branches hung onto the last weeks of green leaves over the path before the group. Emma liked to lean her head back under these canopies, take a deep breath, and close her eyes as her bicycle travelled past the cookie cutter pattern that the sun made on the road. There was something about feeling the beams of light and warmth, between the shade, on her eyelids that made Emma somehow at peace with the day.

About a half hour into the ride Bo's, bike gears began to grind, metal against metal. He slowed down to a crawl on the extended stretch of country road. His bike chain had fallen off the track and begun to gum up the gears.

"Ut ohs, sucks for you, Bo," Emma said, speeding up. "Come on, Ciara."

"Hey! What the...wait up! My bike is broken..." Bo's voice faded as the air whooshed past Emma and Ciara's ears. They pumped their legs, travelling further and further away, leaving Bo as a speck of waving arms in the distance, and then nothing. Though Emma knew this would without a doubt get her in trouble, she was well aware that the path Ciara and her were on was about to come to a dead end.

After gliding down a road that stretched over a long bluff, Emma saw the sight of what brought her much joy, and to Ciara, much amazement – the edge of the Moonlight Wood.

Emma and Ciara turned off the road, their bike tires cutting a clear path into a wide-open field filled with prairie grass that brushed past the skin of their forearms.

A wide wall of redwood trees, each of them over a hundred feet tall, stood side-by-side, aligned like soldiers in formation at the forest edge. Only a measured space of about five feet existed between the trunks of every tree. As Emma approached, cautious, still in awe of their size, she looked north and south, noticing that the forest continued endless in both directions. Here, Emma could almost feel her mother's voice calling out.

"You're not allowed near there!"

Soon, she chose to ignore that Adacia's rules even existed. The majesty of the forest was too hard to ignore.

"These trees are huge!" Ciara said, hoping off of her bike. Emma dismounted and dropped her bike onto a small rock that jutted out of the ground.

"I know!" Emma craned her neck back to see the thin branches at the very top waver in the breeze of that afternoon. "They're beautiful."

She looked past the thick trees, guarding like rooks on a chess board to the forest interior. The forest had great depth, almost looking to Emma like a hazy mirage of alder, pine, and oak all coalescing into an endless bounty of the American wilderness. Yet, no creature stirred in the bracken. No bird sang from the branches. There was little but the sound of the wind making the trees creak and moan in the eerie presence of the guardian redwood trees at the edge of the wild.

"I've wanted to come here so many times," Emma said, touching the layers of sodden bark on the nearest tree. Her fingers felt electric, not far off from the feeling of sharp static electricity one develops in the dry air of winter. She drew her hand away, her nerves feeling the oncoming of a shock. "That's weird."

"What is it?" Ciara said.

"I don't know. The tree just felt like when I got shocked on a bad toaster plug when I was a kid." Emma rubbed her fingertips together, the numbness fading.

"Really? Let me see." Ciara touched the tree as Emma did. With a sharp fizzle, Ciara at once she drew her hand away, shaking. "Ouch!!!"

"That didn't hurt that bad," Emma said, giving Ciara a look. "How can a tree...wait...what's that?"

"What? Ciara looked around, still shaking her hand.

"There," Emma said, pointing to Ciara's feet. "You're standing on a metal sign in the ground."

Stepping back, Ciara revealed a small metal sign poking out of the dirt, appearing as if it was buried by a cadre of mischievous boys. The girls grabbed what they could of the exposed sign and with several tugs and grunts the rusted metal emerged from the earth to come into full view. Using her right palm, Emma wiped away the caked in dirt to reveal the full warning in faded letters.

> Property of the United States Government
> Visitors entering the forest will be prosecuted
> Keep your distance for your own safety

"I knew it," Ciara said, tapping the sign in satisfaction. "The forest is an Army base."

"That can't be. I've checked the maps at the library. There were no roads going in or out of the forest."

"Okay, maybe not an Army base. But still, why do they have this sign?"

"I don't know. Why was it buried instead of hanging up somewhere?"

Ciara closed her mouth soon after her lips parted to speak, looking quite perplexed. "Yeah, you've got me on that one. Maybe it's an abandoned base or something."

"The forest is not an army base, Ciara. The forest is something else."

Ciara began to saunter forwards to the space between the nearest guardian trees. Emma remained back, scanning the ground for any possible source of electricity or a monitoring device of some kind. Her keen eyes could see nothing save for their footprints in the dirt.

Ciara began to trot inside the woods. "I wonder if we just…oooof!" Ciara's walk between the nearest two trunks stopped the moment she reached the middle with a dull pang resonating through the air. Her body flew back into the small patch of dirt, as if she had collided with a window pane.

"What the? What just happened?" Ciara said, looking up from the ground, dumfounded. Emma reached out and pulled Ciara up by her wrist. "I'm good," Ciara said, spreading her arms out to find her balance. "Ummm, don't walk straight in."

When Emma was assured Ciara wouldn't tumble into dizziness again, she let go. Careful, Emma edged up to the spot that flung Ciara to the dirt.

"What are you doing?" Ciara said.

"A test," Emma said.

Her fingers spread out wide on each hand, Emma held them up in the heavy air before her, between the redwoods. A soft vibration began to flow over the skin of her hands and forearms, akin to feeling an auto engine through a dashboard. In her mind, Emma imagined the invisibility of this force unseen to be like a stone that could be moved. She pressed her hands inwards. Inch by inch the resistance grew. Having moved a mere few feet where her hands began, Emma's upper body trembled like that of a body builder having met his match. When she could no longer take the stress on her bones, she relaxed her muscles, only to have her arms slingshot back.

"I think this is a shield…or the worst practical joke a mime has ever played." Emma regained her composure and stepped back to observe, shoulder-to-shoulder with Ciara. "They don't need roads to keep people out if they have these things."

Ciara picked up a small stone and flung it at the invisible wall. The stone shot back and missed Ciara's head by mere inches.

"Ghesh! How do people get in here?"

"Tunnels? Catapult? Parachute?" Emma drifted to thoughts of all the padlocks and closed doors in her life. Her mind clicked, opening an ocean of logic and reasoning. "If people are kept out then there has to be someone inside playing guard."

"How could they? Didn't you say the forest was huge?"

"Yep. I did the math in the library. It's over 2,000 square miles."

Ciara's jaw dropped. "Oh my God, you remembered the math lesson? You are a geek."

Emma shrugged off Ciara. "Shush. My Dad always said the 'geeks in school will one day be the bosses' or something like that."

The thought of that entire wilderness, uncharted by thousands of Americans, Europeans and Native American's over ages of history in northern California weighed on Emma's mind as she paced. They soon sat on a patch of rock in the grass to contemplate the gravity of their circumstances; their eyes never left the darkening light of the wood within.

Time had fallen through the hourglass of the afternoon since they had departed from the house. Daylight had come to shine only on the tops of the mighty trees, ready to bring about the night. A half moon was out, floating near the horizon of the sky. The moon beams were ready to illuminate the dancing constellations that became visible. It was a harsh reminder that the girls had already broken too many rules.

And then, Emma saw deep in the distance of the dimming light of the shaded forest, flickers of light through the trees. The light was reminded her of the sunshine that warmed their faces through the leaves earlier on their bike ride.

"Did you see that?" Emma said, pointing to the light within.

"See what?" Ciara squinted, leaning her head forward. "I don't see anything."

"You don't see that silver light?"

Ciara shook her head. Emma could feel Ciara study her face next to her. Emma's blue eyes concentrated even harder, focusing on the certain illustrious silver points over one hundred yards into the wood. They taunted her, the light reminding her of an infant she had seen eager to grab silver garland from a towering holiday tree at a department store. There at the edge, Emma could see her theories about the Moonlight Wood were coming true.

Then, a beastly roar, deep and guttural, tore through the forest. The creature unseen startled the girls so that they jumped back, the skittish Ciara even more than Emma. The echo's of the beast carried on throughout the thick growth, reminding the girls that underneath the layers of the forest there were souls that had not been seen, and perhaps did not wish to be found.

Once again, the roar tore through the forest to the edge, this time even more ferocious, sounding like a horrific mix of a wild gorilla and a bear. Ciara tripped over her own feet as she ran to mount her bicycle. Emma remained, her senses fixed, still scanning the dim interior.

"Let's get out of here," Ciara said, her feet bouncing on the pedals.

"I don't see anything in there," Emma said. Touching her star, she felt sure that there was no beating heart in that area making that sound. "There's nothing there."

Ciara swallowed, her fear apparent to Emma. "What if it's a wolf? Or worse…what if it's a…"

"What? A Sasquatch?"

Ciara made a mousy squeak as she looked over her shoulder into the forest. Her chin was trembling. Emma's sympathies gave in and she mounted her own bike.

Along the road, across the prairie, a familiar figure stood, flailing his arms to get the girls attention. He started bending over to yell his lungs out.

"GET-OVER-HERE!" Bo shouted.

"Oh no. You think he's mad?" Emma said, with a nervous laugh.

Ciara fixed her face into a stare, tilting her head. "Of course he is. Why do you always gotta make a joke?" Ciara said.

"EM-MAHHH! NOW!"

"Okay!" Emma said, cupping her hands to her mouth, shouting.

Ciara peddled her way out of the grass with a fright that would accompany one in a nightmare. Emma remained in those first few moments that Ciara flew away. The glittering silver light within had never stopped. The radiance grew stronger once the moonlight had taken over duties for the sun.

The unseen creature's roar silenced, the breeze and creaking tree trunks returning to fill Emma's ears. The wood had awoken. Pumping those heavy pedals took much of her strength to ride away and meet Bo. The temptation of wanting to traverse through that invisible barrier, unchecked and unharmed, was stronger than anything Emma had ever felt in her life.

"Are you stupid?" Bo said, as he pedaled along Ciara and Emma, leading them back through the winding country roads. "We live out west. There are wolves and coyotes all over the hills here."

"We were a hundred percent safe, weren't we Ciara?" Emma said.

Ciara didn't utter a word. She huffed at the idea of safety.

"I have to tell Mom, you know."

Emma grabbed both of the brake handles. Her tires screeched to a halt. Emma made a point of staring down her brother. Bo made a circle back to stop his bike, positioning his front tire to hers.

"You can't tell Mom. I'll get a life sentence in her prison."

"Sorry, but I have to."

"Why? Because of the forest? It's no big deal. Don't tell me you've never looked inside. You know you've been to the edge." The tapestries of memories were already flooding back, making Emma so excited she shook her hands in mid-air. "The forest is so beautiful. I swear I saw something glittering inside."

"I don't know what you're talking about. I've never seen the forest," Bo said. His voice was soft, weak and his blue-green eyes of his father, though never wavering from Emma's, seemed sad and defeated.

"Ciara," Emma yelled, "Hold up a minute."

A good ways ahead on the road, Ciara had pulled over to the shoulder, as if she expected the confrontation between brother and sister. "Okay. Just don't pull me into this, guys."

Bo gave a tug on Emma's handlebars. Her body and bike took a sharp lunge forward. "Come on. You know Mom and Dad are going to kill us already for being out this long."

With one furious fell swoop of her left hand, Emma dislodged Bo's grip from her bike. She leaned in, her cerulean eyes, almost incandescent in the failing light of the day, were ready to burn a hole through her brother. "Why are you lying to me?"

Bo avoided Emma's intense gaze. "About what?"

"Everything these days. You made up such a crappy excuse for the vision I had in class. Don't you care anymore?" She waved her hands about to do a horrible impersonation of Bo's voice. "'Yep, Mom, you're right. She sleepwalks. Well…off to being a whiney dork again.'"

"Nice touch on the whiney. And you know you fell asleep that day at school," Bo said. Emma thought raised voice sounded forced to Emma. "You lucid dream, remember? I've fallen asleep tons of times in class."

"That wasn't a dream! MY VISION WAS REAL!" Emma said, her fists pounding down on the rubber handles of her bike, bending the wrought iron underneath with every smash.

Bo feigned a shrug and threw up his arms. "What do you want me to say?"

"That you'll believe me like all the times before."

In the awkward silence that followed, Emma and Bo stared each other down, neither willing to break. Realizing after minutes had passed that this impasse could not be crossed Emma moved her bike aside and walked the wheels forward.

"I don't know what's wrong with you the past year. You are so pissed off sometimes. When you send off those college forms, make sure you also put out a missing ad to find what the heck happened to my brother."

Without delay, Bo turned his bike around and moved alongside Emma. "Hey. Maybe I'm going through a lot lately. I've no idea what the hell I'm supposed to do with my life when I graduate next year."

"Yeah, but…urgh! You're such a nice guy. Why do you have to be this way?"

"Alright, sure, I could work with Dad but then I got to swallow the laundry list of rules for living under them all over again. Maybe I'll join the Army."

"That's not safe. And you only join the Army if it's a for sure, not a maybe."

"Whatever! I can't keep this up - you know you weren't supposed to go into the forest, Em!"

"What does the forest have to do with you?" Emma stopped her bike, cringing as she looked at Bo, his enraged voice still filling the heavy space between them. "And seriously, why are you yelling at me?"

Bo, as if he had caught a look at his face in the mirror, began to look remorseful, the corners of his mouth drooping in disgust. Without a word, he peddled ahead of Emma.

Ciara glided over with her bike and skidded to a clumsy stop next to Emma. "What was that about?" Ciara said.

"I think my family is keeping secrets from me."

"What is it? What's the secret?"

"I don't know. That's why they call it a secret."

"Alright," Ciara said, moving away, throwing on her social armor. "You don't have to be a crab about it."

"Come back, I'm sorry," Emma said, jumping back on her bike and catching up with Ciara. "Listen, I'm going to need your help."

"Sure. As long as I don't have to worry about being eaten by a bear in the forest!"

Emma's smile faded in that tiny moment. She then realized more trust had been solidified in Ciara than she had in the past months with her beloved Bo. Emma's mind was clotted. This realization of abandonment dug like a hook into her heart the entire ride home as she looked from time-to-time at the navy blue sky fading away to the black curtain of night in the east, dotted with a flickering veil of stars.

Chapter Five
A Coffer Delivered

In years past Adacia and Jonathan would have subjected Emma and Bo, for whatever trouble they had caused, to draw a scrap of paper from an old pickle jar. These fortune cookie sized strips of paper did not grant goodwill or advice. An assigned chore was scrawled, with Adacia's illegible handwriting. To their relief from parental duties, dinner would be cooked one night and the bathrooms cleaned the next, almost wishing at times that Bo and Emma got into trouble more often.

For some time that glass jar sat collecting film and dust in some random cabinet in the house. Bo was the first to refuse punishment. As Jonathan and Adacia had expected, Emma would follow suit. For the transgressions Emma committed in her forest adventure that September, Adacia pushed the jar further back into the cabinet and did the true damage of grounding Emma, limiting everything she did from watching television (which she did little of anyway) to an abolition of spending time with friends. Deliberating with some desperate empathy at a thought of losing her friendship with Ciara, Emma won over her father, knowing he was her ace in the hole to reducing the impact of Adacia's verdict.

Sparks flew up into the air with the flames that smoldered a set of logs and crumbled twigs. Nicholas had been stoking the fire with the iron fire poker he borrowed from the fireplace of his daughter's home.

Emma watched him rouse up the embers for some time from the screen door on a night where a blanket of cloud cover made the backyard bleak. But there, Emma could see just as well as in the daylight, her eyes able to adjust between light and dark like a nocturnal creature that dwelt in the fields and patches of trees around her home.

"Have you come to join me? Nicholas said. He straightened his posture at the first sight of Emma crossing the yard to join him at a fire pit, near a patch of trees.

"Yep. I brought some smores."

"Are those the jam and jelly sandwiches on cheap bread?"

Emma giggled, remembering Grandpa could be a little slow at times. She handed over the box of graham crackers and torn bag of marshmallows.

"Oh, I see. I love those wafers, chocolates and sugary puffs!"

"They're marshmallows, Grandpa."

"I don't know what you…you kids call them."

After grabbing a few sturdy sticks from the grove of trees behind them, Emma and Grandpa Nicholas skewered the marshmallows and dangled them just above the fire.

Emma loved sitting around an immaculate campfire that her Grandfather had put together. In the past the whole family would come outside and roast fish or kebabs of beef and vegetables on fire racks and thin iron rods. Satisfied moans would follow when they used either French bread or warm tortillas to pick the succulent meat straight off of the cooling rack, still steaming with a soft shade of pink in the center all due to the attention Nicholas gave to them.

"Where is your brother?"

Emma shrugged, wishing she knew. "He goes out a lot. One time he told me he just drives around. I was hoping he would play Risk or something and drink some of his hot cocoa he loves making."

"The only thing he can cook."

"I know! I always hated when he drew the 'cook dinner' slip from the punishment jar. Remember the boiled turkey dinner?"

Nicholas shuddered, removing his mallow from the fire. "Please, do not remind me when I am having something delicious." The melting chocolate dripped onto his fingers as he popped the smore into his mouth. "Mmmm, yes. That was worth waiting for." Nicholas patted his paunch in delight.

"So do you want to know what's been going on?" Emma said, removing her marshmallow from the touch of the flames to let the confection cool in the autumn air.

"As always, I am listening," Nicholas said, prepping another smore with two layers of chocolate.

"Did Mom tell you that I biked up to the edge of the Moonlight Wood with my friend, Ciara?"

"She did. You do remember why some of us think that you shouldn't be going near there, don't you?"

Emma bit her lip, forcing herself to be civil. "Did she tell you about my vision I had in school."

"Of course. Adacia told me straight away. That was quite strange."

"What? That Mom told you or that the vision was weird?"

"Both, I suppose. I was glad she told me. Trying to talk to your mother otherwise is…" Nicholas poked the fire a few times, showering the air with sparks. "Let us just say that Adacia is too sensitive. Her greatest strength and yet greatest weakness is that she cares too much."

Emma nibbled at her blackened and blistered marshmallow on the smore, loving the bits of milk chocolate that melted the rest of the way onto her tongue. "Cares too much? Smother is more like it. Oh, by the way, I finished the book you brought me last week."

Nicholas slapped his thighs. "Good! Now, you will be ready for this." He reached into his nearby knapsack to pull out another book. The binding was so worn it looked to have been on a shelf for decades. Emma took the book, running her palms over a picture on the cover of a glass orb, a plume of smoke forming within like with a crystal ball.

"*The Slaying of Verago*, English translation," Emma said. "Translated from what?"

Nicholas snatched the book away to glance at the cover. "Oh, I imagine some sort of Celtic or Native American language."

Emma held out the collection of tales to her Grandfather. "So, are you going to read it to me, Grandpa?"

"I will. Lay out. I have one particular good tale that I think is appropriate."

Emma popped the last of her crunchy smore into her mouth. Moving away from the fire, she started her part of the ritual. Once she adjusted her fleece hoodie, she laid stomach down on the grass, the palms of her hands propping up her head. Her attentive eyes watched her Grandfather read with a voice made to lift the elements of fantasy from the page and deliver them to reality.

Nicholas opened the first few pages, the sound of the bending paper filling the air along with the sizzle of the fire. Clearing his throat, he began to read by the light of the flames.

"'The New World was tamed by the tribes, not by the sea-farers. The five paths to Elysium revealed by the Horned Serpent became history, only to be lost. The healing of the wounds of natives in the enchanted waters of the inland seas became myth, soon thereafter draining away when the land was tainted. Their survival in the wake of the colonizing of people of their blood and the Europeans from the Old World became legend. However, all were threatened in this endless land when Verago was awoken in the Great Stony Mountains.

Her flames scorched the Earth. Her wings beat with a concussive fury, greater than any Thunderbird could muster. And when she consumed the great Sorcerer, Lord Eoin Boldger, fear gripped natives and settlers alike. It seemed the Erebys had reformed descended onto the now untamed west of the New World.

In this time of great challenge, a hero from Glencar Aisling arose to lead the people to victory – The Lady of the Beacon…'"

Emma perked up at the name. "Who's that?"

Nicholas never let his eyes leave the page. "A great Sorceress of holiness from Ireland and Scotland."

"What kind of powers does a Sorcerer have?" Emma said, imagining an old wizard, a craggy gray beard, holding a magical staff made from an old tree.

Nicholas looked long upon Emma, nodding. "If you must know…a Sorcerer, according to these stories anyway can wield magic, conjure and manipulate all of the elements, including gravity and space. They have the ability to sense the changes in nature, have their mind map their surroundings by the use of their senses, anticipate thoughts and emotions, and see the future with their exceedingly developed minds, three times the brain capacity of a human like yourself."

"Cool! So they're magicians?"

"Magicians are charlatans and entertainers, like the Great Oz. Sorcerers are of this world and yet posses what in ancient times devolved into idol worship. They were living Gods. And they were to be feared."

"Why? Did they try to rule the world or something in these stories?"

He cleared his throat, regaining his composure. "Not exactly...and ruling the world? There are far more deceitful and selfish matters than that. Now wait until I am finished!"

As the many times in the years before, Emma stayed awake as long as she could. Her Grandfather's readings seem to pump caffeine into her veins via osmosis, leaving her ears peeled to the next scenes. Jonathan had once joked that these sessions required a bucket of popcorn due to the heightened, unbreakable splendor of the sweet honey of words that filled the ears of whoever was lucky to be present.

The late hours of the day began to wear Emma down. The cozy feeling that she had in her jeans and hoodie, thanks to the warm embers of the fire, took her down for the count. When Emma laid her head down upon the grass, half-listening to Nicholas' voice echo in her drowsiness, Emma fell asleep with one thought on her mind.

"I wish these stories were real."

One afternoon, a few weeks later, when the autumn leaves had become a cornucopia of vibrant oranges, browns and yellows, the Grant family sedan dogged a few reckless sport utility vehicles and luxury foreign cars to pull up along the sidewalk of Woodland

Academy. Emma waved goodbye to Ciara as her friend still waited for her mother by a lamppost. Plopping herself inside the car, Emma was in for a surprise that afternoon.

"Hey, Mom...Bo, what are you doing?"

Bo checked his mirrors as he edged out from the space, slow and steady. He slammed on the brakes when a white SUV with no concern for the low speed limit or the lives of grade school kids, shot past, with Pace Angles in the passenger seat.

"What the?" Bo honked on the horn, only to get a suggestive hand gesture back out of the driver's side window SUV. "What a jerk!"

"Yeah. Well, at least it's a nice change," Emma said. "Mom is the always the one to almost kill people with her driving."

"I'll take that as a compliment," Bo said. He maneuvered the car out of Woodland Drive and onto Madison Avenue, leading into town.

"Why are you driving?"

"I had a half-day. I was running errands too. And, to be honest, I think Mom was sick of me begging her to drive the car," Bo said. He proceeded to smack Emma's thigh without looking. "Hey, get your seatbelt on, already."

"Oh, nice! Let's first get some milkshakes at Emmitt's," Emma said, taking longer to get her seatbelt on because she proceeded to bounce in the seat with the excitable memorized sensation of malted milk on her taste buds. "I hope the milk shortage didn't happen this week. I hate having to wait for things like that."

Bo laughed to himself, shaking his head as if he knew better. "Sucks to be American, doesn't it?"

"Not really...oh, whatever. Sorry! I have enough money this time so that you don't have to pay for me for the millionth time."

"Millionth time? We'd be five hundred pounds after that much ice cream."

"You know what I mean." Emma looked out her window as the car passed through the intersection of Norris Avenue and Center Street, moving west and away from civilization. She tapped on the glass. "Bo, the downtown is that way."

Bo reached over to flick on the radio to an AM news station. "We're going home, actually. Sergeant Mom's orders."

The soft crackle of radio waves met their ears before a correspondent spoke.

"From NPR news in San Francisco, I'm Nabel Gross. Congressional leaders spoke today about how they would consider returning to old World War II style ration books in light of the worldwide economic depression, coupled with the growing famines and armed conflicts in Africa, Asia and the Middle East."

"So much for no shortage's," Emma said.

"In local news, the town of Forest Lake in northern California, had a bizarre incident the other day..."

Hearing this, Emma and Bo glanced at each other in curiosity. Bo turned up the sound.

"Matthew Tours, who was evicted from his house, attempted to force his way onto a Government held property which locals call the Moonlight Wood, after the sheen the air has in that area during a full moon. Mr Tours, who now sits in the town hospital in critical condition, said he tried to tear down one of the trees and live inside the forest where no one would bother him. An improper placement of five sticks of dynamite later on a redwood tree later resulted in fifty-five year old Tours being peppered with wooden shrapnel. He said the redwood tree still stood, to his amazement, as he limped back the five miles into town. Desperate times coming to our shores indeed. Weather and traffic coming up next…this is NPR…"

"Holy cow!" Emma said, running the scenario of the man the radio program spoke of through her mind. "Even this guy couldn't get into the forest."

Chewing the hangnails off the ends of his fingers, Bo didn't speak for a good minute. Emma tilted her head as she glanced at Bo, feeling his uneasiness fill the air. Out of the corner of his eye, he glanced at her, never totally allowing himself to become distracted from the road.

"What? I'm listening to the news," Bo said.

"Are you going to say anything about that story or are you just going to tell me the present below the seat?"

Bo pounded the wheel, looking dumbfounded. "Okay, come on! That was the surprise. Are you reading my mind?"

"Nope. But if I could, I would."

"Creep," Bo uttered out of the corner of his mouth.

"Dork," Emma said, like a reflex.

Bo turned the radio dial off. Emma's hands met with smooth wrapping paper over what felt like a book. Pulling out the present, Emma proceeded to tear past the polka dot wrapping.

"It's September. You know my birthday is March 7th."

"I know. Just thought you might like a new book."

A copy of *Fantastic Tales of America* rested in Emma's lap. She moved her fingertips over the illustration on the cover of a several hundred foot tall brawny bearded man, clothed in buffalo raw-hide. He stretched his body over a Western canyon, allowing an old steam engine train and the seven passenger cars it towed to ride over his back to safety on the other side of the sandstone bluff. Emma remembered seeing books like these in the Woodland Academy library when she tried to find any tales that could match the majesty of Grandpa's books.

"Bo! That was so sweet of you!" Emma said, rubbing her brother on his shoulder. "Thanks, buddy. Why did you decide to give me this one?"

"Mom and Dad think those other ones are too violent for you to be reading," Bo said, almost in forced distain.

"I think Grandpa knows what he's giving me." Emma began to thumb past the vast amounts of illustrations placed before the ten classic American tall tales. The cartoonish portraits featured American legends like Johnny Appleseed tossing out miles worth of seeds in the Ohio valley, to Pecos Bill roping a tornado with a rattlesnake in the old American west. "Are the stories meant for kids?"

"You are a kid."

"You know what I mean. Little kids. Fables and stuff." Emma proceeded to use her speed reading eyes over the text. "Yeah, these aren't like the one's Grandpa gives me."

"They're realistic, I'll say that" Bo said.

"That's why I like 'em," Emma said, turning toward Bo in her seat, bouncing with an excitement to become a storyteller like Grandpa. The most recent story she read from the copy of *The Slaying of Verago* came to mind. The tale had kept her up a good half hour past her bedtime. "There was this one where these ghost souls, after this awesome, super bloody battle, were all floating around a forest. The kingdom's soldiers and magic makers had trick 'em and then cover them in this red dust which made the ghosts turn back into dead bodies. Cool stories, right?"

Bo gripped the steering wheel, tight enough for Emma to hear the gray leather flex under his hand. Emma could see Bo's disillusioned eyes glance at the copy of *Fantastic Tales* that Emma had set onto the dashboard.

"They are not as cool as you think," Bo said. His grip softened with time as his eyes continued the exchange from the book to the stretched arc of the road in the countryside not far from home. "But…it's your choice if you like reading Grandpa's book. I'm not going to stop you."

Emma and Bo soon pulled into their driveway. Emma noticed there were only a few letters in the mailbox, along with an issue of a bluegrass music magazine for Adacia. Emma was about to shut the rusting tin door to the maple strip mailbox when she did a double-take.

Placed as far in as possible in the darkness of the very back of the mailbox, was a small coffer with a brass handle. The coffer reminded Emma of the ones her father had used for his business. Reaching in, Emma grabbed the coffer and began to pull the box towards her. Much to her surprise, the closer the box came to exiting the mailbox, the larger and heavier it became.

"What the heck!" Emma said, pulling her hand out. No neighbors were around. Bo had parked the car but was too preoccupied to notice Emma as he listened to music with the doors closed.

She peered inside the darkened box to notice a letter jammed in beside the coffer. Emma reached in and pulled the letter out, careful to not tear the envelope. There was no return or mailing address. The letter read...

William

Emma knew this second letter, at least from what she has seen, had to be from the girl he was writing back and forth from. Her fingers fluttered along the golden sticker with the initials M.R that sealed the back, beyond curious to open the envelope.

"Stop. Stop," Emma said to herself, as she shoved Bo's letter amongst the other mail. "It's none of my business."

She peered back inside to press the coffer with her forefingers. The box decreased in size by a few centimeters. Emma then pulled on the handle and the wood seemed to expand by several centimeters. Emma did these back and forth maneuvers a few more times, giggling like the goofy kid she could be at times. After her fun, she took a firm hold of the brass handle and gave the box a sharp tug.

The wooden coffer flew out of the mailbox, increasing in size to two feet long and six inches high by the time the brass and wood hit the open air. The sudden change in weight threw Emma off balance. She fell backwards and landed on the rough pavement, the now fifteen pound coffer landing on her chest, sharp corners and all.

"Whoa!" Emma said, the air from her lungs escaping. "Death by treasure chest." Her rib bones would ache for a good few minutes afterwards. Pushing the coffer off of her and standing up, Emma stretched, feeling the impact points strike her nerves from her neck to stomach. She pulled out her star, touching all of the points – no damage.

"How did that happen?" Emma said. She reached her hand all the way back into the mailbox, touching the back piece so dark, spiders liked to crawl on the tiny metal wall. Her hand and arm did not change in size like with the coffer. Emma began giggling as she looked from the mailbox to the coffer on the black pavement. "This is so cool!"

Grabbing the coffer by the brass handles on either side, Emma walked up the driveway to the front porch, the mail tucked between the box and her body.

"Hey, Bo! You got a letter!"

Bo sat up from the reclined driver's seat to turn down the volume and lower the window a crack. "What?"

"A letter from a girl, you dope. And look what I got!"

Emma dropped the coffer down with a clunk onto the narrow sidewalk that ran from the driveway sideways to the front porch. Tossing the rest of the mail aside, she held out the letter to her brother.

"Take it."

Bo exited the car with his and Emma's book bags thrown over his right shoulder. He bent down at the sight of the coffer. "Where did you get this?"

"In the mailbox. Did you know this thing can expand in there? So cool."

"Give me that!" Bo snatched the letter away to look at the engraving upon the sticker. "Why would she…oh…stay here, Em! Do you think Mom is still home?"

"I don't know. We just got here."

"This is so weird. Stay here and don't open that!" Bo darted across the driveway to fly through the front door and into the house.

"Why not? Okay, thanks. Man! Ghesh, what is up his butt?" Emma said, shrugging off the more than usual oddness of the family.

Sitting down on the front steps before the coffer, Emma lifted the latches and tilted back the lid. Inside was a smaller wooden chest, almost identical to the larger counterpart.

"Is this a joke?" Emma had not forgotten a similar act that Bo pulled for her birthday a few years ago. He had hid a book in a series of cardboard boxes, all fitting inside one another like a babushka doll.

She lifted out the small coffer and rested it on her legs. Inside, was a letter tucked in an envelope tied to a crystal vial with a cotton ribbon.

Emma held the vial up to the sunlight. Swishing the crystal like a snow globe, the liquid sealed inside seemed to shine. In the water, tiny silver flakes like a fish's scales and a red dust both seemed to light up once they hit the sunlight that had just peaked through the clouds. A little slip of paper was attached to the vial in a white ribbon that Emma read.

Corrosive materials. Use against foe when in peril

Emma set down the vial. Picking up the letter, she noticed the envelope was sealed at the back with an emerald wax imprint. The symbol on the imprint looked to be of a comet streaking across the sky.

Using her forefingers, Emma tore the envelope open to pull out a letter written on fine parchment in professional calligraphy.

Dear Emma,

With anticipation for the journey
Companions will bring the answers
Be aware of the apparitions.
They dwell this season in the nightlight.
And beware of the howl of the undiscovered demons
For they seek the heir to the Lady of the Beacon.
Use your strength in the abilities you wear, Alastar
And in your journey, be stealthy amongst the leaves of silver.
Find Esylltora, and if she be absent, befriend Siobhan.
The world is changing. You will be here for proof.

There was no signature. Emma held the letter, her hands almost shaking as she pieced together 'Lady of the Beacon' and 'Alastar' in the vast canvas of her mind. Placing the coffer inside, Emma sat up and began to pace along the porch.

"The Lady of the Beacon..." Emma said, thinking out loud. "That's from Grandpa's book, the Slaying of Verago." Was he pulling an elaborate prank on her? Two facts soon convinced Emma otherwise. One, she knew her Grandpa's handwriting was much too messy for this letter. Two - although she had shared her vision of a phantom with her family, never did she mention to any of them that the creature referred to her as "the Alastar."

Her rapid eyes scanned every word, twice over, committing them to her near photographic memory.

"Emma?"

"Over here!" Emma said from the front porch.

From around the corner, a wide-eyed Adacia scanned the yard for sight of her daughter. Her face was flush, concerned.

"Hey! Look what I found," Emma said, holding up the letter.

"Put that away, Emma." Adacia was now running up to her. Bo lingered not far behind on the sidewalk, watching the drama unfold.

"What's wrong?"

Adacia ran up to the two open coffers near Emma's feet. Snatching the envelope from Emma's hands, Adacia stared at the wax imprint. Her face twisted into a confounded bitterness. Her shaking hands gripped the coffer on both sides

"I don't believe this!" Adacia screamed. With a violent heave, she threw the larger coffer against the brick wall of the north side of the house, shattering it like a tinder box. This froze Emma in her tracks.

"Oh, great! Chill out, already!" Bo yelled, marching forward. "What the heck are you doing?"

Adacia handed Bo the envelope. His eyes widened at the sight of the imprint.

"Wasn't who you thought it was, huh? Looks like she couldn't resist," Adacia said, her fists clenched.

"Is the name on there?" Emma said, approaching. "Let me see that again."

"Give me the letter, Blue Eyes." Adacia snapped her fingers in succession. "Give-me-that-letter."

"No. It's addressed to me."

Adacia held out a demanding hand. "Don't turn into a brat, now. Give that to me."

"Mom. Take it easy," Bo said, the plea falling on deaf ears.

Adacia took the letter and tugged in one direction and Emma the other. The tug of war between mother and daughter ended when the paper tore in half.

"What are you doing?" Emma said, balling up the letter without thinking.

"This is all unsafe for you," Adacia said, snapping her fingers to Bo and pointing to the coffer. "Bo, take them inside."

"No," Bo said, folding his arms.

"You'll take that inside, William Bo."

"Maybe when you stop acting insane, I will."

"Enough! I have had enough of your attitude," Adacia said, pointing her long, right forefinger in Bo's face. "You want to be a big man, go try and live with your Grandfather then for a few days. See how you do without us."

"Fine. Let's do it that way," Bo said, smirking. This made Adacia speechless as she backed up, quite stunned. Emma shook her head, surprised at Bo's audacity.

"Emma, go inside and get in your room. I need to speak with your father when he comes home."

"And then you'll talk to me?" Emma said.

"No. Stay in your room."

"Like a prison," Emma whispered. Emma couldn't take the injustice anymore. She balled up her half of the letter and tossed it against the front picture window. "Stop hiding things from me!"

"Emma," Adacia said, holding out calming hands. "Please don't get angry. I don't want you to pass out again."

Emma's voice then rang out, piercing the ears of Adacia and Bo. "I didn't pass out! It happened because I can do things no one else can. Why don't you believe me?" Emma hadn't noticed in her rage that though Adacia and Bo had their eyes fixed on her before her fever pitch of frustration, they averted her gaze, almost as if they were afraid to make eye contact with her.

"Look at me!" Emma's voice seemed to carry weight with each word, like an echo that could cause an avalanche. When Bo and Adacia did not reply, Emma turned to the window, looking for her paper and instead, catching a glimpse of herself in the reflection that made her scream. "My eyes! What's wrong with my eyes?"

Radiating out from Emma's eyes was a cascade of sapphire light. Her pupils had turned blood red, no longer holding their previous beauty. Her whole body seemed to emit an otherworldly aura. "Mom…Bo? What's wrong with me?"

The mother and eldest child held out their hands at a dead sprint. Emma had only turned to see the panic that had gripped their faces. She was falling off of the porch. The darkness blacked her out a mere second later.

The bedside lamp lit Emma's room since night had fallen. The digital music player on her dresser played the 2nd Movement of Beethoven's 7th Symphony, the type Emma like to listen to when she was invested in such deep thinking. When the movement began with the short blare of horns, Emma shot awake from her bed with a gasp. The room was empty.

Emma turned her head to the window she had left ajar a few inches. The aura around her eyes had faded, returning her blue eyes once again. She crept over to the open space where the chilled late October air flowed in. In the near distance, perhaps on the other side of the house, Emma's ears could hear what sounded like a lock and bolt being fiddled with. Thinking her black dress shoes might make noise, she slipped them off.

The window quietly lifted. Emma slipped out onto the lawn, wet with dew, to sneak along the edge of the house. Crouching down, Emma held tight to the wall, avoiding contact with any light from a window. She froze on the spot when a silhouette formed at the window to the dining room. As Emma stared at the shadow on the grass from her hidden space under the window, she could tell her mother was just beyond the wall.

Adacia's fingernails began to tap on the glass in rhythm of a musical medley Emma was unfamiliar with. Emma did not leave her mime-like post, nor try to breathe heavy, for she knew she would be heard. Then, Adacia then drew the drapes shut with one swift movement. The light from the kitchen turned off. Emma was alone in the darkness.

Not being a fool, Emma waited a good minute under the window, not desiring to be caught and thrown in a cage in the attic for all she could imagine. When Adacia did not return, Emma moved again, making her way to the bushes around the corner. The sound of shifting metal and the soft concussion of heavy freight being dropped had returned.

Emma knelt down behind a thicket of lilac bushes, her body well concealed. A mere fifty feet away was Jonathan. The shed doors were wide open, the only light coming from a glowing lantern hanging on a branch of a twenty-year old ash tree adjacent to the shed. The lantern was not powered not by oil and flame, but by a bizarre yellow ball of energy that hung in mid-air in the glass. From around the base of the tree, Jonathan picked up Emma's coffer.

"That's mine," Emma whispered, soon after hoping it was said quiet enough.

Jonathan walked up to the shed entrance. From a brick on the shed landing, he produced a chipped metal key and placed it onto a specific location on the floor. After a few seconds, a gritty sound of stone on stone filled the air. When the noise ended,

Jonathan took his lantern in one hand and the coffer in the other to enter the shed. Emma jerked her head to the side in wonder as she saw her father descend a set of stairs inside the shed, the lantern light going with him.

"There's a cavern inside," Emma said. Springing her body back upright, Emma went on her tip-toes to get a closer look. "What's down there?"

When she was about twenty-five feet from the moss covered shed, the light of the lantern began to return.

Emma's heart stopped, the fear crippling her. Boot steps were coming up now. Emma forced herself to turn on a dime and run across the lawn back to her room. Her hips brushed against the untrimmed arms of the lilac bushes as she ran past.

"Is someone there?" Jonathan said, his voice carrying across the lawn covered with flecks of dew that shone in the jets of light from the full moon above. From his waist, he produced a small rod with a trigger on the handle. "Show yourself!"

"Nope, no one is sneaking out and about to get grounded," Emma whispered as she found her window on the other side of the house. Jonathan's boot steps approached from around the corner. Emma wasted no time jumping in on her belly and then rolling onto the floor, soft and graceful. The lantern light became brighter from around the corner. In one quick push, Emma lowered her window down to allow a tiny opening.

She dove backwards into her bed and threw the covers over her body. She lay on her side, face towards the window, and shut her eyes. From under her eyelids she could sense Jonathan was beyond the glass, just outside her bedroom by the light that now poured inside. For what seemed like the longest ten seconds of Emma's life, Jonathan lingered. When Emma remembered that she left the window unlatched, she clenched her teeth, praying that she wouldn't be made into a hermit for a few stupid secrets. Those lies, those mysteries - Emma did not hate them as much as she wanted to solve them and bring about days where she did not have to hide from her father and mother anymore.

Emma counted to sixty in her head before she opened her eyes. Jonathan soon had moved away, his lantern with him. Nothing remained but the grass and shrubs outside her window where moonlight did not shine.

Chapter Six
The Door in the Floor

Emma had a way of separating her thoughts in unique ways. While able to examine numerous thoughts in a balanced, simultaneous fashion, much a well rounded chess player that focuses not only on a rook or a bishop, she could see the whole board, at times even the next moves. Her deductive reasoning fed off of these thought processes, often earning her astonished remarks from her science, math, history and English teachers as her grades soared with each new challenge that baffled 99 percent of the school. The girl with the bright blue eyes and a star necklace to match her mystique never ceased to amaze.

The night that Emma snuck out of her bedroom window, her mind once again became that chess board, attempting to solve the mystery. When the morning light came just after six a.m, Emma was wide awake, aware of the challenge that awaited her from the decision she made in the darkness before the dawn. That afternoon, when the family wasn't home, Emma would break into her father's shed.

The bedroom door opened without a sound. Emma turned around to see Bo mosey in and shut the door behind him, as if he thought Emma was still asleep.

"What do you want?" Emma said, sitting up.

Bo dropped his messenger bag, packed to the hilt, onto the floor. He attempted to sit down on the bed, facing Emma. She stretched out her legs, not allowing her brother a comfortable place to sit.

"Alright. I won't sit on you this time." Bo stood upright, his hands in his pockets, rocking back and forth on the ball and heels of his feet. "Why are you still wearing your school uniform?"

"I've been thinking all night," Emma said, crossing her arms.

"Yeah, me too." Bo grabbed the back of his neck, rubbing the muscles.

"Are you going somewhere?" Emma said, gesturing to the bag.

"Yeah. That's why I came to say goodbye."

Emma released the tension in her crossed arms and turned to her brother, concerned.

"Goodbye?"

"Not goodbye, goodbye. I mean that I'm leaving for a few days."

Emma remembered their mother's strong suggestion to Bo from the previous afternoon.

"Are you going to stay with Grandpa?"

"After school, yeah. I'll be at Grandpa's from Friday until maybe Monday. Who knows. Maybe a whole week. We'll see what happens."

"Well..." Emma said, her interest percolating amidst her remaining frustration with Bo. "...at least tell me what Grandpa's place is like when you get back. Let me know if he has a huge library full of fairy tale books!"

"I'm not stealing any for you, though." Bo picked up his bag and threw it over his shoulder with a heave. "I guess I'll see you next week."

Emma held out her hand. "Wait! Tell me one thing before you leave."

"Is it what I think it is?"

"Probably not. What's your girlfriend's name?"

Bo laughed and tugged at the shoulder strap on his chest, loosening up. "Meira. And she's not my girlfriend. We're just...I think we're close to dating. Well...maybe not if we're just writing back and forth. But yeah, I like her." Bo's smile was precious, epitomizing a bashful, red faced teenager in the subject of romance. "She's nice to me so, you know, don't be you and write a letter back in my voice."

"What is that supposed to mean?" Emma tossed aside her covers to stand toe to toe with her brother, the top of her head meeting him at mid-chest.

"You know what I mean," Bo said, giving Emma a forceful shove in the shoulder, sending her back down onto the mattress.

"What did you think I was going to ask? About my eyes?" Emma said.

Bo nodded, mustering courage to look into her eyes. "I'm not gonna lie to you."

"That would be a nice change!" Emma said, folding her arms. "So? Mom tell you I have some sort of infection or something?"

"No. We both know that's not true." Bo bent down and with his right hand he tapped Emma's star to her chest. Emma moved closer, her ears cautious for a lingering parent outside of the room. He took a sharp breath and shook his head, fighting a demon. "This star is the key," he said at a whisper. "I don't know how or why but it taps into your soul."

Emma took hold of the crystal star. "You mean...this turns me magical?"

"No. This makes you even more of what you are. When you landed on your head on that fall from the bleachers at school last year...it was because you were chasing those kids that ganged up on you and tried to steal your necklace, right? Even without it, you stood right up from the fall, no injuries. Nothing! With this...things...even more fantastic things happen when you wear Grandma's star."

Emma held fast to her star, her eyes never wavering from the sight of Bo. "I've never heard you talk like that. Why now?"

Bo stood up and threw his backpack on, pulling the straps tight to his shoulders. "I'm on your side. Don't think I haven't had a hard time doing what I was told and fighting what I've always wanted to say." Hesitating for a moment, Bo gestured on his chest for Emma to place her necklace under her shirt.

Emma followed Bo's suggestion, surprised to see him smile as she did. "What?"

Bo turned right around and spoke over his shoulder as he sauntered out of the room. "Good to know my little sister still listens to me."

Her hand over her heart, the fingertips touching the star underneath her shirt, Emma's mind did cartwheels at the thought that her star had to be protected. "What the heck am I supposed to be?"

"Star girl, over here!" Ciara said aloud.

Ciara's lack of volume control prompted a series of shushes from the librarians in Woodland Academy who policed the library, their index fingers placed before their lips. Coming into the library for her free period, Emma made a bee line past another eighth grade class to where Ciara sat at one of the computer stations.

At lunch, Emma had poured out the details of the past day to Ciara. Being the good listener she was, Ciara hardly bothered to chew her ham and cheese sandwich as Emma unfolded her story. Emma couldn't help but to laugh at this, reminding her friend to stop chewing her lunch like a stick of gum.

Ciara had already begun her investigation online during the free period, promising to be the Watson to Emma's Sherlock Holmes.

Emma trotted over to Ciara's computer, noticing she had several tabs open on the internet searches. She couldn't help but notice a man's name typed into one of the search engines, next to an equals sign, followed by 'Moonlight Wood'.

"Who's Jabari Inaya?" Emma said.

"Nobody," Ciara said, using the mouse to close the web page in an instant. "You wanna see what I found?"

"Sure, show me," Emma said, sensing Ciara was in another one of her closed off moods that afternoon.

From a table of chatty, high maintenance, girls that Emma recognized as the Pace Angels Pied Piper-like followers, Emma stole their last chair and slid it across the carpet and up to Ciara. Emma reveled for a hot minute in hearing the clique hiss.

The screen displayed a map of far northern California. Clicking the mouse, Ciara zoomed in.

"Oh, so you found Forest Lake on an online map?"

"No. I found this." Ciara pressed the left arrow on the keyboard. The satellite image of the rural town and country roads met an abrupt end when the Moonlight Wood came into view, each magnified panel turning gray, reading NO IMAGE AVAILIBLE. "Why are there no images of the forest?"

Emma leaned in to play with the arrows. Even when she zoomed out over the great space that the forest covered on the map, the shrouded, inconclusive evidence remained.

"Weird, right?" Ciara said, using the mouse to move the image along the edges of the forest on the map. "And you were right. There's no roads going in or out."

"Is there anything else on the internet about the forest?" Emma said.

"Nope. Just all of these conspiracy theory websites, like that weirdo you heard who tried to break into the forest."

"Oh, the kind of sites created by geeks who live in their mother's basements, right?" Emma leaned back in her chair, trying to forget the image of that poor, curious man, loaded with shrapnel from the tree. The puzzle came out again in her mind. She remembered the line from the mysterious letter in the coffer.

Companions will bring the answers

"Emma," Ciara said, shaking her friend back into reality. "Are you okay?"

"Ciara," Emma said, her eyes pleading. "I need your help after school."

Emma and Ciara waved goodbye from the driveway of the Grant home.

"I'll be back at seven," Michelle said, calling to Ciara from her open window of her ramshackle pick-up truck.

Emma turned on her heel and moved for the yard. Ciara pulled her back by the strap on her backpack.

"Wait until my Mom is gone," Ciara said, continuing to wave, flashing a fake, wide mouthed smile as Michelle gingerly backed out of the long, sloping driveway.

"Sure, because that creepy smile would convince anyone that we're not about to do something wrong," Emma said.

When Michelle pulled out of sight, Ciara gave Emma a playful shove.

"What? You make it too easy," Emma said. She led Ciara around the ash tree at the end of the driveway over to the slab of red clay bricks encased in the soil that led up to the front door of Jonathan's shed.

"How are we going to get in?" Ciara said, staring at the oversized, 19th century padlock.

Emma bent down on the brick landing, pointing with a forefinger. "One down and three from the left." Emma pointed to the one brick free of mortar. "That's the one." Using the tips of her forefingers, Emma removed the brick from its companions. Flipping the brick over onto Ciara's open hands, Emma was surprised to find a worn metal key, no larger than a ballpoint pen, wedged into the hallowed out inside. Removing the key, Emma held it up, looking to the lock on the shed.

"That's an old key…oops!" Ciara said, losing control of the brick. The block fell and split into three pieces on the slab walkway. Emma breathed in a sharp intake of air, aware of this now dead give-away of her rooting around.

"I'm sorry, Em," Ciara said, collecting the pieces. "We can glue'em."

"It's fine. Let's not panic. We should get inside before my Mom comes home."

Turning the key in the lock, the gears click open inside. Emma could help but to envision the stern eyes of her mother and deliberate, irate voice of her father. "We're in."

Emma threw the lock onto the grass and removed the latch to swing the right door open wide.

"You don't trust me to handle the lock?" Ciara said.

"I do," Emma said, smirking. "Just don't touch anything else."

There was no light bulb to be turned on inside the shed. Sunlight from beyond the door shone in on a few dusty boxes and empty crates, making the space feel like an abandoned property.

"Didn't you say there was a door in the floor?" Ciara said.

"Don't know." Emma grabbed a lantern from the floor. From the pocket of her Woodland Academy green buttoned jacket, Emma removed a box of matches. Lighting one with a strike across the combustible black strip, Emma turned the gas nozzle and placed the burning match inside the open glass. No wick needed lighting for the space in the middle of the glass began to glow like a floating ember.

"That's so cool," Emma said, staring at the lantern as she extinguished the match on the cement.

"What's that under your foot?" Ciara said, pointing.

Looking down, Emma moved to see. In the dust, putty colored cement on the shed floor was a porthole for a key.

"Let me see the key," Ciara said, her hands reaching out to Emma. Once Emma handed the key over, she placed it flat against the design on the floor; a perfect fit. After a few seconds of staring at the key in place, the girls jumped back in shock. The metal of the key began to bubble and break down just before the key dissolved into the porthole in the floor as it is had been smelted into molten iron ore.

Emma held her lamp high to spread the light out over the floor. From the key porthole, clean cut lines spread out two feet on either side and then went down about five feet to the center of the shed. A pattern of a door emerged, the keyhole now a handle.

Passing the lantern to Ciara, Emma lifted up on the handle, pulling the door out of the floor. A rush of damp air blew back Emma's chestnut hair. There was a dark cavern below and a set of mud stained wooden stairs leading down into the pitch black.

"We are going to get into so much trouble," Ciara said, looking down the hole with Emma.

"Probably." Emma took the lamp, holding it out as she began to descend the stairs. "But I have to know the truth. I'm sick of being lied to."

Each uneven step creaked under the weight of Emma and Ciara's footsteps. The lantern swayed the light out in front of Emma's outstretched arm. A small rock cavern, no larger than Emma's bedroom, came into view. On either side of the dozen steps were wooden shelves fastened into the stone wall, all of them clotted with knick-knacks and sheets of parchment, stacked inches high with labels that read as such: Domestic Orders - Foreign Orders – Transportation - Customer Correspondence.

"I think you were right, Emma. You're Dad is a trade goods seller," Ciara said.

Emma couldn't resist examining an orange and green collection of shredded herbal leaves encased in a black metal design of an oak leaf that had slits run up and down to allow air to pass through. Holding the metal leaf up to her nose, Emma took a sniff. The overpowering scent of tropical citrus fruits poured into her sinuses, strong enough to make Emma shiver.

"What is it?" Ciara said.

"Strong," Emma said.

"Really?" Ciara leaned in and breathed in the encased leaf. The intoxicating smell forced her into a coughing fit. "Oh, that's like biting into a lime."

"Warned ya," Emma said, placing the potpourri holder back onto the shelf.

"Check this out, Em," Ciara said. She took hold of what looked like a Chinese finger trap, except that these had a pull string on the bottom. "What does this do?" Ciara yanked down on the string.

A fizz, faint at first, emanated from the tube. Then a bang erupted from the top end, sending out an array of multi-colored jets of phosphorus materials. An opus of fireworks and flares shot throughout the cavern. Ciara panicked and threw the blazing firework aside. Emma pulled Ciara into the corner and ducked down. A stench of sulfur poured out with searing jets of light that bounced and encircled the room like fireflies flying around at the speed of sound. The air of the echoed cavern seared with the high pitched squeal of the fireworks.

Once the firework burned out, leaving the lantern to light the room, Emma peeked out from beneath the arms she held firm over her and Ciara's head.

"Don't pull any more strings," Emma said. She had to fan the clotted air with a book from one of the shelves to see through the smoke.

"I won't touch anything else, I promise," Ciara said, her voice muffled as she remained crouched, hands covering her head in the fetal position. "Can I get up?"

"Nope. You stay there," Emma said, picking up the lantern. Emma could hear Ciara scoff behind her. She paid her friend no mind. The light of the lantern highlighted a pool of water that came into view against the back wall made of pitch-black granite. The shallow pool, a few inches deep and a few feet on either side was crystal clear, as if it was a rainwater puddle. Holding the lantern over the water as she knelt before it, Emma could see hundreds of glittering pieces of golden dust.

"Ciara. Check this out," Emma said, waving her friend over.

Ciara crouched down next to Emma. "What is that in the water? Is that gold dust?"

"I'm not sure." Emma then touched the surface of the water. From where her left forefinger made contact, perfect ripples spread out in continual bursts every second, a dull ping accompanying each ripple. The gold dust then began to move. They joined together to create words that spelled out upon the surface of the water in a written script.

What communication do you desire?

Emma and Ciara's eyes shot out of their little teenage heads. Emma was the first to break, giggling as she spoke.

"That is so cool!"

"What is this?" Ciara said, slow and still amazed.

The words broke apart and the golden dust formed new letters.

I am a Ripple.
All is clear for channeling.

"Channeling what?" Emma said, presuming the pool was able to take answers and perhaps commands.

The words reformed.

A correspondence
With whom do you wish to speak?

"The President," Emma said, having a bit of fun. "Yeah. I wanna speak to the President - in the White House!"

Connection to the United States of America Executive branch not authorized...

...Producing lists of the Office of Presidents

A long list of names in a registry came into focus. Each name, from Aldus Andreaeson to Zacharias Zeal, held a title and location at the end of their lines. Emma thought the name King Augustus IV was an interesting one.

"The Kingdom of Augustus. Appalachia. The Republic of Avenmore. I've never heard of any of these places," Ciara said. "Tocantis? Is this like one of those fantasy games that geeks play?"

"Probably not," Emma said, considering the advanced technology. "Ripple - no more presidents or leaders." The names disappeared into the water. "I think it's like a visual telephone."

"Awesome! I totally want one now."

"I don't think its pocket size." Emma leaned forward when the letters began to reform.

Reverting to common point of channeling

The golden letters fell away as a series of images came into focus, emanating light like the beams of a television in the dark. Within seconds the water rippled a few more times and then fell still. On the surface was the image, as woven together as tight as any high resolution video, of a series of shelves and wooden table, organized with decorative trade goods that looked quite similar to the ones in the cavern.

A voice called out from the water. "Jonathan. What can I do for you, boss?"

Emma grabbed Ciara. "Someone's there." Just in time, Emma pulled Ciara to the cold, uneven cavern floor with a bone crunching thud. "Ouch!" Ciara whispered.

"Jonathan? Are you there?" the deep voice of the man said, even louder this time.

Emma held Ciara tight to the rock and stone, still out of the light of the pool.

A glass crashed to the ground from inside the watery image. "Ack! Don't worry, that was nothing." The man proceeded to whisper to someone off screen. "Clean that up, you fool." The man cleared his voice. "Jonathan, let's have a talk before I close up the shop for today. I know Bo has you in knots. But trust me – I can tell he's a good kid from all the times we've talked after hours in the shop. He's your only child after all. See ya, boss." The voiced echoed and the girls could hear the water move.

Emma sat up to see the images fading away into the clear pool again with a series of ripples. For a good minute she rested her hands on the edge, staring into the water.

"Only child?" Emma said, standing up.

"I know. The guy seemed as if you don't exist," Ciara said, getting up.

"Don't exist. Why would my Dad act as if I don't exist?"

Ciara shrugged. "Bo has to know about this. I mean, if your parents are in on this, so is your brother, right?"

Emma remembered her brother that morning, how sorry his eyes looked. "Not anymore." Emma drifted away from the pool over to the shelves, her heart heavy at the thought of her father denying her existence. Her mind was awash with doubt. "I don't understand. He said last week that 'I brought so much joy in his eyes.'"

"Hey, don't feel bad," Ciara said, hugging Emma from behind.

"I do feel bad. My Dad and my Mom only care about Bo."

"Or…your parents don't want to tell people about you."

Emma turned around, releasing from the hug to stare at Ciara with a sudden realization. "They don't tell people about me. That's it!" Emma removed her star from under her jacket and held the crystal out to Ciara. "All because of this."

"Your necklace? You know that's just a piece of jewelry, right?"

"No. It's not. This is special," Emma said, her train of thoughts winding up in a dead end. She began to pace, still holding her star, seeing if her theory of the star would find a connection somewhere else. "Maybe this is all because I'm special and they want to hide me."

"Someone's getting a big head don't you think?" Ciara said.

"I'm not being arrogant. I'm serious. How come these mysterious people write to me and my parents hide the letter? How come I've never been sick or really hurt with all of the accidents that I've had? How come I have visions and sometimes even know what a person is going to say and do before they even do it? Last night my eyes were shooting out light! Explain that!"

"I can't, Emma," Ciara said, sympathetic. "I want to help you. I just have no idea why you can do things that nobody else can."

Emma appreciated Ciara's candor but her blood was still worked up. "What's that in your pocket?"

Poking out a few inches from Ciara's back pocket was a roll of parchment. "This," Ciara said as she unrolled the sheet. "I think it's a map of the forest."

Emma jumped alongside Ciara. Holding the opposite ends of the parchment, the girls surveyed the map by the dim amount of sunlight that found its way down the stairs.

"I think this shows us how to get into the forest," Ciara said. "And look - Alastar. That's your house."

"Alastar," Emma said, letting the grandeur wash over her tongue. "Alastar…that's what the phantom called me in my vision."

"Ummm, phantom?" Ciara said, taking a loud swallow. "Like a ghost?"

"Sort of. Like a demon, ghost mix. The letter said also said – Emma Alastar."

"But your name is Grant."

"I know! Maybe this Alastar thing is a nickname?" She pulled out her star from under her shirt, realizing as she did that she was breaking a promise to Bo. "Maybe this is called the Alastar? People want to find this!"

Ciara pointed to the top left corner of the map. "Isn't Jonathan your Dad's name?"

"That's him. But 2402 N.C.A? What is that, a year?" Emma's eyes scanned over the whole of the aged map, committing it to her excellent memory. "Footpath…" Emma took her right forefinger and moved along the drawing of a footpath by her house all the way to the road. "Crossing boughs…"

"They look like two trees, you know when they lean over each other with their trunks," Ciara said, her voice getting excited. "I think that's your way in."

Piled amongst endless pieces of parchment – the map to get inside the forest was there all along. Emma looked beyond the crossing boughs to the Eastern road and then the entrance. Though she could not make sense of their purpose, journeying past these redwood guards into the woodland of her dreams had become much more hopeful of an endeavor. With the thought of the recent denial of her existence, the mounting lies and now the absence of her greatest ally in Bo, the choice was clear for Emma.

"Ciara," Emma said, sincere. "Can you please sleep over tomorrow and stay on until Saturday."

"Sure. I thought that was the plan."

"That's half of the plan. But I need your help on the other half. I need you to go into the forest with me."

"The forest?" Ciara said, her voice becoming a little meek. "What about those phantoms? And what about the roars we heard? There has to be wolves and bears in there."

"Lions and tigers too," Emma said, amusing herself. "Come on! The letter said *'companions will bring the answers'*. I need you to go with me tomorrow night. We'll sneak out with our jackets and backpacks all stuffed with supplies and go on an adventure."

"What if we get into trouble?" Ciara said, a troubled look about her. "You don't know how angry my Mom gets."

"Can't be any worse than my Mom. She's not going to stop me from going through that gate made of trees." Emma caught Ciara's glance and held it with her mesmerizing eyes. "Please. Bo's gone and I don't trust anyone else but you."

Ciara let go of the map and took a few pensive steps along the floor. She glanced at the ripple and then paced over, not a word coming out her mouth. Emma knew Ciara's mind was full. Emma concentrated on Ciara's head, and could feel her friend's thoughts percolate into the damp air of the cavern. Emma sensed the word 'Jabari.' Ciara held out her hand, those dark eyes scanning her precious ring.

"Do you think there are people there that don't want to be found?" Ciara said.

"If everything is kept a secret, probably, yeah. Why?"

Ciara shook her head, almost to herself, and then took a deep breath. "I'll go with you. I'll go into the forest."

So overjoyed at this victory in a gallery of defeats, Emma wrapped her arms around Ciara and lifted her off of the ground in a bear hug.

"Air!" Ciara said, gasping.

"Oh, sorry," Emma said, removing Ciara from her clutches, setting her down.

"What the hell!" Ciara said, clutching her chest, catching her breath. "How are you that strong? I bet you don't even weigh a hundred pounds."

Emma touched her star, her face delighted and her hopes soaring from a near tumble down a well of despair a mere few minutes before. "I think this is one of those things we have to find out tomorrow night."

A few minutes later, Emma and Ciara emerged from the cavern. Ciara was quick to tear a sheet of paper from the shelf and place it into her pocket before ascending.

"What did you take?" Emma said.

"Who cares? Let's move! Grab the lantern."

Emma extinguished the lamp with a turn of the nozzle. The map pressed into eight tiny folds and stowed away in Ciara's pocket, next to the torn bit of paper. The stairs fell dark with the closing of the door in the floor. The liquid metal key returned to the solid state on the imprint once the door sealed shut. The edges disappeared into the cement. Emma was swift to return the key to the space under the now broken brick. She did her best to place the three shattered pieces back into the walkway amongst its brothers. Ciara closed the door and sealed the lock.

But before they were in the clear, Emma and Ciara turned the corner, around the massive ash tree to be stopped in their tracks. Ciara let out a loud, deep gasp.

"What are you girls doing?" Adacia said, sauntering over from the house.

Emma so wished to speak but the muscles around her mouth felt paralyzed. This old habit she had formed around her mother in those situations.

"Is everything alright, girls?"

"Fine," Emma said, forcing the words out. "We're fine - just looking for the soccer ball."

Adacia pointed over to the ferns that surrounded the base of the ash tree. "It's right over there, Emma."

The roughed up, worn down soccer ball was wedged between two bristled shrubs. Emma could feel this fear bubble with a sudden incitement to snap at Adacia's existence in that tiny moment. Instead, she bit the inside of her cheek when the annoyance of her mother became too great to handle. She moseyed over, plucking the ball from the shrubs.

"Ha. Got it! Thanks for always…always watching out for us."

"Of course, sweetie," Adacia said, crossing her arms at Emma's change in mood. Would you girls like some dinner?"

Ciara looked like tea kettle, ready to burst out a scream. Her voice was frenetic. "Dinner? Yeah, I'm down for dinner. Dinner is awesome. I love dinner. What are we having for dinner?"

Emma stared at Ciara in disbelief. "Really? That many dinners?"

"Yeah, I know!" Ciara said, talking out of the side of her mouth, looking more obvious than she realized. Ciara then yanked the ball from Emma's hands and threw it into the back yard. "Bet you can't catch me, Em." Ciara then ran after the ball, not looking back as she drove her foot into the rubber, driving the ball into the far reaches of back yard.

Emma remained, Adacia and her looking at one another with an air of suspicion. The tension ebbed away for Emma as her nerves filled with a distain for Adacia's stare.

"What? Want to ground me for something else, now?"

"Why would I ground you again? Are you doing something over here which entitles a grounding?"

Emma put her foot down, let out the most convincing sigh she could muster, and turned away to join Ciara. "I didn't try and get into the shed. I know the rules."

"I know you know the rules…" Adacia said, losing Emma's attention. "Blue Eyes, listen."

Emma stopped, swallowed and turned to face her mother. "What?"

"Sometime soon your father and I would like to speak with you," Adacia said. "We have to talk about your future."

All the pickle jars of punishment couldn't stop Emma from her mission now. Even this olive branch of peace Adacia tossed Emma wasn't good enough. The doors of acceptance were shut in Emma's mind.

Emma shrugged her shoulders, forcing a feigned interest. As she turned away from Adacia to join Ciara, Emma could sense an odd resonance in the air, as if Adacia's scrutinizing eyes scratched at the wall of Emma's mind.

Chapter Seven
The Forest of Silver Leaves

A thin layer of fog had begun to settle that night, obscuring the fringes of the forest. Emma and Ciara had crossed the last road before the forest like cautious nocturnal animals. Along the prairie grass fields they went a good half-mile north, maintaining a visible distance from the edge.

"Are you sure your Mom won't check on us?" Ciara said, looking back, the Grant house so many miles behind them.

"She will in the morning. That's why I wanted you to move back there. It took us an hour to get to the forest gate," Emma said.

"Sorry! You know I have asthma," Ciara said, taking a few controlled breaths.

Ahead, Emma could see a tight grouping of the dewy vapor between the boughs, thicker than the rest of the mild fog. The unseen mystery beyond gave her even more reason to want to look before leaping inside.

"I think that's the entrance," Emma said. The map was open, spread out over Emma and Ciara's knees as they bent down in the field. They did not need a light for the full moon was cascading its concentrated rays downward. Emma placed an old compass, stuffed away in a drawer for years, on the map. Opening the top, the needle spun in concentric circles, never settling on true north.

"Compass's don't do that, do they?"

"They shouldn't," Emma said, giving the magnetic guide a shake. "Maybe the wall of trees, or whatever that is between them, is throwing them off."

"So do we go between the cross boughs?" Ciara said, reading the map. "What's on the other side? I can't see anything."

"Me either," Emma said, standing up, breaking down the map into pocket size form and stuffing it away with the compass. "But that's not gonna stop us, right?"

"Eh, maybe. When's the last time you stepped into a creepy fog?" Ciara said, her eyes glancing at the wall of imposing, colossal redwood trees.

"Come on, you big baby," Emma said. She tugged at Ciara's jacket, beckoning her friend to follow.

A mere five feet before the entrance, Emma and Ciara stood shoulder-to-shoulder, their necks craned back to look at the place where the two aged, withering birch trees bent over each other, leaving a space wide and tall enough for two adults to walk through. An inscription was carved into the bark in the dead center. Ciara squinted to read in the dark. Emma sharp eyes scanned the warning with ease.

Pure of heart – People of old – Enter with risk – Far from home

"What does that mean?" Ciara said, taking an ominous step back.

From the pocket of her black wool jacket Emma pulled out Bo's pocketknife and drew out the blade with her thumb.

"Enter with risk. That's what it means!"

Taking a deep breath, Emma closed her eyes, and stepped into the fog.

A few paces in and Emma found her body, from head to toe, surrounded by the mist, separated from the forest and Ciara as if she was in some sort of limbo. She could feel the concentrated moisture from the vapor on her cheeks. As Emma passed further through the entrance, she could feel her blood in the veins of her arms and hands, as if all of those red blood cells were alert when she was not. Though the sensation had passed within seconds, leaving her fingertips tingling as if her arm fell asleep, Emma was not prepared to stop her calculated march forward.

"Emma?"

"Ciara? Are you okay?"

"I can't see you!"

Emma could feel her friend behind her. "Follow the sound of my whistling."

"Whistling?"

Pressing her lips together, Emma began to whistle *Twinkle-Twinkle Little Star*. Emma's rendition seemed to carry through the hanging cloud, her high pitch bouncing off of tree trunks that were coming ever so closer.

A brittle crunch beneath her sneakers stopped her dead, ending the whistle. Her mind formed an image of a pile of bones. Looking down, there were no bones of small animals but a twig scattered amongst dried leaves. Two more steps and Emma began to see the fog part with a breeze from the path ahead. In a matter of seconds, the mist had lifted, remaining then behind Emma in a tunnel between the trees.

An endless cobblestone path lay out ahead of her. Twenty feet wide, the foliage covered lane cut through the forest. Trees of pine, oak, and the occasional redwood were peppered between the green flora and hidden fauna on both sides. Not a danger in sight, Emma folded up the blunt end of the blade against her jacket, placing Bo's pocketknife inside her jacket.

"EM-MAAAA!"

Emma turned around, trying her best to see Ciara in the fog. "Sorry. Sorry." Emma once again whistled the notes of *Twinkle-Twinkle Little Star*, swaying from side to side like a chirping sparrow on a branch.

"Okay. I think I'm here."

The cloud lifted around Ciara and she came into full view. Her arms were outstretched, waving about in circles like a blind woman. Emma continued whistling as she stepped forward to grab Ciara's forearms. Ciara let out a quick, shrill scream that made Emma wince.

"Stop! It's me. It's me."

"Sorry," Ciara said, clutching her heart. "Did you know you scared the hell out of me!"

"Nope. Couldn't tell."

The girls looked ahead. The path continued on, the end even beyond Emma's eyes.

"Do we know what's up there?" Ciara said

"Nope." Emma said.

"Well, thank God there is at least a path," Ciara said, adjusting her backpack straps and walking ahead, with purpose. "You coming?"

Emma blinked in shock at this sudden change in Ciara before following with equal vigor.

Since the cloudy sky had obscured the moon at that point on the night of October 30th, the girls found their way by the beams of their flashlights. Emma thought how odd it was that the lowest level of clouds seemed to zip across the sky with the occasional breeze, like a low flying airplane.

Five minutes after Emma and Ciara left the vapor tunnel, they came upon the end of the path.

"What is that?" Ciara said, pointing.

The path opened into an oval clearing, devoid of the forest. In the middle, one tree stood - a hefty young tree that looked like a mesh between a gigantic bonsai and a sequoia tree that dwarfed the girls. The branches were massive enough to hold what looked to Emma as a series of wooden platforms, enclosed from higher branches in hanging sheets of white muslin. Not a soul was stirring.

"Hello?" Emma called out, her voice echoing. No answer. The muslin drifted in the soft night breeze. "Shouldn't there be guards here?"

"What? Guards?" Ciara said.

"Yeah, that's what the map said." Emma began to walk into the clearing. Her eyes and ears were on alert for even the smallest movements in the tree above or in the brush that surrounded the clearing on all sides before the forest began once more.

Along the bonsai sequoia's trunk were a series of thin wooden steps that wound up and around the platform. Emma removed her star necklace and so that the jewel could lay upon her thin gray sweater. Giving the crystal within a rub for good luck, Emma ascended the stairs.

"What are you doing?" Ciara said in a sharp whisper from behind.

"Nobody's home. I'm just taking a look," Emma said, making her way.

"No! No! This is what happened in Goldilocks. The bears found her and kicked her out of their home."

"Nope. They ate her."

Ciara's eyes widened. "They what?"

"In the original story the bears ate her."

Ciara let out a soft, nervous laugh that continued for far too long. She placed her back to the tree and crossed her arms, tighter than needs be, her eyes shifting about.

Reaching the first branch, Emma stepped off the stairs and onto a wooden ledge. A few steps more balance beam like cautious steps and she reached the platform. She pulled back the white muslin screen.

Inside the platform a few pillows and woven wool blankets were tossed about, as if those who slept there rather in the past hour had gotten up in a hurry. On the floor was a glowing ember, flashing on and off in a tiny, coal like glow. Holding the palm of her hand above the ember, Emma found that no heat seemed to emanate. Too curious to step away, Emma took the ember in hand to find that the device was cool and solid as a stone. The instant she wrapped her fingers around the ember, the device shook and then set out a substantial puff of white smoke.

Dropping the ember in surprise, Emma watched it fall between the muslin and the platform down to the hand trimmed grass below. The ember began to release strong jets of smoke that drifted into the air and began to take shape.

"Um, Emma! This rock is starting to spell."

Emma flew herself down the steps to join Ciara. "A smoke signal!" Emma said, watching the letter take a recognizable shape in the smoke. Each line of smoke was replaced the previous.

Quadrant One high alert!
Spiritual disturbance
East by Southeast, thirteen point two miles
Edge of Silver Thicket
Dispatch two Watchers

"Spiritual disturbance? Is that us?" Ciara said.

"Maybe. But if that was us, we would have been caught, right?" Emma said, waving her hand through the letters. The smoke letters fell apart and floated up into the air, evaporating into the sky. Emma picked up the ember, no longer glowing nor emanating smoke. She placed the device into her pocket, next to the knife.

"That thing is going to fill your coat up with smoke."

"I know. Then we'll know if another message is being sent out. "Emma adjusted the straps on her backpack. "Should we go?"

"Sure, let's go back," Ciara said.

Emma tugged Ciara back like a rubber band by the strap on across her shoulder. "We're not going back. Not yet."

"Fine," Ciara said, swinging around to look at the foot path that lead back to the forest entrance. "I don't see any…ah….Emma, look. Look!"

Emma turned to see at about three hundred feet or so down the path, two rather large men, their clothes a mix of forest green and brown camouflage, running towards the girls with all speed. They carried rifles, the hammers cocked back, ready to be fired.

"Run, Ciara!"

The rapid boot steps came closer, and louder in the silent forest.

"Instigator! Halt this instance," the one guard called.

Emma and Ciara took off running across the glade, away from the armed men. When the girls re-entered the forest, their feet flew like great athletes, passing by endless trees and what looked like two mounds with doors that led to some cavern below the forest floor. Puffing every usable ounce of oxygen in the fresh air, they pressed their muscles for all of their worth. Emma and Ciara dashed deeper into the forest, not daring to look back at the guards who ventured no further in their chase from the edge of the oval glade.

"Intruders! You will not journey far. Our confounders will trap you," the one guard said.

"There is no way you cannot escape their power. And then you shall answer to our company, you fools," the other guard said.

The further Emma and Ciara ran, the guards booming voices grew fainter, fading away into echoes. Then, with the silence in the forest that held an aura beyond this world, the girls felt as if they had stepped out onto the surface of the moon. They did not stop running through bracken, over fallen limbs and trunks of rotting trees until they were a little over a half mile from the glade.

Emma's lungs recovered from the sprint right after they stopped to rest. Ciara's chest was heaving, her breathe coming out in a wheeze.

"Are you okay?"

Ciara shook her head, trying to control her breathing. "Grab my inhaler...it's in the...side pocket."

Emma reached into Ciara's satchel to produce the medicine.

"Thanks. Cold air helps." Ciara took a few strong coughs and returned to controlled breathing.

"Maybe I shouldn't have pushed you too far, too fast."

"So far away from the guys with rifles?" Ciara said, shooting Emma a look.

"Alright, you got me there," Emma said, laughing to herself. "Who are those guys?"

"Like you said," Ciara said, her mouth muffled by the plastic inhaler tip she wrapped around her mouth. "They're guards." Pressing down on the medicine, Ciara breathed in the slow relief, tilting to the side for a second as her body balanced out.

Emma removed the canteen from her backpack. She took a long, satisfied chug before passing the cool water to Ciara.

"We should keep going," Emma said. Her eyes scanned for any sign of movement between the trees from the trail that they had just blazed. "Do you think those guys were soldiers? You know, like in the Army?"

Ciara shrugged, wiping water from her chin once she took a few satisfying drinks. The forest was still, ominous, the branches barely groaning, the air tight, scarcely moving in that area. Emma could sense her uneasy nerves. She couldn't shake the thought that in the tight grouping of ash trees ahead that there were eyes, following their every move. The light was close to pitch black as in a cave in that section. Emma's nerves couldn't ignore an unseen monitor watched every move they made.

"Why are those trees so close together?" Ciara said, turning her flashlight beams on the trunks of the massive ash trees ahead. They had grown in a patch that ran left to right in unseen distances to the north and south. The web of protruding bark on the bottom twenty feet of each limbless pine, save for the top, set off alarms in Emma's head, the puzzle of the security making sense.

"The trees are another gate," Emma said, shining her flashlight as well.

"What is?" Ciara said, placing her things away, her every step a cautious one as she joined Emma.

"Those pine trees. They are like the wall of redwoods outside the forest. This has to be another barrier."

The girls were beginning to see how small the space was in-between the gathering of ash trees, placed there not organically, but by careful genetic manipulation of nature by whomever resided beyond the wall of wood.

"Are we going to fit?" Ciara said

"We should. Take off your backpack."

Emma led the way through the maze, holding her backpack behind her, making herself as streamlined as possible in order to fit through. Ciara followed, struggling to keep up with Emma who bent and twisted her body as she side-stepped past the tree trunks. The further they went, the tighter the pine web had become, so constricting that an adult body would have felt a corset-like squeeze on their ribs. The girls could feel their shoulder blades and elbows scrape against the ragged bark that when torn from the tree in the dead air, seemed to echo like a demon's scream in a cavern. Emma couldn't help but to feel the goose bumps on her arm rise up, no matter how she ignored the faint, torturous screams of nature unkind.

"I can see the end," Emma said.

"Give it to me in feet!" Ciara said, huffing and puffing. "Ouch!" Her knuckles had scraped against the nearest pine, ripping her skin open. "Cripes! The bark is sharp as a knife."

A fifty-foot wide strip of grass and grouping of small shrubs laid in-between the ash tree maze and the next normal stretch of forest. At the last pine tree in the maze, Emma's bag became wedged in a space small enough for an infant. Stepping over her bag into the strip of grass, Emma pulled her bag through with a tearing sound. The jagged bark had ripped open the leather.

"What the? This bark IS sharp."

Ciara stepped onto the grass, flashing the flesh from her torn up knuckles. They were bleeding. "Yeah, I know!"

"Ghesh, Ciara. Let me see your hand," Emma said. She removed a thin white kitchen towel from her backpack to tear it in half, lengthwise. Getting her canteen back, Emma poured the cold water onto Ciara's hand, following up by pressing the cloth onto the wounds, making Ciara wince.

"Sorry. That stings," Ciara said, taking the cloth and wrapping it around her hand to secure the temporary bandage. "Thanks, Em."

"Sure. Come on, you had to admit this is an adventure so far."

"Totally an adventure," Ciara said, hesitating. "But no offense, we now have more questions than we did before. And now, we're off of the map. Do you even know where we are?"

"We're probably only a mile in. There are plenty of things to see. Besides, we're not even at…huh," Emma said, consulting an old pocket compass from her jacket. The needle did not fluctuate like a spinning top as it did at the entrance. The true north was clear, stable.

Emma held up the face of the flea market compass to Ciara. "This old piece of junk now works. Guess we're still going west!"

"Weird," Ciara winced, placing a finger in her ear. "Ouch, that's loud. You hear that, right?"

Emma looked to the forest beyond that separating strip of grass. A pitch, so disturbingly high, began to fill Emma's ears. "Are your ears ringing too?

Ciara looked around, a puzzled look about her face. "Yeah, they are. Kinda hurts." Ciara stuck her fingers in the other ear.

"Any better?" Emma said, copying her friend by plugging up her ear canals.

Ciara shook her head, her face showing the disturbance. "Okay, this is really starting to…OH MY GOD!" Ciara screamed, dropping to the ground, covering her ears.

The ringing, like when one's eardrums vibrate from some vociferous loud music, intensified in Emma's ears as well.

"My ears won't stop. NO! Please don't hurt, Emma." Ciara was in a fetal position on the ground, her face in a horrible mix of absolute emotional and physical pain. "She's my best friend. PLEASE DON'T HURT HER!"

"Ciara, I'm fine," Emma said, touching Ciara for comfort, her calm hands doing no good. "What's going on?"

The tenacity of the ringing increased, making Ciara whimper. Emma covered her ears and tried to focus through the pain. She closed her eyes and felt the strength her star gave her through the string that touched the skin of her neck. Then, an image, hazy and translucent, began to form in the darkness of Emma's mind, as if she was looking into a prism of the future. A voice, chilling and guttural, spoke to her.

YOU ARE NOT WELCOME

A flash of the Grant family home shot across her mind. Flames licked every room, torching every book and sacred nesting spot. She could almost hear the searing sound of flesh.

CONTINUE AND YOUR FEARS WILL COME TRUE

A flash appeared of Emma looking at an older, teenage version of herself in a graveyard. She stood before the headstones of Jonathan, Adacia and Bo, all six feet under freshly packed dirt.

I CAN SEE YOUR MIND

"No. No. This isn't real," Emma said, trying to keep her concentration. The ringing became fierce, to the point of an unsafe decibel level.

Another flash appeared in Emma's mind. She was no more than a year from her current age, her clothes torn and tattered, wandering in a field alone. Her face was gaunt, eyes bloodshot, sores on her skin bleeding; her body was quite close to death.

LEAVE AND DO NOT RETURN

"No! You're not real."

LEAVE THE FOREST

"NO! I WON'T!" Emma screamed, her voice shattering the connection of the horrible visions. The demonic voice did not return. However, the voracious ringing in her ears remained. Ciara was still on the ground, her body beginning to convulse. Emma knew she had to act. She knew there had to be a source. Touching her star, Emma looked amongst the trees beyond the rim of grass.

Woven between two branches of an oak tree was a tight grouping of string and copper wires. They seemed to twang and vibrate like plucked piano strings, despite the absence of wind or a visible hand. Pulling out Bo's pocket knife, Emma ran across the thorny juniper bushes in the strip to the trunk of the tree. Noticing there were notches in the bark to set her toes and fingers, Emma climbed and clawed her way up to the branch with the device.

"You must be a Confounder," Emma said, eyeing the device, remembering what the guards had shouted at her. Close up, the Confounder looked more like a Native American dream catcher.

The strings vibrated again. Ciara began to scream, tearing pouring down her face. "Please. I just want to see my Daddie...I'm sorry. We'll leave. We'll leave."

Emma drew the blade on the knife. Touching her blade to the star for good luck, the metal on the knife began to glow with a silvery/blue light. The neon glow filled the night, chasing away the shadows of this new world.

"That's new," Emma said, her eyes having gone wide.

Ciara screamed again. Her cries became so terrifying to Emma that she raised the knife up high. With one swift swipe, the glowing blade cut through the vibrating Confounder, heaving the device in two. Emma made quick work of the support strings, severing those as well. In a second, the ringing faded and then stopped altogether. Ciara's misery ended.

"Ciara!" Emma called, her legs wrapped around the limb. "Ciara?"

Standing up, looking woozier than an inebriant, Ciara regained her posture. Sniffing and wiping away tears, Ciara returned to her normal self.

"Emma? Are you okay? What happened?"

"Yeah. Look. I stopped the stupid thing!" Emma held up the dangling Confounder; a spoil of this journey. Cutting a piece of the brass string, Emma stuffed it in her pocket as a keepsake.

Ciara grabbed Emma's bag and dragged it over to the tree. Emma cut off another piece and let gravity take it down to Ciara below.

"This was making me cry?" Ciara fiddled with the odd looking monofilament string, a fine weave of golden wires mixing together.

"Has to be. The Confounder is another barrier or something." Emma slid herself backwards off of the limb. Careful, she climbed back down to Ciara.

"What was I saying?" Ciara said. "I swear I heard myself. I just don't remember."

"Seriously? Well, you said something about me, and then your Dad…"

"I said something about my Dad!" Ciara said, cutting Emma off. "I think I did…yeah. I wanted to see him."

"Where? In here?" Emma said, gesturing to the forest around them. "That's why you came along, isn't it." Emma remembered the name of the man, Jabari Inaya, which she sensed from Ciara's mind in the cavern of her father's shed and on that internet search at the school. "You think your Dad is in here, don't you?"

"No! That wasn't the only reason." Ciara said, hanging her head, looking embarrassed. She handed over Emma's backpack.

"Ciara, don't worry about that. I won't tell anyone."

"I know. I should have told you." Ciara dug her balled up fist into her jacket pocket. She produced that torn piece of paper she stole from Jonathan's cave. Emma's eyes went wide at the sight upon the page – a pencil sketch of a ring that was an exact match of the one Ciara wore on her finger.

"You think your Dad is in here, selling these somewhere?"

"Maybe. I kinda put two and two together I guess."

Emma threw her backpack on, placing her arms inside the snug straps. With care, Emma tucked the sketch of the ring back into Ciara's pocket.

"You ready to keep going?" Emma clicked on her flashlight.

"As long as there's no more of those torture machines." Ciara hit the tree with the butt of her flashlight, looking a bit exasperated.

The two girls trekked on into the forest. Their artificial beams from their flashlights were about to prep them for the sight of the next obstacle.

Emma and Ciara walked on for close to a half hour. Though nighttime, the girls had seen no more than a few nocturnal animals rush through the batches of leaves. From time to time an owl hooted across the expanse, placing Ciara on edge.

The trees had begun to change from ash to scatterings of smaller trees amongst the redwoods and hundred year old oaks. Emma shined her flashlight upon the small trees, which resembled the gigantic bonsai sequoia which she came across in the entrance glade. Though autumn, the leaves had not fallen from the branches.

Emma turned the flashlight in the nearest mystery tree that sat at the edge of a small patch of prairie grass. A fair amount of breeze came in and down through the wide open space between the networks of tree tops. Emma's light showed what her eyes had managed to catch in the wood of this mysterious tree. The bark appeared to be infused with hundreds of silver stands, comfortable resting into the wood as if they had grown that way from seed.

"That is so cool!" Emma said, touching the silver tree. She found that the thin layers of bark twisted around the tree and then about every branch and limb like a candy cane. Emma rapped her knuckles on the wood. "Holy cow!" Emma said, drawing her wounded bones back. "That tree feels thicker than iron on a tank."

Ciara leaned forward and tapped her wrapped, healing bloody knuckles on the tree as well. She drew back her hand, shaking and bouncing on her toes, wincing.

"Why did you do that?"

"I don't know. I thought you were kidding."

Letting out a small giggle, Emma looked up as the next soft breeze that came in from above to blow her hair back. Using a tie from her coat pocket, Emma placed her hair, now stuck up with a bit of a leaf or two, into a pony tail.

The clouds had begun to part. The full moon reared his face. The celestial light reached the silver trees, and the strands of silver in the wood began to glow. Then, like a light bulb gaining strength, the leaves infused with even smaller strands of silver filaments, began to shine, mirroring the moonlight.

Emma and Ciara's jaws dropped when they witnessed every silver tree light up in their vicinity. Close to thirty in all came alight. Emma clicked off her flashlight. There was no need for them now that the forest was illuminated so well that Emma and Ciara could read by the soft light.

"This is what I was looking for!" Emma said. She ran her curious fingers along the glowing bark. "This light is what I saw all these years. This is it. Silver trees!"

The forest of silver leaves was beginning to speak to Emma. In her nerves, and even deeper in her blood, she felt the world of her dreams, of tales, come to fruition. Connected to some deep chasm within this nature, Emma's body warmed to the thought of this enlightenment. The wood had already awoken and yet then, with an abyss of tranquility in her soul, Emma felt her mind peak into another plane of existence, another layer of this Earth. She did not hear Ciara until her friend shook her out of the easily achieved meditation.

"Emma. Emma. Look! Over there. What is that?"

In the distance to the west, between the scattered redwoods and silver trees, were three spheres of blinding indigo and emerald lights that travelled through the air.

"Quick. Hide," Emma said, pulling Ciara down by her jacket.

The girls took cover, crouching behind a trunk of a silver tree. They watched as the spheres of light, flush with familiar colors of the forest, flew closer.

"Should we run?"

"No," Emma said, her instincts feeling certain, her nerves and mind calm. "I think we're alright."

The lead sphere began to flicker and combust like that of a firework after the wick had been lit. In a flash of silver and sapphire light that almost blinded the girls, the ball of energy disappeared.

In the place of the light was an eight-foot tall woman, holding a bow. Her sallow skin and radiant beauty was fairer than anyone Emma had ever seen. She was adorned head to toe in a warrior outfit, made of individual plates of finely polished armor above a tight blue fabric. Her eyes, devoid of pupils, were luminous, glowing like the moon. Her skin gave off a glittery sheen, as if energy was pulsating just below the stark white skin.

"Who is she?" Ciara whispered.

Emma removed her Grandfather's book from her backpack. From memory, she flipped to one of many pages bookmarked with scraps of yellow paper. There, in the illustration on page thirty, was a creature that then stood before Emma and Ciara that night. They noticed the mighty woman's narrow ears that led up to pointed tops and the visible blue aura that surrounded her, drawn no different than on the page.

"Ciara...I think she's a Faerie."

Chapter Eight
The Watchers of the Wood

The Faerie woman's faultless posture seemed to extend her frame and dwarf the girls, even at the distance of twenty feet. At first, her eyes scanned left to right, more microscopically aware of the surroundings than Emma was. The girls did their best to hide behind the trunk of the silver tree. Their stealth was to no avail. The Faerie began to stare in their direction.

"Come out, children," the Faerie woman said, her soft voice resonating with distance, like when ones shouts are faintly heard over a outstretched field.

Ciara nudged Emma forward, already holding up her hands in surrender. Emma pushed Ciara's hands down and remained, preventing the feigned attempt at admitting defeat where there was none.

"We can see though water, wood and the silver leaves, and of course, we can see you," the Faerie woman said. "I can feel a familiar heart, there. Come out to see mine, little Emma."

"Emma," Ciara whispered. "How does she know you?"

"Dunno. Stay here for a minute," Emma said, no longer able to resist coming out.

Appearing on the other side of the silver tree, Emma made direct eye contact with the Faerie woman. Emma knew this creature of fantasy had finally come true when the blue pupils of the Faerie's eyes danced like starlight amongst the gleaming whites of the eyes. For Emma, a dimensional window, an abyss of knowledge and nirvana, existed in those abyssal eyes that never wavered nor blinked.

"I want to ask you, that is, if you don't mind," Emma said, a bit uneasy in the woman's commanding presence.

"Indeed, I am a Faerie, as you call us. Esylltora is my name."

"Nice to meet you," Emma said, giving a little bow. She remembered from one of her books about Faeries that one should give a courteous bow. The gesture seemed to work. The astute Esylltora bowed back to Emma.

"You are fairer than I remembered," Esylltora said.

"Than you remember?" Emma said, her mind shifting into that chess board of hers, sorting out the facts. "So, you know my name. How long have you known me?"

"All of your life, little Alastar."

"All my life? Wait! You just called me Alastar!" Emma edged forward to confront Esylltora.

Ciara took in a sharp breath, whispering. "Emma! Don't piss off the giant woman!"

"Shush! What does that mean, Esyllktora? Did you write me that letter?"

Esylltora did not answer back. Her eyes and senses became fixed on a faint sound in the distance of the darkened forest.

Emma turned to view north into the darkened forest with Esylltora. "What's that sound?" Emma said.

A faint drone of howling came from the north. As the howl increased, Emma could see little patterns, of solid black and gray vapor clouds flying towards them with an alarming speed.

"Take your friend, Emma, and lay close to the ground," Esylltora said with urgency. Removing her bow from a pack on her shoulder, Esylltora drew an arrow from the tight bundle of quiver. Placing the arrow on the bow, she drew back on the string. The arrow turned from a crafted piece of wood into a fiery crimson deliverer of death.

"Ciara. Come here," Emma said, waving her over. Ciara ran over and grabbed Emma for protection at the sight of white and grey shrouded creatures that approached. Their blood curdling screams from wide open mouths and loose jaws, loud as the piercing ring of the confounders, shattered the beauty of the pristine forest air. Getting within fifty feet of Emma and Ciara, darkness cascaded and the silver trees went dim.

Esylltora fired her radiating arrow at the charging patterns of grim shadows. Her arrow hit the first of what looked like ten vapor creatures square in the chest. The crimson punisher set the creature ablaze, making it scream a deflated cry. The demon evaporated into piles of ash that collected on the forest floor like at the bottom of an extinguished campfire. Emma caught a glimpse of its face – bony, drained of life, and with eyes the solid color of running blood. The memory of her vision at Woodland Academy had crept back. They were the Phantoms.

"Get down!" Emma said, pulling Ciara down flat to the ground. Just as they hit the hard ground, the nine surviving phantoms flew past, tossing up the fallen leaves as they glided a few feet above the forest floor. When the shrouds passed over the girls, Emma swore she could hear the faint, muffled voices of desperate men and women screaming for liberation.

"Stay safe, Emma. And use your star," Esylltora said. Her body became a blinding pattern of translucent light once again. With this order to Emma, Esylltora changed from the humanoid/elf form back into a small sphere of glowing blue light. In a split second, Esylltora took off, her white and emerald companions flying after her.

Standing up, Emma could see they flew faster than the phantoms. The faeries were beginning to surround them in a triangular ambush in a low area up ahead where the forest dipped down.

"Come on," Emma said, taking off after the faeries.

"Wait up," Ciara said, grunting as she got up. "You really threw me down."

"Didn't I save your life?" Emma said, slowing to a jog to wait for Ciara.

"Fine! You're 2 and 0 for tonight."

Emma and Ciara ran a good hundred yards to a spot in the forest where the elevation dipped with a tiny sloping ridge, down to a wedge of open land where the hill turned up thereafter to the regular forest floor. Much like with a fireworks show, the girls were amazed as the three faeries shot jets of their unique colored light from a triangular defense position, trapping the phantoms in confusion.

"Are these the phantoms...from your vision," Ciara said, trying to catch her breath.

"I think so. Looks like the faeries are at war with them."

The phantoms then developed an attack position, forming a phalanx with their mangled, undead spirit bodies. They charged the nearest faerie, Esylltora's emerald companion. The phantoms overwhelmed the faerie to a crumpled up place on the ground, pushing west into the forest with all speed. Esylltora and her remaining glowing companion fired their energized arrows from their spheres of light, giving chase once more. The overwhelmed emerald Faerie floated up from the ground in a daze to cathartically follow in the wake of his superiors.

Emma and Ciara followed, taking care to not tumble down the small ridge. As they powered their way up the other side, their legs burned. They were blind to the danger that stayed behind.

Like an itch in the back of her mind, Emma threw out her arm to stop Ciara from advancing. Emma felt a reverberation in the air that was unfamiliar, cold, and malevolent.

Up ahead, a phantom glided down from the darkness of the canopy. The flesh torn feet, bones sticking out, crunched as they landed upon the ground. With his back to the girls, this phantom, more an emaciated human form than a vapor spirit, threw its dead, pale hands out, feeling his surroundings. His lungs were gasping and rattling with long, deep breaths.

Then, Emma couldn't help but to shudder when blood dripped down the hand from inside the black cloak, pleasing the creature as his fists clenched with a deep, satisfying breath.

The phantom turned on an axis and reared his death's head. Ciara screamed; her face contorted into absolute fear. The eyes, so piercing and volcanic in their stare, began to radiate heat - what Emma thought might be radiation. With one swift movement, the phantom leaned forward to not give his own battle cry but an exact, if not shriller and more terrifying version of Ciara's own scream.

"It copied my voice!" Ciara said, beginning to tremble. "Emma! It copied my scream!"

"Not good. Run!" Emma pushed Ciara back to where they came from. The girls took off along the ridge into the north of the forest. Remembering Esylltora's advice, Emma took out her star.

The phantom screamed out in Ciara's voice again, so loud the piercing decibels could have broken glass. Emma glanced back to catch the phantom's gaunt, decomposed feet tramp the ground harder with each step, gaining on the girls.

"Uh oh. Run faster, Ciara!"

"I'm running as fast as I can."

Emma took one look back at the phantom and let out a little yelp. Her feet began to fly with no concern for her muscles.

Emma kept up a few feet behind. She could feel the air change on her skin, in an insufferable heat and density like that of pressure on one's lungs as Emma knew the phantom was closing in. One look over her shoulder confirmed this. Knowing that she and Ciara would soon be overcome, Emma reacted.

At about the time the phantom with its blood stained, terribly thin hand was about to claim another prized soul, Emma jumped on Ciara's back and using the weight of her body and backpack, to send her and Ciara's bodies tumbling down the diagonal ridge to the bottom, thirty-feet below.

The phantom, flying with tremendous speed, too concerned with the hunt, did not expect Emma to be so spry. When the girls tumbled down the ridge in an instant, the phantom did not look ahead. The half-alive demon collided with an oak tree, the translucent form shattering in a kinetic crash with nature, cutting through the tree and landing in the dirt on the opposite side with a tremendous thud that echoed throughout the forest floor like a minor tremor. The severed trunk, with outstretched branches, came crashing down within an arm's reach of Emma and Ciara. The phantom remained in several clouds of structured vapor on the forest floor, wounded but not defeated.

"Are you nuts?" Ciara said, shoving Emma and spitting out a leaf as she spoke.

"3 and 0 for tonight. You're welcome," Emma said.

The girls moaned as they stood up to stretch their battered bones. Leaves and bits of shrubs from the forest covered their jackets and hair.

"Should we go back? I mean, is that thing dead?" Ciara said, casting a frightened look over the crest of the ridge.

Emma looked east to the other end of the ridge. Slow and steady, she raised her hands up in surrender. "I think moving is a bad idea right now."

Ciara turned and jumped back at the sight of a husky man of what looked like Scandinavian ethnicity with shoulder length blond hair tied back. He wore autumn colored camouflage, pointing a steady rifle in their direction from the top of the ridge.

"We surrender!" Ciara said, throwing up her arms to the sky.

The guard held up a long finger and shushed them. He gestured over to the opposite side of the ridge where the phantom began to reform from the dirt.

"The phantom?" the guard said, his voice in a near whisper.

Emma and Ciara nodded. The guard urgently waved the girls over, lowering his rifle. Picking up their backpacks, the girls hurried over. Up close Emma could see beyond the three days of stubble and distinct jaw bone, a gentle face. Out of his front vest pocket, the guard removed what looked like a small, narrow firework and handed the mechanism over to Emma.

"I don't know what you children are doing out here," the guard said.

"We came in the forest, Mr..." Emma said before the hurried guard cut her off.

"Captain Erik Rasmussen of the Eastern Watchers of the Wood. Stay here. I need you to set off that flare while I subdue the phantom. Can you do this?"

"Yes. Hurry up. It's re-forming," Emma said, pointing over to the phantom rising from the soil, close to collecting itself into one, cohesive form yet again.

Taking careful aim with his rifle with a slow exhale, Erik pressed the trigger. A bullet sliced through the air with a white phosphorous trail and collided with the chest of the phantom like a stone being thrown into water. The phantom became frozen as its body swayed in the breeze like a kite on a lazy Sunday.

"Light the flare, girl!"

"Right here?" Emma said, pointing the flare up.

"No, not like that," Erik said, lowering her arm.

"See, you have to tell me these things."

Erik sighed, short on patience. "Hit the bottom with your opposite palm, wait a few seconds and then point the flare to where the signal lights can make it beyond the canopy...like over there." He pointed a section nearby them where the open sky and stars could be seen.

Emma ran over to the tiny opening under the trees. Erik reloaded his breech loading rifle from the back with a red bullet that seemed to contain a jelly-like substance inside. Rifle at the ready, Erik went over to the paralyzed phantom.

"Can I fire it off? Ciara said, standing beside Emma, looking up as she did.

"Did you forget that you and fireworks are not good friends," Emma said, holding back a laugh.

Ciara's eyes widened, looking frustrated. "Do you have to be right about everything tonight?"

"Pretty much. Here we go."

Hitting the bottom of the flare with her palm, the device began to shudder. Emma vibrating arm held tight and pointed to the sky as the tip began to light up. Like a round from a military mortar, the flare pumped out a shot up past the canopy. At about a few hundred feet above the forest, the round exploded with the resounding boom of a firework, sending out dozens of little beacons of flashing red and blue lights in every direction. As they illuminated the night sky, the little flashing flares fell to Earth. The flare shuddered and pumped out another round, exploding with another round of beacons.

Emma and Ciara looked up, their faces capturing the light that gravity lowered to the ground. The majesty of night turning into day lasted for a mere few minutes when another gunshot shattered the serenity.

The girls turned to see a trail of smoke emanating from Erik's rifle. He had just fired another round of the subduing substance into the chest of the phantom. The demon growled with the sound of suffocation as it fell to the ground, stuck to the dirt.

"Did you kill it?" Emma said.

"No. My troops and I merely paralyze them," Erik said, as he reloaded his rifle. "Remain where you are, girls. My patrol will be here in due time."

True to his words, within ten minutes the in-step march of boot steps from platoon of about twenty men and women, dressed in similar military camouflage of the forest that obscured their approach, came running to Emma, Ciara and Erik's position. Their rifles were armed and their fingers on the edge of the triggers. As Emma watched these soldiers approach, she couldn't help but to sense there was a different aura to their bodies; a more earth bound presence.

"Two Watchers, regolith bullets at the ready. Come to my position. Others, take care of the girls," Erik said.

"Take care of us? Whoa, wait!" Emma said, holding her hands out, protecting her and Ciara.

With trained precision, the guards surrounded Emma and Ciara in a circle. One skinny young man, not a day past nineteen, raised his rifle, prompting Emma to wrap her arms around Ciara at the sight of the cold steel of the barrel staring them down. Ciara turned her head inwards to Emma.

"Don't shoot!" Emma said, holding tight to her best friend.

All of the sudden a whooshing sound, similar to that of a sword slash, sliced through the air, moving past Emma's right ear. The anxious soldier had his rifle thrown from his hands by some invisible force.

"Now you've done it, rookie," said one of the Latino looking female guards, hissing at him. "You knew that wasn't right, even when Erik wasn't looking."

"Yes, Sergeant," the skinny man said in compliance though his teeth, shaking a bit as he stood at attention, aware of the woman that approached.

Walking towards them was a woman in her late thirties with long, wavy black hair and high cheekbones. She held a small crystal orb, outstretched in the palm of her hand.

"Do not harm these children. They are pure souls," the woman said, a clear presence of an Irish accent about her.

"With respect, they are not, Vice-Governor. They look human," said the pig faced, trigger happy soldier.

Forcing out her orb at the subordinate soldier, the woman, by some spell, removed the belt of bullets from the soldier, letting them fly over to the nearest obedient soldier. "We do not shoot humans. By the Gods, where is this hatred coming from these days?"

"Please don't kill us," Ciara said, her fingers holding onto Emma's arms like glue.

"You need not worry, little miss. What is your name?"

"Ciara."

"And you, blue eyed girl. What is your…wait," the woman said, hesitating to respond for Emma could sense a premonition on her lips. "Your face is familiar to me." The woman placed her orb in a leather pouch that rested on her hip. "How do I know your face?"

"I'm sorry. I've never met you before," Emma said.

"I think we have…" the woman pointed her long fingers to Emma's neck, her eyes beginning to widen. "My God!" She whispered.

She sprung forward and tucked away Emma's jewel underneath Emma's sweater. "Oh dear, child, haven't I told you to not leave the house of Joseph."

Emma and Ciara gave each other confused looks in unison. The lady held Emma even closer with one hand as she gestured Erik over with her free arm.

"Siobhan?" Erik said, looking as suspicious as the rest of the curious troop. "Do these children belong to you?"

"Of course, I have only had them in foster care for a few days between me and Chief of Staff Joseph. Hardly recognized the little cherubs…"

Siobhan's voice trailed off in Emma's ears, only to be replaced by whisper of this elegant woman in her head. Emma swallowed hard for she knew, for the first time in her life, that she had found another that possessed similar abilities.

"You would do well with your friend to keep calm, quiet and carry on with my lead. Do not let them see your star, little Emma!"

Chapter Nine
A Guardian's Midnight Tale

Siobhan's eyes were a mirror unto her emotions, absent of any malice when they graced Emma, stern and commanding for the troops who were at times wary of staring back. Nodding along to the telepathic directions Siobhan poured into Emma's mind, the little Blue Eyes whispered to Ciara.

"Do what I do. This woman is her to help us."

The guards stood down, holstering their weapons. Some of them mumbled phrases that Emma could pick up about the degenerate nature of "those human girls."

Erik approached Emma and shook a stern finger at her. "You should not be leaving your caretaker, little human. The Vice-Governor was at least kind enough to take in your homeless souls."

Siobhan slapped a hard hand on Erik's shoulders. "I thought we had talked about this last week? Enough already. They are nothing more than lost, confused girls that need some shelter."

"I am sorry," Erik said, shooting a glance at the soldiers in his platoon that started snickering at the less than professional interactions of him and Siobhan. "We should escort the children back to Adoette."

"I could not agree more," Siobhan said, allowing her guard to come down as she rubbed Erik's shoulder. "Come girls. Let us be off."

Emma knew she had to play the orphan part. Thinking back to a Charles Dickens novel she once read, Emma glanced at Siobhan with dough eyes and tugged on her sleeve. "Our tummies are so empty. Where are you taking us, Miss Siobhan?"

Siobhan looked hard at Emma as if she was stifling a laugh. "We will walk just under a mile to the Eastern outpost. We will leave other matters to the Republic's finest," Siobhan said, looking over her shoulder to the ridge where the subdued phantom laid.

The company of soldiers split into two squads at a whim at Siobhan's glance. The one squad made a bee line through the trees to the phantom. The one female sergeant, who Emma could see on her shoulder tag next to a flag patch, designed with a tree, was named Sergeant Morales.

"Execute the burning of the body immediately, Sergeant," Siobhan said.

"Yes, Vice-Governor!"

"Remaining company, let us depart."

The Watchers, led by Siobhan, fell into formation. One of the guards was careful to load a clear bag of red powder into a handheld mortar. Emma guessed this to be the equalizer that would eradicate the creature. Soon, the danger of only a few minutes before was left behind in a maze of trees in the northbound trek into the massive forest.

Moonlight guided the way of the company across the forest near the midnight hour. As much as Emma would have liked to admit she was a girl of boundless energy, her legs were beginning to get heavy and sore. She could tell Ciara was well past this point, yawning so deep that Emma swore the air was being stolen from her own breathing space. Emma made sure to tease Ciara when her eyes watered every time she yawned, as if she was crying.

After a short hike up an incline in the forest, Emma and the troops made their way past two jagged boulders that sat at the edge of a small, elevated plateau in the forest.

After passing these rocks, complete doorways leading to subterranean storehouses, the outpost came into view.

The Eastern Outpost was a wooden complex, the timbers gleaming in a maple lacquer and from the silver trees in which they were carved. There were three levels of the outpost with two gated doors that led to the forest floor and a long staircase that snaked around the building like a vine, stopping at certain platforms that led to rooms on the second and third floors. Emma took special note of the triangular roof, shaped to look like the tip of a pine tree. Sticking out of the top of the roof, being tossed by a lazy wind, was an emerald flag. On the flag there was a full moon surrounded by a constellation of four stars on the top left. In the middle, a shimmering silver tree stood – the beloved symbol of the land as Emma had guessed.

"Is it time for bed?" Ciara said. Emma covered her mouth before she unleashed her grizzly bear yawn again. "Stop. I don't care if I sound like a guy. I'm tired."

Siobhan spoke to a few guards near the entrance. She gesturing from the girls to the trees did so.

"What are they saying?" Ciara said. "And when are you planning on telling me what's going on?"

"I can hear her voice in my head. I can read thoughts she sent to me on purpose," Emma said.

"Whoa! Kind of like you can do?"

"I think like that, yeah. Now shush! Let me hear them," Emma's audible ears began to tune into Siobhan, even though she was more than a hundred away. From what Emma could pick up, she could tell Siobhan did not wish to follow through with protocol and give the girls "a memory dusting." Before Siobhan left, she ordered the guard to make contact with a woman that Emma became more and more curious of.

"I imagine you two are tuckered out," Siobhan said, her arms swaying as she made her way to the girls.

"Who's this Lady Eleanor?" Emma asked.

"Lady...wait, how did you hear that?" Siobhan said, looking amazed.

"You should have whispered."

"We were whispering."

Ciara let out a tiny, almost dunce-like laugh, looking at Emma with admiration. "Nice! So cool."

"Cool," Siobhan said, shaking her head. "You people and your slang."

"You people?" Ciara said, her eyebrow raised at Siobhan.

"No offense, my dear. I am glad you followed my lead back there," Siobhan said, her eyes studying Emma. "I suppose you have questions, yes?"

Emma remained adamant to discover more and she stepped forward, her eyes never wavering from Siobhan's. "So who's this Eleanor?"

"The Governor of our land," Siobhan said, quite proud. Siobhan hesitated to speak as she tossed Ciara a sympathetic glance at another yawn, her eyes watering yet again. "Ciara, I can understand if you wish to get to bed. Come now."

"What about Emma?" Ciara said, being led away by Siobhan.

Siobhan held her hand out to Emma, inviting her to follow. "She and I have to speak in private. Hand me your bag, Emma. I'll bring it up to the room we reserve for guest travelers at Fort Miwok. Will a goose feather bed be to your liking?"

Emma and Ciara looked at each other, a little surprised. The glint they caught in each other's eyes, followed by a devious smirk, championed their desires to push their good accommodations.

"I like hot chocolate before I go to bed."

"Yes, and a bubble bath," Ciara said, "with massages and room service."

Siobhan placed her hands on her hips, so very aware of the girls playing her. "Room service, huh? What do you think you are, a Queen?"

"No," Ciara said, letting out a tiny, nervous laugh. "We were just kidding. Can we still get cocoa?"

"I believe that can be arranged. I hope the bed will be comfortable enough."

"You could lay me on a rock right now and I'd sleep on it," Ciara said.

Siobhan laughed out loud, her lungs grabbing at the air as she chuckled. For the first time that night, thanks, to Siobhan's genuine ear-to-ear smile, Emma began to relax for the first time in days.

After slipping off her shoes and tossing her coat onto one of the four carved oak bedposts, Emma slid her body under a white as snow blanket. Siobhan was kind enough to draw the cozy wool up to Emma's neck.

"You have become such a beautiful child," Siobhan said, placing aside a strand of hair that feel over Emma's left eye.

"Thank you." Emma thought at first that this stranger that she had just met was being rather forward. Naturally, Emma defected into inquiry. "Do you have a girl too?"

Siobhan shied away. "I do not have any children."

Seeing how this bothered Siobhan, Emma sat up. "Is that why you said we were your new foster children?"

"Perhaps," Siobhan said, her voice terse. "I take in foster human children before they are adopted by people who can take care of them. This sets a good example as well in my Vice-Governor position."

Siobhan removed the book of tales, *The Howl of the Undiscovered*, from Emma's open backpack. "Read yourself to sleep. I am sure these tales will get you to a slumber land."

Emma took the book, opening it to a place in the middle, bookmarked with a scrap piece of yellow construction paper from school. "Ever read this book?"

"Yes, I have! That was one of my favorite books when I grew up in Glencar Aisling."

"Glencar...wait, I've heard that name before!"

"I am sure you have," Siobhan said, tucking in the covers closer to Emma's body. "We shall leave that all until tomorrow. The last thing your mind needs before sleep is a bounty of questions."

Emma leaned up, unable to resist. "Siobhan, you know who I am, don't you?"

"So much for the questions."

"Tell me...please. Am I a freak? An alien? A beast?"

Siobhan forced Emma back down under the covers. "A beast? At your petite size? Emma, beyond a human and a perceptive telepath, I am unsure of your true nature as you are. Just keep that jewel hidden. I cannot say if one of my soldiers will be villainous and try to steal that valuable jewel from your neck if you continue to parade it around."

Emma tucked away the Alastar under her sweater, patting it down. "Safe and sound."

"Good. I will help you on your journey, little Emma…starting tomorrow! Now be a good girl and sleep."

Siobhan departed from the room and walked down the winding steps of the outpost to the forest floor before Emma could initiate her usual rapid fire inquires further. Emma felt like wishing Siobhan "good night". Yet, she didn't want to keep her from her obvious duties on a night rife with domestic security issues for that forest.

Across the room Ciara snorted in her sleep, turning over in a bed identical to Emma's. Ciara was well into her dreams. Over the next hour, Emma stifled giggles at Ciara, not desiring to end Ciara's unawareness of the midnight speeches she gave in her deep sleep. "Okay, let's get that cat and put it into a ball….of course I love chicken strips…You're so funny Emma, you should do dancing on Broadway." Eventually, Ciara ended her ramblings to give Emma concentrated peace.

Emma ran her fingers along the headboard adorned with stars that were alight with a soft light was imbedded amongst the carved branches, fashioned out of wood by some master craftsman. After endless minutes of distraction, Emma shut the book and placed it back on the loose top of her backpack. The autumn air drifting in was a fair reminder that she was far too enticed by the land that Emma suspected so little had seen.

Pulling the smooth wool over her shoulders, Emma slipped down and onto her side on a bed so accommodating to the curvature of any body, her muscles were at ease. As her head rested on the pillow, drifting to sleep, Emma began to hear a rag-tag group of voices below, just beside the outpost. Emma listened to the Watchers of the Wood as they serenaded the night, accompanied by a guard plucking a guitar, with a bluesy song from a world Emma was just beginning to greet.

> Down in the Silver City
> Walking down those roads so free
> Down in the Silver City
> The rivers seem to flow just for you and me
> So many memories through the years
> Ain't no place in the New World I'd rather be…

Soon after the serenade, Emma had fallen asleep into a series of dreams she would not remember come morning. In her slumber, she did not notice *The Howl of the Undiscovered* roll off of her backpack and onto the floor, propping open to an unread chapter called the *The Firefly Hills*. The chapter illustration was of three spheres of light levitating from a glittering cavern. A young Sorcerer stood before them in awe as he touched a metal necklace, designed with an image of angelic light pouring out from underneath the ocean, leading up to the Giant's Causeway in Ireland. The lead sphere was turning into a Faerie, who wore a golden crown and bore translucent gleam of blue and silver. The Faerie was Queen Esylltora.

A stone's throw from the outpost away a rather angelic voice carried throughout the forest. The ethereal light of the creature became a lamp in the midnight.

Down a series of hewn wooden steps placed into a rough angled ridge, Siobhan waited alone at the apex of a flat, oval glade. A great sphere of blue light rested on the highest branch on the opposite end of the glade, waiting like a perched owl.

The singing, harmonious, deep and transcending, carried on in a language of ancients.

Éist leis an paidir Sorcerer's!

Is féidir leat a chloisteáil trí fhiáine;

Beidh siad ag sábháil ndán dúinn despair.

Is féidir linn Sábháilte codlata thíos faoi chúram thy

The creature descended into the circle under the veil of stars between the wood. The song grew faint in the descent. All was silent save for the graceful breath of the forest.

In one instantaneous flash of a blinding white light so stark that Siobhan had to cover her eyes, the sphere disappeared. A beautiful faerie woman stood, her dress a series of intertwined blue and white fabrics that glowed like a candle. She wore a crown of translucent gold.

"We have had some surprises tonight, Esylltora."

"As I have seen. They are watching for her."

"I've had my suspicions too of curious eyes these past weeks. I will reach Governor Lady Eleanor when the sun rises."

"Please do my child. We must keep Lady Emma secret and her Alastar jewel safe. We cannot have others corrupting her abilities before we can harness them."

With a bow, Siobhan held a sincere hand to her heart. "On my honor, for the Republic, I will earn Emma's trust and keep her close until the revelation is made."

Chapter Ten
Further into the Forest

A mere few hours after the dawn of the new day, Emma and Ciara sat at a dining table wedged in a corner between two windows at the lower level of the outpost. Emma had let her damp hair down to dry out from her visit to the cleansing room. Both Emma and Ciara admitted in their individual visits to this bathroom of sorts that they had little understanding of how the sink, toilet and warm stone basin for cleaning one's self much like a bathtub, operated. Siobhan was kind enough to show the girls how to operate these. She had also brought each of them flower petals that emitted unnaturally strong potpourri in which to rub on their clothes. Much to Ciara's luck she was stopped in her confusion just in time by Siobhan for not using the sink like a bidet.

The detectable scents of a hearty breakfast filtered over to the dining tables. When a rather lanky middle aged man came out of the kitchen holding up a plate of eggs with fresh herbs and a hollandaise sauce on one plate and a colorful variety of fresh fruit on another, the five Watchers of the Wood dropped their conversations and parked their bottoms onto the benches next to Emma and Ciara. The girls held up a fork and knife in each hand like the hungry orphans they were playing with saucer eyes, ready to devour. However, the much larger and forceful hands of the male and female guards pushed past the girls, filling up their plates.

"Ease up, ya vultures," the tall chef said, his voice rather high-pitched. "Allow our guests to take the first choices."

"Too late," said the boyish guard from the previous night, his mouth chomping on runny eggs, some of the yolk spilling onto his chin.

Erik took a seat across from the girls, greeting the boyish slob with a look of distain. "Private Ignatius, your table habits are worse than your trigger finger as of late." Erik held out his right hand; several fingers bandaged up with a white medical tape of sorts. "Serve yourself, girls. You're capable."

"Thanks, Erik," Emma said, spooning and egg and fruit onto her plate.

"We apologize for being hasty," said Sergeant Morales. She was kind enough to be courteous and fill up Ciara's dish.

When Emma and Ciara both had their meals, they did not eat for the size and splendor of the giant single egg in the center, three times the size of an over easy chicken egg, looked intimidating.

"Eat up, girls. We have a fair march ahead of us today." Erik began to follow his fellow Watchers by digging into the carbohydrate filled plates in-between downing glasses of clear water and golden juices. "Humans can be weaker, you know."

"Are these people aliens?" Ciara whispered to Emma. "Why do they keep calling us humans?"

"Maybe cause we are and they aren't? Dunno," Emma whispered back, her hand over her mouth, acting as if she was chewing.

Emma and Ciara used their fork to break off a piece of the egg. They turned to each other's delighted faces once the bite was taken, all of the untainted, unique flavors of the land, set apart from the world they grew up in. Emma couldn't hold back her manners as her taste buds experienced the sugared cranberries, the apple tarts, and milk that was fresh enough to taste the grass the animal ate - each flavor was distinct, almost devoid of any man made chemical. During this bliss, Emma made a point of eavesdropping on Erik and Sergeant Morales.

"Why did it take two hours to notify Lady Eleanor about the girls?" Morales said.

"You know why," Erik said, grumbling.

"Marrigain…I don't know how a Mage like her can be so unprofessional and yet appear as if she's made of gold to the public. Remind me why we have elections again?"

Erik tore off a piece of soda bread and used it to soak up the yolk left on his plate. "The right people are in the right places," Erik said, waving the bread around. "At least in most cases."

"Like Siobhan?"

"Yes, like Siobhan. Thank God she won the Vice-Governor role. She needed some happiness after that fool Hector broke her heart."

Morales laughed and nudged Erik, whose bulky body, wide shoulders and all, moved but an inch. "So are you going to sweep in there and finally take Siobhan off of her feet?"

"You like Siobhan?" Emma said, flat out loud, a piece of tart still in her mouth.

The entire table fell silent. All eyes were on the red-faced Erik, who proceeded to fidget with his napkin. Morales gave Emma a little appreciative wink.

"Ah-hem!" Erik cleared his throat, not looking up from his food. "Mind your plates, ya nosy bunch."

"Yes, Sir, Erik," the troops replied, doing a horrible job of holding back their laughter as they finished their breakfasts.

"You," Erik said, pointing to Morales, "You are lucky we are friends. And you, little Emma. You're lucky Siobhan has a kind enough heart to take in you and your friend."

Emma nudged Ciara to play along. Ciara, munched down her slice of apple.

"Oh yeah, we are. Siobhan is so nice with her maids and feather pillows...ouch!"

Emma elbowed Ciara as she coughed into her hands. "Over the top!"

Erik didn't seem to notice. He leaned into whisper to Ciara. "So Siobhan finally bought those feather pillows, eh?"

The company, near the brink of tears, held back their laughter about as well as a dam ready to spew water. Erik growled and slammed his hand down, rattling the girls glasses on the table.

"All of you be ready in ten minutes," Erik said, marching away.

"Oh, Captain, come on..." one of the soldiers moaned.

"Nine minutes, now."

"Yes Captain fluffy pillow," one soldier whispered, making the others squint with intense laughter.

Emma returned to eating, feeling guilty for her big mouth.

"Do not feel bad, Emma. You just helped us dig out something from Erik we have been waiting to hear for months," Morales said.

Ciara chimed in as she licked her fingertips clean. "Is he is love with Siobhan?"

"I would say so but even with Erik being one of my close friends, I still couldn't get him to confess..." Sargent Morales' eyes fixed on Ciara's hands. "My, what is that on your finger?"

Confused, Ciara looked to her ring. "This? It was a gift from my Dad."

Emma leaned in, knowing she had to do her part to pry. "Is this ring special or something?"

Morales held out her hand to hold Ciara's steady, her eyes studying the symbol.

"The imprint of the symbol is old; looks like from the Augustus III age back several hundred years ago. Though, the ring itself does not look old," Morales said.

"Do they still make these rings?" Ciara said, leaning in.

"They might. There is a jewelry shop in the Silver City named El Dorado."

"The golden country," Emma said, remembering the legend.

"Precisely. I don't care what people say, your kind isn't stupid," Morales said.

This prompted Emma and Ciara to look at each other in confusion as they mouthed "your kind."

"I mean humans," Morales said, catching the girls.

"Are you not a human?" Ciara said.

"I am not!" Morales said, scoffing.

"I don't know if I'm supposed to be insulted or curious," Emma said.

"Oh…this is no offense to you girls, of course."

"None taken," Ciara said, her face having gone sour.

"This will be hard for you to understand now but human beings have been the bane of a Croatoan's existence for thousands of years." With that, Morales stood up from the table and gestured to her troops. "Move along now, Watchers."

"Croatoan," Emma whispered, watching Morales leave. The puzzle was beginning to form again in her mind.

"What?"

"Croatoan. These people are called Croatoans!"

"That sounds like the people from those fairy tale books your Grandpa gave you, right?"

"Uh, I think it is those people in those books," Emma said, elated that the word was no longer a dead end in her mind but a long cavern, the doors just beyond reach. "Croatoan. That definitely shows these people aren't human. They're a different species!"

Emma and Ciara followed Siobhan's lead on the trek away from the outer ring of the forest. Twelve Watchers of the Wood, including Erik and Morales, accompanied them. Each of the guards were quite loose in spirit, cracking jokes and singing unfamiliar and yet delightful rhythms to the ears of the girls. Emma loved the one tune called *The Wind and I Shall Fly Away*.

> The Wind and I shall fly away
> Fly Away, when they're mourning
> Fly Away, in the morning
> To lands of golden fields
> In the valley of our dreams
> The Wind and I shall fly away

Emma found it curious that these Croatoans looked no different than any human such as Ciara and herself, aside from being to some extent taller in their frame and studier in posture. The Croatoan's did seem to have sharpened senses, ever more aware of the very soul of the forest. The guards, perhaps from their training, made sure their footsteps were light, almost silent, against the wooded trails that were of such a low impact on the nature they weaved around in the trees and hills as if they were in fact living in harmony with anything that lived under the sun. Emma also did not miss the fact that these men and woman also had a rifle, pistol or bow with a quiver on their uniforms, ready to be drawn at the slightest hint of danger to this platoon. Loaded to the hilt with weapons of antiquity, Emma was keen to learn more about the pocketsize digital devices Siobhan and a few guards used to triangulate positions, communicate and complete logistical responsibilities.

The forest had begun to change as well. Where before the trees were woven like a spider's web and the hazily seen precautions planted in the first few miles had given away to a forested land so rich and detailed, Emma swore any line lifted from one of her fairy tale books would do all of this justice. Hundred year old oak, willow, cypress and pine trees looked to be in their infancy amongst scattered groupings of silver trees that seemed to defy the ages and live as long as the redwoods that were peppered alongside the forest trail, heading due west.

Emma craned her neck back to feel the sunlight on her closed eyelids. The light, now more abundant because of frequent gaps in the canopies, let the forest breathe. Though the temperature was dropping, hovering in the low forties, Emma liked how a strong beam of sunlight could warm her skin better than any man-made heater.

Opening her eyes, she watched Siobhan lead the troops ahead. Just then, she figured that Adacia had panicked at the sight of an empty bedroom and screamed loud enough to rattle the window panes. She had so wished to tell Bo about the forest adventure and in believing her, perhaps he would come along with Ciara and her once again, becoming the brother that she had faith in all these years.

Siobhan turned around and smiled at Emma. She returned this gesture to Siobhan, feeling again comfort in that there was nothing fishy behind this black haired Mage.

"We should talk to Siobhan," Ciara said.

"About what?" Emma whispered back, attentive to the fact that Siobhan was ten steps ahead.

"About Erik or that guy Hector. She doesn't have anyone to talk to."

"A woman like Siobhan isn't gonna talk to us about boys."

"Whatever. She totally connected with you," Ciara said, snapping her fingers, stressing the mental connection. "Then once she has your trust you can find out what she knows about you."

"Ehhh, I don't know. Remember that crystal ball she had? What if she gets mad and uses it on us?"

"Ugh. You're being paranoid," Ciara said, nudging Emma.

Emma gave Ciara a shove back, sending her off the path for a second.

"You should talk! And I'm not paranoid. There's no way I would have left my house and gone into this big scary forest if I was scared. What a bunch of junk."

Ciara shot Emma a puzzled look. "Okay, one – blood covered ghosts and machines in the trees that make me cry are scary. Two – If you weren't afraid to come in here, why can't you just walk up to Siobhan, who's so nice by the way, and ask her a personal question?"

"Believe me, I tried last night. She's mysterious."

"Mysterious? No way," Ciara said, shaking her head. "She just doesn't want to share anything personal. That's why she seems mysterious."

After another half hour of walking at a gentle pace, the group came to a series of caves that began in a tight patch of hills. The rocky edges had become overgrown on every side for years with trees and shrubs. As the dim caves came into view, their entrance a slight decline from the forest floor, Siobhan drew out her crystal ball. Holding her conjurer up and out to the subterranean world, Siobhan's magical intermediary let out several visible white pulses that shot out into the caves, echoing with the sound of a ringing bell.

"That is the coolest doorbell!" Ciara said.

Before Siobhan could respond, a mighty roar came from the caves, making Ciara let out a tiny yelp in fright.

"Do not worry, Ciara," Siobhan said, still holding her crystal ball. "He is but a simple Sasquatch."

"Sasquatch? Sasquatch!" Ciara said, her voice getting breathless. She stepped back a few paces and hid behind Emma.

"I'm not a brick wall, Ciara," Emma said, trying to move Ciara aside.

"Just use that thing of yours if it gets mad." Ciara crouched down behind Emma's shoulders, peering over, her hands shaking.

"Chill. Be cool," Emma said. She touched her star beneath her shirt, just to be sure. As one of guards looked suspiciously at Emma, she shoved her hands into her pockets, remembering what Siobhan warned.

A second roar, this one much tamer and lazy in execution, was the precursor to a dim lantern light in the cave becoming blocked out by a ten foot silhouette. Emma could feel slight vibrations under her feet, the weight of the creature causing a low grade tremor.

Ciara moaned again when the sunlight's beams revealed what looked like a ten foot tall, upright ape with horrible posture. His body was covered in a matted, overgrown tan fur. The eyes were bloodshot. He could have roared his mighty head, bearing his beast-like teeth and tore a tree limb apart and flogged the entire company with ease. Instead, the hairy beast scratched his butt and burped loud enough to rustle the leaves. The scratching and expelling of gas continued for close to ten seconds. Emma's soft giggles at this kept Ciara from running away.

"Wow, man. Morning, I think," the Sasquatch grumbled. "What day is this?"

"Good afternoon, Bigfoot," Siobhan said, being polite. "You did check in last night during the spiritual disturbance, did you not?"

"Whoa, whoa, whoa, slow down! You mean I slept through breakfast?"

The girls couldn't contain their giggles any longer. The squad, however, sighed, trying to keep their patience. Emma guessed they were never quite use to this lackluster beast.

Siobhan stepped up, looking dwarfed by comparison, and took his Frisbee sized hands and looked into the giant's enormous black, dough eyes.

"Am I in trouble?" Bigfoot asked, looking as if he shrank under Siobhan's glance.

"No. Do not worry. My squad needs to rest before we get to Adoette. May we make a travelling lunch in your cave?"

The Sasquatch let go of Siobhan once he caught sight of Emma, rubbing his eyes. He leaned in and stared with his eyes as big as saucers.

"There is something special about that girl with the blue eyes."

"Bigfoot, meet Emma Grant," Siobhan said, gesturing over.

Emma waved back, Ciara halfheartedly following suit.

"How did Siobhan know your full name?" Ciara whispered.

"I don't know," Emma said, tossing another mystery into the ever growing list in her mind. "Save that for later."

"Later! Ask her now," Ciara said, loud enough for Siobhan to hear.

Emma continued to wave at the dazed and confused Sasquatch. "Ciara, I have a hairy beast waving back at me. I don't want to ignore him and then have him get angry and rip off my arm."

Ciara's eyes widened and she ducked back behind Emma, all of the sudden aware that could occur. Siobhan struggled to pull back Bigfoot's hand back from his starry eyed wave. Bigfoot then shook his body and yawned loud enough to make Siobhan cover her ears.

"I'm sorry, Vice-Governor Hewens," Bigfoot said. "I only slept twelve hours last night."

"Aye. That is a shame," Siobhan said, covering her mouth to stifle a laugh. "May we come in?"

Bigfoot nodded and waved his arms at the Watchers, changing the wind direction. "Come in, weary travelers. My stove is warm."

Ignatius and Morales exchanged a whisper which Emma caught.

"Bout time the brute had a clear thought," Ignatius said.

"I'm not saying anything," Morales said, covering her mouth. "I heard he ripped off the fingers of Watcher last year."

"No, not that bad, it was the guy's ear," another Watcher chimed in.

"Oh, that's right! They sewed Jedediah Smith's ear right back on," Morales said. "Smith shouldn't have asked how much Sasquatch fur goes for.

With this the Watchers made their way into the cave, taking out their day packs and prepping their mid-day meals. Emma moseyed up to Bigfoot with a cautious Ciara creeping behind. The gentle beast seemed twice as tall as Emma. His head, not a tuft of fur combed or groomed, blocked out the sun like an eclipse. Bigfoot reached out his hand to shake Emma's. Siobhan had to step in to stress the ease that Bigfoot should give to this little girl.

"Nice to meet you, Erma," Bigfoot said, a rather juvenile way about him.

Emma tried not to wince both at the horrible use of her name and at the fact that that it felt as if the bones in her right hand were shuddering under the light touch of the woodland giant.

"My name is Emma."

"What is...?"

"My name."

"My apologies. Nice to meet you, My Name is Emma."

Siobhan waved off Emma, well used to this with Bigfoot. "Shall we have afternoon tea? Girls?"

"I picked some tea leaves last week," Bigfoot said, gesturing for the girls to follow. "That little girl is nice, Siobhan. I'll have to help her sometime."

"You should," Siobhan said, giving Emma a wink and a smile. "We will all be helping Emma one day."

As this notion rolled around in Emma's noggin, making her wonder why she would ever need help from a Sasquatch and a Mage, she and Ciara followed into the cave, continued their reserved amusement of Bigfoot.

"Have you been hot this week, Siobhan? This winter fur of mine has me roasting!"

"I've been better, if that is what you are getting at. What do you do with that coat when the summer sun starts cooking you?"

"Oh, my wife strips me naked and shaves me."

"Yes," Siobhan said, shuddering at the thought. "I could have gone without knowing that!"

The afternoon tea accompanied with biscuits smothered in honey and butter turned out to be much longer than Emma expected. For close to two hours they remained at Bigfoot's home, eating, taking cat naps and attending to routine security measures with the Sasquatch's assistance.

Throughout all of this frustration with the beast, Emma noticed how these Croatoan's seemed much more level-headed, less worried to have to complete a task for fear of failure, guilt, or stressful deadlines like with a human. It was during this act of being a fly on the wall that Emma felt someone tap on her shoulder.

"Hey, Siobhan," Emma said, before turning around.

"How did you know it was me?" Siobhan said, kneeling down next to Emma.

"I don't know. I just felt you there."

Siobhan nodded, her smile reserved, which seemed to Emma as if she was amazing this Mage once again.

"Would you and your friend like to accompany me? I would very much like to show you something."

Emma looked over at Ciara, who to her surprise over the last hour, had torn down her walls and had taken a liking to Bigfoot. The two were in a rock throwing contest. Bigfoot was flinging the stones so deep into the distant view of the forest that he looked like an Olympic shot-put champion. Ciara laughed ever time he gave a mighty growl and outdid her distance by at least fifty yards with every attempt.

"Ciara, come here," Emma said, waving her over.

"Do you two make the decisions together?" Siobhan said.

"No, I can think for myself…" Emma said, cupping her mouth. "I'm sorry. That came out rude."

"No bother," Siobhan said, helping Emma up. "That sharp tongue reminds me of someone I once knew long ago."

Ciara jogged up with a giddy Bigfoot in her wake, a stone in each other their hands. "Where are we going?"

"Now, what would be the point of spoiling the surprise?" Siobhan said, walking ahead. "Come here to me, girls. Bigfoot, you stay behind and gather your things before you leave with us."

"Bigfoot? Is that your nickname?" Ciara said.

Bigfoot leaned over to the girls and crossed his arms in a professor-like fashion. "Well, the nickname comes from my size 31 feet. But my birth name is John Smith."

"John Smith?" Emma said, gawking at Bigfoot in surprise.

"Yeah. But you can call me Jack too…CROW!" Bigfoot broke away from his civilized talk to chuck his stone at over a hundred miles an hour at a devious crow perched on a nearby branch. The spooked bird flew away, certain to not return.

Siobhan, Emma and Ciara could do nothing but gawk at the amused Bigfoot, all of them bemused with this perplexing creature.

"Girls…Shall we go?" Siobhan said.

Siobhan proceeded to lead Emma and Ciara into a golden winter wheat field beyond the caves and the forest. After a good few minutes of taking careful steps past the young, foot tall blonde wheat, they climbed a hill in the middle of the one thousand acre farm field. As they walked up the steep grade, the familiar trees substituted for the wheat grass, making an island of wood, dirt and shedding autumn leaves.

Ciara slipped on the trail's loose rocks near the top. Emma and Siobhan both grabbed Ciara's arms and with several grunts pulled her back up.

"You've got quick reflexes," Ciara said to Siobhan.

"Emma was quicker," Siobhan said.

As the three neared the top of the hill, they all had to use the tree branches to climb for crawling on their hands and knees did no good on such a steep incline and patches of free, eroding soil. Emma allowed Ciara to be pulled up first by Siobhan. When Emma came up on her own, her leg and arm muscles burning, the air seemed to clear now that she was on the grassy, treeless hill top a few hundred feet up the winding trail that started at the level farm field below.

Emma threw her hair back with a tie to avoid the winds from that elevation. From that height, a tad higher than the forest canopy, they could see the Silver Forest extend for many miles into the west, so far that she could not see the end of the mystical woodland. To the north and south more of the same unbridled nature, dotted with lumps of hills and the occasional redwood that poked their mighty bristled head out over the tree line.

"What's that?" Ciara said, pointing to a spot due west.

Emma narrowed her keen eyes, able to see a hazy image of an open field and a set of rivers in a valley that flowed around what looked like a city with a green stone wall and a silver interior. "Yeah, what is that?"

"That, girls, is where I am taking you tonight," Siobhan said, looking out, a certain pride glossing over her face. "See that soaring, stick-like thing sticking out past the two rivers?"

"No. What thing?" Ciara said, copying Emma's move of leaning in and squinting.

Siobhan handed over a small square device to Ciara. The device had a large rotating set of lenses on one side and on the opposite side, a touch-screen interface. The distant image of that section of the forest in what Siobhan described magnified for Ciara's eyes.

"I can see," Emma said, not needed the magnifier. "That looks like a tower. Wow. It has to be like four or five hundred feet tall." She could see the sunlight catching the top of the object that sat like a lighthouse in the hills that later formed into highlands and mountains in the west.

"Not a tower, but a tree."

"A tree?" Ciara said, looking back at Siobhan in surprise. "How big is that tree house? Is it the size of a mansion?"

"No houses there," Siobhan said with a tiny laugh. "And the tree is over five hundred feet."

"That's as tall as a skyscraper!" Emma said.

"Yes. I suppose that a tree could scrape the clouds," Siobhan said, a confused look about her as she sat down at the edge of the hilltop, their feet dangling over the side.

"Crann Móra, one of the last Adoette trees. It is the second symbol of our land and the name bestowed onto our great capital. Folk say that the ten or so trees that remain upon the Earth are the last in the line of the great species. Scientists have for years tried to find a way to duplicate this God send from the days before the coming of Lord Augustus the first, thousands of years ago.

"Why are there only ten left?" Emma said.

"Treasures such as these Adoette trees and sanctuaries for Faerie's and unique creatures like Bigfoot are being encroached not only by humans anymore. Croatoan's are to blame as well with selfish, greed driven developments. Little seems left of the ancient world. The attitude these days seems to be a cruel, take what you will with little regard for your true impact…this is not who we are as a people." Siobhan fell silent, looking troubled as she stared, unblinking, off into the distance.

Emma caught Ciara giving her looks, gesturing with a nod of her head over to Siobhan. Taking the hint, remembering what she and Ciara spoke of earlier, Emma scooted herself closer to Siobhan.

"Siobhan," Emma said, placing a soft touch on her knee. "Are you alright? It kind of seems like something is bothering you."

Siobhan was slow to turn her head and look at Emma. "Do you recall me saying how I thought you looked familiar?" Siobhan said, her voice full of pauses and breaks.

"Yeah. Did you remember where you knew me from?"

"Yes. From Adacia."

"That's my Mom? You know her?"

"Yes. We we're friends when we were kids. Best friends in truth," Siobhan said, stopping for a few seconds to reflect and gather her thoughts. "Our lives were not made for the same roads. No surprise considering my responsibilities here. That and the worry surrounding keeping you and your brother out of harm's way. Adacia and I have not spoken for years now."

"I'm sorry," Emma said, quite aware of how her mother could drive people away. "I left home because of her. Well, I left because of my family. I couldn't stand being lied to anymore."

Siobhan acknowledged this with a compassionate nod. Ciara, listening to this the whole time as if she was watching a dramatic film unfold, leaned in closer. Emma cast an odd look her way.

"You want some popcorn for this show?" Emma said.

"You got some? So Siobhan, if you knew Emma that probably means you remembered her face from like years ago, right?" Ciara said, not pausing to breathe in her speech.

"Yes, Ciara. I used to rock Emma to sleep," Siobhan said, making her arms like a baby cradle. "Here in these arms. Rare ones like you have the most brilliant eyes. Your mother used to rub her forefingers along your freckles and call you Blue Eyes."

"She still does that," Emma said with a sigh.

Siobhan patted Emma's soft hair. "When you were only a little girl, you used to call me Auntie Siobhan."

Emma so wished to throw her arms around Siobhan and embrace her if it not was for the confused puzzle board of her mind roaring back. There was no memory in the wells of her mind being cradled or being loved as a surrogate daughter by Siobhan.

"I don't remember you. I'm so sorry."

"No," Siobhan said, taking her hand away. "I suppose you wouldn't."

Without delay, Siobhan stood up and dusted off the back of her Watcher of the Wood-like military outfit of any leaves and flecks of dirt. Emma glanced at Ciara and winced, hoping she didn't shatter Siobhan's feelings.

"Come on, girls. Tonight's nightfall will bring a great festival to the Silver City," Siobhan said, pulling the girls up gently from under their arms.

"What festival?" Emma said. Her head instantly filled with images of bands and carnival-like games.

Siobhan winked at Emma once again, the smile still drained away. "You'll see. I've already given away too many secrets."

Several hours later the sun had fallen into the Western horizon and the stars had come out of hiding. Siobhan led the way once again, this time with Bigfoot, who carried a series of hastily packed supplies in a massive wicker basket attached to his back by straps. Thanks to another night with a full moon, the Watchers needed not to light any of the lanterns for the illuminated silver trees lit their trail.

After climbing up a long incline, Emma and the group passed between two hills and began to make what the Watchers called "the long, sweet descent between the trees" to the Hetch-Hetchi Valley. Soon the forest came to an abrupt end, giving way to Hetch-Hetchi, a short switch grass, three-mile long valley that was split in two by a river that Erik referred to as the Shikakwa thanks to wild onions and ferns that grew on its banks. Just beyond the river, a short walk across a thirty-foot wide stone bridge, was hands down the most beautiful sight Emma had seen to that point. A stone walled city, littered with thin green shrubberies, shined from every rooftop and tower in the silvery moonlight.

"Welcome girls," Siobhan said, beaming with pride. "Ahead, there lies Adoette, the Silver City, the capital of the Republic of the Silver Forest."

Chapter Eleven
The All Hallows Festival

From the ring of trees at the edge of the flaxen prairie grass, Siobhan led the girls and the troops down a white stone path that cut through the Hetch-Hetchi Valley. Emma had plenty of time to observe her surroundings on the good half mile march from the forest to the LaSalle bridge that hovered over the Shikakwa River, straight into the city of Adoette.

"Siobhan?" Emma said, tugging at the Mage's sleeve, pointing to the forested hills on the opposite side of town. A colossal tree jutted out from the forest like a massive tower. "Is that the Adoette tree? What was its name again?"

"Crann Móra, Emma," Siobhan said, twirling her finger as she pointed from the canopy to the lower trunk of the tremendous freak of nature, sticking out from the tops of the trees as wide as a house and as tall as a mountain. "Do you see the staircase winding up the tree?"

Emma's eyes followed the exterior set of stairs and railings that wound their way up the tree to several platforms near the tip, the one spot on the massive trunk where branches fanned out wider than wings on a massive passenger jet. The railings were visible for they were lit on that night with tiny orange lanterns.

"Maybe one day we will take a peak from the top platform. The observation deck is after all the very best view in the Republic," Siobhan said.

Ciara sized up Crann Móra, which now caught the full moon, the silver tree fibers in the railing illuminating the way up. "How many steps is it to the top?"

"Around six hundred and fifty steps," Siobhan said. She waved the anxious company on past the girls. Erik stood behind with Siobhan, allowing his compatriots pass, each one of them shooting him kissy faces when Siobhan wasn't looking. Erik balled up his fist shook out his anger at them.

"Thank you, Secretary Hewens," Morales said, taking up the train of the troops.

"Of course. Register our arrival with the Defense watch. Then get in there and have some fun!"

"We will. Watchers?" Morales called. The remainder of the platoon stopped and waved either their hats with a salute at Siobhan.

"Thank you, Secretary Siobhan," the troops called back before they turned on their heels for their Silver City. Some of them began to race each other up the path, all of them little children at heart again on this night of alternate identities.

"Come along, girls. I presume you do not wish to miss the All Hallows Festival," Siobhan said, a lighthearted way about her. Emma couldn't help but to notice Erik's effortless smile at the bliss that radiated out of Siobhan.

"Didn't take you long to smile again, Grumpy Gus," Emma said, nudging Erik.

"I'm not that grumpy, am I?" Erik said, looking to Emma as if he was beyond unsure of himself in that innocent minute of his obvious crush on Siobhan.

The closer Emma and her companions came to Adoette, the towers, many leveled tiers of buildings and mighty stone wall, covered from top to bottom in emerald ivy, the city seemed like every street a massive boulevard, every building a citadel. Music and the upbeat hum of countless raised voices in a unique harmony reached Emma's ears before the rustling waters of the Shikakwa flowing south made itself seen. A low stone wall, a mere few feet high, ran along each bank, as Emma guessed, for safety.

"Whoa! Who are they?" Ciara said.

Emma had to do a double take for the magnificence of the city blinded her from two life size statues made from white marble that stood at either side of the LaSalle stone bridge. Erik kissed his fingers and touched the statue of the man on the left who wore a flowing robe with a crown of woven clovers. Emma thought how the image on that Sorcerer's jewel at his neck looked much like an odd natural wonder of basalt columns that she and the family saw years ago in Northern Ireland.

"This is Lord Eoin Boldger, the founder of our land long ago when it was once a Kingdom and a colony of the Union of Kingdoms in Europe," Erik said.

"Is he the King and that Lady the Queen?" Ciara said, pointing.

"No, dear," Siobhan said, kissing her fingers and touching the female statue as her and Erik seemed to share a tiny inside joke. "He used to be King. That was before the revolution of the 2230's, where we transitioned to a Republic."

"Then who is she?" Ciara said, her fist pouncing on the boots of the statue. A sharp sigh hissed out from Erik and Siobhan at this apparent impolite gesture.

"Kiss the statue," Emma whispered, egging Ciara on.

Ciara froze, a deer in the headlights look about her. The kind Siobhan ushered her across the bridge. "Do not worry, Ciara. You will soon know why we kiss the stone idols, these leaders of our land."

Emma stood below the statue of the woman. This striking woman wore a practical Victorian dress. On the head of the woman, above strands of hair braided in artistic ways was a replaceable crown of real silver leaves, freshly picked for this marble idol.

"Are you ready to move along?" Erik said, moving his bulky hands in the air.

"Hold on a minute," Emma said. She noticed that both of the statues, just below the neck, wore a jewel just like with her star. This woman's signifier was small metal jewel of a comet streaking across the sky. Halfway tempted to draw out her Alastar, Emma trusted in Siobhan's advice and put her hands back at her sides. "Umm, they are beautiful statues."

Erik nodded, moving alongside Emma to admire. "This is the Lady Eleanor Lumerious. By my guess she will be in Burnham Square tonight, lending herself to the revelry. Such a woman, she is!"

"She's beautiful," Emma said, moving forward to unconsciously touch the statue. "Oh, I'm sorry." Emma kissed her right two fore fingers and placed them on the smooth boots of Eleanor, the original design worn down by the hand oils of thousands.

Erik waved Emma off, smiled and clapped his hands together, loosening up in an instant. "Just don't touch it in the future! Alright, let's get inside. I have half a mind to drink at least a few pints of J. Bartlett's Seasonal Ale tonight."

"And ask Siobhan out?" Emma said, her eyebrow raised, egging Erik on.

"Let me get some liquid courage first," Erik said with a hard swallow.

Emma jogged across the bridge into Adoette with Erik in tow, catching up with Siobhan and Ciara. A guard, loaded up with a rifle and a curved sword in its scabbard at his side, stood protecting on either side of what looked like a former gate. A set of three hallowed out slits, as high as the outside wall, remained on either side of the entrance way. Emma imagined these produced a set of interlocking gates if they were ever invaded.

"Welcome to Adoette, little ladies," the guard on the right said, giving a slight bow in his old, cricked back as he flashed a set of gnarly teeth.

"Thank you," Emma said, bowing back. "How late are you guys open?" Emma and Ciara exchanged a set of laughs as the guards, Siobhan and Erik looked on, confused by these human girls.

Siobhan shook her head at this and gestured for the nearest guard. "Benjamin. Please take the backpacks of these girls up to Boldger Hall with the orders to place them in my Chief-of-Staff's office for safekeeping."

"Right away, Ms Vice-Governor," Benjamin said, taking the backpacks from the girls before running off. "Enjoy the festivities, girls."

A new festival song, accompanied by a boisterous band, began within the city, soon followed by a tremendous wave of cheering a clapping. Emma and Ciara, both anxious, glanced at Siobhan, the two of them almost unable to keep their feet to the ground.

"Stay to Burnham Square, girls. And be smart, Emma," Siobhan said, taping the nape of her neck, indicating to Emma.

"I will, Vice-Governor Hewens," Emma said, saluting Siobhan like a soldier.

"Oh, will you get already!"

After Emma threw her arm down, the girls took off like short distance sprinters. They ran down the ever widening avenue, the buildings and store fronts on either side were a classical and polished mesh of stone, steel, clear panes of glass and carved wooden signs hanging from the entrances.

"Some of this reminds me of an old Colonial village, like a modern Williamsburg or something!" Emma said, as she found it hard to contain her smile.

"Kind of. Like a mix of old and new," Ciara said.

Down one avenue was a post office, complete with white Corinthian columns. The place looked to Emma like what Ciara had said, a mesh of an old European style, maybe Italian, post-office and an American bank. "We should send out postcards to friends back home," Emma said.

"I'd send my only one to you."

"Yeah, I'd do the same!"

A small silver tree, shining in the moon's beams, stood as a fork in the road. The tree separated their street, Sheridan Boulevard, an avenue to the south named Sierra, and the entrance to the town square. Emma and Ciara choose the path that lead right into the square, under the lowest branches of the silver tree, fifteen feet from the ground, and into a brave new world.

Then, Emma and Ciara came to a screeching halt. Before them was the city square, more than twice as long as a football field and at least half as wide as it was long. Emma imagined that even three soccer fields could fit into the massive open space. In the middle, dividing the two long city promenades was a long, man-made oval pond, a few feet deep throughout. At the near side of the pool, facing the long, rectangular square stood a fifty foot granite statue of a woman. Carved in her left hand, held to her chest were scrolls marked with the words 'Constitution, July 1st, 2230'. In her right hand, held high above her head was a small globe.

Intermixed in the square were over what looked to be a thousand people, not a face among them looking dour in light of all the joyous events on that Halloween night. Some wore elaborate outfits of famous figures in their history like a Mage, some wore costumes creatures of fantasy and reality in the world like werewolves, vampires and witches. Emma giggled as she pointed out that one man even wore a hairy Sasquatch costume, looking like he sewed several thick pieces of carpet together. The dilapidated Sasquatched man tried to hold hands with his equally tall girlfriend, her arms in white wings of a bald eagle, the headdress all feathers. Several teenage boys and girls wore an interconnected dragon costume at the waist, which to their detriment kept tearing for they all had different ideas of where to go. The un-costumed folk wore every color of the season in their shirts and dresses. As these Croatoan souls of Adoette weaved amongst one another, Emma could see from her height at the top of the marble staircase that cut between two sloping roads, leading twenty feet or so down into the square, that the color scheme of these people in this silver city reminded Emma of the collected cornucopia of leaves Bo and her used to dive into every fall in their front yard.

"Whoa, check that out!" Ciara said.

Ciara pointed to the space beyond the stairs where people gathered under and around an immense banyan tree, growing in vibrant patches of soil in the stone. The branches from the singular, age old tree spread around like creeping vines, holding the bottoms of dozens of children and teenagers who climbed up the wood. Various "oohs" and "ahhs" poured out in unison as the space beneath the tree lit up in flashes of light, illuminating the dimly lit, multi-tiered square building with Greek style columns, opposite of the statue in the water.

Ciara grabbed Emma's arm and tugged her along. "Let's check it out that crowd!"

As fast as their feet could fly down the marble staircase, Emma and Ciara ran past a group of little girls in white lace and silk costumes, dressed as Mages and Faeries, before they reached the banyan tree.

The crowd underneath the tree was too tall for the girls, even when they stood on their tiptoes. They caught a bare glance at a woman in the center wearing a crown of autumn leaves on top of her chestnut hair. Emma climbed the nearest free banyan root branch to get a view several feet above the heads of the crowd.

Once she had a good view with Ciara, Emma could not look away from the crowned woman in her mid-40's that wore an eye-catching dress of seasonal orange and brownish leaf yellow. This woman's radiant green eyes seemed to enchant every man.

The crowd surrounded the woman, with young ones crouched down with brother, sisters and parents, arms around their little waists in the ring around the lady. The taller, older Croatoan adults and teenagers stood around them, paying special attention, almost leaning in as the woman captured their imaginations.

The woman appeared to be controlling several floating incandescent images of what looked like a dragon and a much younger version of herself, both of them radiant as a light bulb. Upon the neck of the lady was a bronze and silver jewel in the shape of a comet. She wove her holiday story around the crowd's minds with her engaging, commanding voice that sounded like muddled mix of Scottish and American English.

"Verago was persistent and though wounded by the trap set by the colonists, I too was pinned down like my cousin Eoin when he met his demise," the woman said, speaking with a suspenseful cadence. "My people could have fallen and the west would have remained wild if I did not remember…"

The image of the dragon snorted out a shot of steam from its nostrils, ready to rend the flesh of the younger woman, who struggled under rocks on a dry riverbed that appeared with a wave of the storyteller's hand.

"What happened next, my Lady?" said a curly red haired, squeaky voiced little girl, her eyes full of concern.

The crowd laughed at this adorable little child. The Lady smiled as well at her, winking. "I will tell you. I remembered the mind is always stronger than the body."

The woman waved her hand and the dragon stepped onto the long pile of river rocks, losing its balance under the mighty claw.

"The pride of the beast was no match for good acting and the skills of a young, ambitious conjurer as I was."

The figure of the woman disappeared from the pile of rocks as the beast fell into the trap, pulling the dragon down into a massive hidden hole beneath the rocks. The woman reappeared on the hill top above the river bed.

"The weight of the shattered rocks was too much for the beast and as I reappeared, I broke the dam and released the lake, drowning Verago."

With a wave of her hand, a translucent image of water poured over the pinned dragon as it let out a roar of defeat. The water extinguished the flame of the beast and its evil beating heart in a torrent of steam. The beast lay subdued under the water, never to rise again. The small figure of the woman shot up a flare of sorts into the air, which exploded and hung in the air with the design of a comet, like her on necklace.

"And that…that was how the west was won!"

The woman shot out both her arms from her body and the three dimensional images flew apart into a hundred sparks. In mid-air, the sparks formed into little wrapped candies that flew into the hands and laps of every nearby child.

"Happy Halloween!"

The crowd roared and clapped their hands raw at the performance by the woman. She took a few respectful bows and with grace in every step moved past the seated crowed into the square with purpose in her direction.

"Please do come up to the promenades and the stage for a treat for your ears," the woman said, hesitating back for a brief second, as if she sensed a presence behind her.

"Are you playing, my Lady Eleanor?" a man called from the crowd.

"Always for my people," Eleanor said with a smile and a wave before she crossed the massive square.

From her banyan branch, Emma noticed how every person she passed, from the curtsying little girl in a cherub costume to a gruff, rather plainclothes man in a leather vest, all paid their respects to this woman so great, they carved her in stone. Emma felt a rush of life about her as she was nestled in that tree now having seen this great, enchanting leader, the Governor Lady Eleanor.

When Emma hopped down the tree, Ciara opened one of the orange magic candies and handed half of the sweet to her.

"What is this?" Emma said, sniffing the candy shaped like a pumpkin. "This smells like pumpkin pie."

"Tastes like it too," Ciara said as she chewed.

Emma popped the candy into her mouth. The juices flowed with hints of baked pumpkin, a dash of sugar and a taste of a flakey, buttery crust.

"The candy needs whipped cream," Ciara said, swallowing the last of the sweet. "We should try and find some sweet potato pie candies."

"Oh and maybe some apple and French silk pie," Emma said, hoping on her toes. "I think those are food stands in the middle of the square."

The delectable scents of the food stands filled Emma's acute nose before she and Ciara reached them. Strong culinary perfumes of frying sausages with onions, ladles full of sautéed wild forest mushrooms in butter and red wine, hot mulled cider steaming in the cold air, and an assortment of vegetable and fruit pie-like candies – they all pulled Emma and Ciara from stand to stand, walking past each one with hungry bellies.

"How many bucks do you have?" Ciara said, digging into her jean pockets.

"I don't think they take American dollars," Emma said. Her eyes caught a sign nailed to the post of Saccharin's Desserts.

One Silver Dollar per candy

Ciara moaned. "Ohhh! I wish Siobhan gave us money."

A rosy cheeked, chubby woman in a white apron leaned forward from the opposite end of the stand. "Would you girls like a candy pie?"

"I'm sorry, miss," Emma said, digging into her own pockets. "We don't have any money."

A lanky Watcher of the Wood pushed past the girls. Emma immediately recognized him as Private Ignatius.

"You can give the poor blue-eyed girl a soul cake," Ignatius said, whispering the last part as if it was a dirty little secret.

"So one soul cake then," the chubby woman said, holding out a sort of cookie/scone hybrid of what smelled to Emma like cinnamon and raisins.

"My friend gets one too," Emma said, throwing her arm around Ciara's shoulders.

The woman shifted her eyes to Ciara, looking at her with caution. Again, she held out the tart, only for Emma. "Take your treat, pretty one."

"Are you serious with this?" Emma said, her anger bubbling up.

"Don't take this too seriously, little human," Ignatious said, "That's enough for like the likes of your poor lot. You'd probably die if you ate too much too quick."

Emma moved away with Ciara, almost a bit too forceful. "I'd probably say the same for you, you pig!"

The woman covered her mouth as she whispered something to Ignatious.

"You don't have to defend me," Ciara said.

"I know. But that was so rude!"

"I know," Ciara said, tapping Emma on the shoulder with a well-seasoned attitude in being treated with rudeness in her past. "I know. Come on. Let's check out that show."

Emma cooled off as Ciara and she made a bee line for the stage past dancing circles and portable wooden tables where countless people enjoyed a Halloween feast of roasted and juicy beef brisket, slices of gamey lamb, and late-season vegetables like squash and corn. The sight of what Emma guessed was roasted lamb with gravy with garlic mashed potatoes at one of the tables was enough to make her forget her troubles.

Emma took note on how the public square was constructed with very clean cut lines. On the south side of the square was a white stone building complete with an entrance that jutted out with columns, a small dome at the center, and was covered in temporary autumn colors. Dominating the north side of the square, on the other side of the pond, was a singular massive building that took up a ¼ of square space. It was hard for her to even ignore the Beaux-Arts styled oval shaped building on two story square basin, which stood upon several large square shaped levels at the end of the square, right behind a stage that was temporarily erected.

"That building has gotta be the capital," Emma said.

"Probably. Come on," Ciara said, grabbing Emma by her hand. "Let's get closer so we can see the show."

After weaving past the Croatoan men and women that seemed slightly taller than the average Americans Emma grew up around, Ciara and she found a space about thirty feet from the stage with a few kids around their years. A few of the nearby teenagers, who had just become of age to drink alcohol, sang along with the band on stage in a haze of slurred words. They waved their mugs about, the ale sloshing out and onto their feet, lost in their last bastions of youthful carelessness. Emma and Ciara were quick to pick up on the lyrics, with Emma doing her little bounce from side-to-side as they sang along to the Croatoan version of a pop song.

> Love your life
> Give all you can to 'em
> The city of dreams wants to
> be founded

The song faded out. Emma whipped her head around to the stage to see Lady Eleanor two-step her body onto the platform. A wave of bows and choruses of appreciative applause roared out from the crowd. Emma and Ciara followed suit, not wanting to look out of place. Emma even placed her two forefingers in her mouth to whistle, not noticing that the high pitch she delivered caused some nearby partiers to clasp their ears.

"Happy Halloween, Adoette!" Eleanor shouted. Her voice amplified as if it was spoken into a microphone. With a wave of her hand about ten carved Jack-O-Lanterns appeared from behind the stage to rise and hover above the crowd. "Let's welcome the departed spirits back."

The crowd joined Eleanor in song.

> Hallowed Spirits
> Departed from the living
> Glow in your memories
> Light this night on Earth

With this uniform chant the air above the square became thick with fog. Emma could tell that there were objects moving inside the mist that looked like little half skin/half skull heads with a trail of light following them like a comet's tail.

Eleanor holstered her fiddle to her and played a slow and inviting tune that filled the square, silencing the crowd. Then a jet of light shot out of the fog in a neon trail, followed by another, then another. Ten dancing patterns of phosphorous-like bands of white light in all floored the crowd.

"What are they?" Ciara said, ducking as one of the lights flew by a mere few feet above the crowd.

"I think they're ghosts. Everyone was singing 'Departed from the living,'" Emma said, her eyes following the acrobatics of the spirits.

"Ghosts?" Ciara said, crouching down a bit. "Like phantoms?"

"I don't think these are the same. No one seems to be afraid of them."

As the sweet bow slid across Eleanor's fiddle strings, the other band members on stage picked up their bongo drums, flutes, Celtic pipes and a Croatoan guitar-like instrument to join in with her.

"Welcome back the spirits, dear citizens for Halloween, 2409!" Eleanor called.

The audience erupted into cheers. As they did this the illuminated spirits fells into formation with each one holding a spot above one of the floating Jack-O-Lanterns. The audience counted down in unison, like on New Years, as the spirits little-by-little lowered themselves into the carved pumpkins.

"Three – Two – One!"

With this, the spirits became a hot, blinding white light for a few moments. Their stem caps closed the tops. The white jet of the spirits gave way to the gentlest amber light that flickered here and there like a candle.

"My, my," one of the Jack-O-Lanterns said in a rather squeaky, frail voice of an old woman. "I thought I'd never get a chance to come here."

"Look at all these people," another one bellowed in a rough, grating male voice. "I swear Adoette has multiplied since we were here last. Hey, watch out, buddy."

One of the other Jack-O-Lanterns floated by, bumping the last pumpkin on its way down to an adoring crowd. "That's because you died a hundred and ten years ago, dummy."

Eleanor's band ended their set, dragging out the last note in a fade. During this, pockets of the crowd, including the one Emma and Ciara were in, were being greeted by the presence of one of the ten spirited lanterns.

Emma had no fear of the spirit as it drifted down to her with a smile that bore a single tooth and a crooked triangular nose on the skin of the Jack-O-Lantern. Dozens of nearby partiers watched Emma as her fingertips glided along the spotted orange shells of the pumpkins.

"Who is the spirit? Who do you think it is?" some whispered in the crowd.

"Hello," Emma said, staring at the flicking light inside.

"Ello' there, little one," the Jack-O-Lantern spirit said in a broken, almost Cajun accent. "Wha' would you like to know about da' past, eh?"

"Are you dead?" Emma said, trying her best to sound kind.

"I certainly 'ope so. Otherwise those 180 raw oysters I ate are gonna be awful when they pass."

A man in the throng of citizens called out to everyone else. "It's that champion eater, Eugene Delacroix." Half of the nearby crowd nodded in recognition, some of them scowling at this cultural figure that Emma had never heard of.

Eleanor's band struck up another tune, this one fast, much like a frenetic mix of traditional Irish and an American bluegrass song. Emma and Ciara turned with the crowd to the stage, many of them dancing in place or joining hands with others for a little jig. The girls couldn't help but to let out a joyful little giggle as they bounced from side to side with the rhythm of the music.

The world slowed down for Emma, all her senses much more acute than the revelers around her. As Eleanor took the front of the stage, playing her part with ease, she looked out over the crowd and met Emma's eyes. The hair rising upon her arms like the seconds before a lightning strike, Emma felt a deeper connection to this Sorceress with bright green eyes. Eleanor stared back at Emma, slowing her playing and losing her posture. Then, Eleanor smiled at her, not in a pleasing way but more relieved, puzzling way.

"She knows me," Emma said to herself.

"Oh! I'll be right back, Emma."

In her wave of bliss Ciara brushed past Emma as she joined a rung of dancers moving through the multitude to the music, all of them not a care in the world as old hands held tiny ones.

"Ciara!" Emma said, falling on deaf ears.

Emma turned back to the stage to find Eleanor had moved to the back to allow the bagpipe player to shine for the adoring fans. Even at a distance, Emma could see Eleanor glance over her fiddle at her. The stunning eyes of that woman shined with curiosity.

Though the music stirred everyone's soul, the music softened in Emma's ears as she knew how removed she had felt just then. The unanswered questions flooded back, the puzzle board of questions and solutions appeared back in her mind, and in those tiny moments, she couldn't explain why she didn't want to be around anyone.

She gently pushed past the crowd over to one of the footbridges to cross over to the right side of Burnham Square. Digging her hands into the pockets of her wool coat, Emma made way for the string of storefront business, tucked into the façade of the gigantic Marshall Building on the north side of the plaza. The itch to ask Siobhan about Eleanor floated around in her head. Looking all over, even over the pond to the other side of the festivities, the diligent Mage was nowhere to be found.

"Why do I have so many questions?" Emma said to herself, just then beginning to understand the phrase 'The more you know, the less you know.'

As she walked alone, her head a mile away from the revelry of the festival, Emma's mind drifted in and out of these memory puzzles. She found pleasant distractions in the stands of children's carnival games and storytelling circles. Around one of the circles were two teenage kids laying down a frenetic rhythm of lyrics off the top of their heads. The teens and young adults, gathering around in a semi-circle, cheered them on. The one boy started with…

Ya'll know my name, I'm a pro at this game

The other boy chimed in with…

Outcast in the country, but alive on this night
Laying down who I am 'cause I was taught what is right

As Emma began to move along the battle of poetic words, a long, rectangular picture window caught her eye. The storefront was one of six tucked into the front of the massive Marshall Building.

"J.W's International Trade Goods," Emma said, reading the wooden sign that hung above the entrance to the door on a set of metal rings.

Walking up to the door, Emma could see through the glass that this business had closed down shop for the night. Pressing down on the handle, the door did not budge. Remembering the power her Alastar jewel had given her when she destroyed the Confounder fear machines in the forest, Emma removed the necklace from underneath her sweater. Touching her fingertips to the metal, Emma wrapped that hand around the door, the muscles in her hand already feeling much stronger. She pressed down on the handle again and pulled. The door flew open with a tearing sound of wood, destroying the trim.

Emma looked around, a nervous laugh bubbling up as she stood, amazed at her own strength. The citizens of Adoette were too consumed in the music catch Emma breaking and entering the shop.

Once Emma entered with extreme caution, her eyes widened and her smile returned at the sight of several long wooden tables filled with trade goods for every purpose. A large globe rotated on its axis with no assistance. A little, miniature orchestra on a stand, assembled like those found on a coo-coo clock played a tune that reminded Emma of either Mozart of Beethoven. With that thought of her parents, Emma thought it was odd on how all these devices looked all too familiar.

As her hand touched the casual rotation of the globe, her heart stopped in her chest for her mind's eye could sense someone behind her, approaching the picture window. In the dim light that poured out onto the stone sidewalk in front of the shop from the lanterns that hung above, a man stood, staring at her in the shadows.

Part of Emma's nerves told her that if she was to flip her head around, Siobhan would be there. But as the figure approached, Emma turned to see that the light of the shop window illuminated certain handsome youthful features of a teenage boy who looked back at Emma in disbelief.

"Bo?"

Chapter Twelve
A Grant Family Secret

Fireworks cascaded into the sky above the square, flashing their hues of red, yellow and orange light onto Emma and Bo's cheeks. Emma did not know how long she and her brother stared at each other through that picture window. Bo waved for her to come outside. Emma stood firm and with a stern look about her, she pointed to the floor. Bo nodded with his sagged head, admitting defeat as he made his way to the door.

"What the? Emma, did someone break in?" Bo said as he bounded inside, his eyes darting between the torn trim and Emma's awaiting face.

"Sorry," Emma said, timid. "That's my fault."

Bo walked up to the door and played with the little broken splinters of wood. "How did you do that?"

Emma threw her hands to the side, shaking them in mid-air. "That's your biggest concern right now? Bo, what are you doing here?"

"How did you get in?"

"No!" Emma said, raising her voice. "You first."

"Fine," Bo said. He grabbed a nearby chair and flipped it around to rest his forearms on the tall backing. "This isn't gonna be easy."

"Please just tell me," Emma said. She scanned his puzzled face, trying to follow his darting eyes that bounced around the room, each look seeming to hold a memory. He toyed with the spinning globe, his finger running along the equator line.

"Our name isn't Grant," Bo said, pointing to Emma. "Now you go"

Aware of the private ritual she engaged with her brother over the years when the chat was too good to keep all on one side, Emma gave in a little. "I ran away from home before last night with Ciara and went into the forest.

"What? How did you…"

"Nope. No judgment yet. Now you go."

Bo shook his head in disbelief. "Fine! Our last name isn't Grant. It's Alastar."

Emma touched her star. "Does that have to do with this?"

"No questions until we're done," Bo said. "Your turn."

Emma balled up her right hand and pounded her thigh, wanting to know more. "Siobhan found us with a company of Watchers and brought us here."

"Siobhan brought you…sorry. These people are called Croatoans. They are an offshoot species of humans. Mom is one of them. Dad is a normal…I mean, a human."

"Then that means you and I are half-Croatoan then," Emma whispered, the realization fitting together. "So that explains…do you want to just skip *You Say, I Say*?"

Bo blurted out, shaking his chair from the frame. "Yes, please! Tell me everything!"

Like a frenetic gun battle, Emma and Bo rattled off how they both arrived in Adoette. Bo had arrived a few days before, entering through the same western bough Emma had snuck into. Yet, Bo had an authorized entrance pass and was allowed a Watcher to escort him to the Silver City.

Emma replayed her journey, scaring Bo enough to grip the back of his chair, when she told him about the encounter with the phantoms. When Emma finally told Bo about their parent's arrival sometime the next day, he had to stop Emma with a wave of his hand.

"Wait a second," Bo said, standing up. "Mom and Dad are coming? Why didn't anyone tell me?"

"I thought you knew."

"No. Grandpa didn't even tell me."

"Grandpa is here? Where?" Emma looked out of the window, trying to pick out his face in the masses.

"He lives on the west side of Adoette. I should find him," Bo said, scratching his head in a pensive stare.

The front door flew wide open from the kick of a boot, bolting Bo out of his chair, placing his body square in front of Emma. In rushed a rather portly man, his breath thick and wheezy.

"Oh, its…you…ugh, seriously, I'm about to pass out here," the man said, his hands upon his knees.

Emma, her courtesy a mere reflex, picked up Bo's chair and set it before the man.

"Thank you, little one," he said, taking a seat. Emma recognized the man's deep, throaty, voice from the ripple in the cave below her father's shed. He shook a handheld device in the air that flashed on the liquid crystal display. "I saw there was a break-in. And who is this girl, Bo?"

"Kugel, it's fine," Bo said, his hands up in admission. "Totally my fault. Leaned too much on the door."

"And her? Your Dad doesn't appreciate you bringing girls in here after hours. Besides, she's too young for you!"

Simultaneously Bo and Emma dry heaved at the thought.

"She's a friend of a friend, Kugel," Bo said, patting him on the shoulder. "Help me find my Grandfather if you can. We'll get this sorted out."

"Of course." With a snort and a grunt, Kugel pushed himself up and out the door.

"So I'm a friend now?"

"Emma!" Bo shouted, cutting her off. "I'm being safe. Siobhan told you to keep quiet on who you were, right?"

Emma folded her arms, nodding along to the truth of secrecy.

"Can you stay in Dad's shop for a few minutes while I find Grandpa?"

"Dad's shop? Oh, see I knew he had one. Where is it?"

Bo gestured with a wave of his arm at the dozens of knickknacks, furniture and antique books for sale all around them. Every item looked unique to a girl still looking at this world with human eyes.

"I'll be right back. I promise."

Before Emma could respond, Bo left through the broken door. He disappeared amongst the throng of the crowd, who gallivanted on as before.

Emma picked up the nearest lantern by the metal handle, and turned the knob to get the floating light in the center to allow her eyes to better investigate the room. Her fingers graced a stone tablet, about the size of a textbook. The ancient words, written in a language Emma couldn't begin to decipher, began to sing with the voice of an old man, worn out and beaten down by life and the meandering ways of love. The song was titled *Eisht as Nish*.

> Keayrt va mee aeg,
> As mish ta mee shenn;
> Keayrt va daa aym,

> Agh nish cha vel nane.
> Kys ta ny guillyn aegey
> Hurranse liorish mraane!

Deciding the song sounded too sad, Emma tapped the stone again. The weathered voice fell silent. Nearby, on a bookshelf stand against the wall, were various covered tins of teas. She took the nearest one marked *Congestion Eucalyptus* and unscrewed the round cover and took a long sniff. Her sinuses, esophagus and every airway in her lungs began to expand under the power of the clarifying, almost overpowering eucalyptus leaf.

On a table to the left of the teas were a variety of wrapped chocolates. Her stomach contracted at the sight of a bar marked *70% dark cocoa with pomegranate*. Then aware that this was her father's shop, Emma took the bar and ravenously ripped the paper wrapping, hoping her father would understand that she, and not a rat, had torn into the decadent dessert. With the first resounding bite into the bar, the intoxicating combination of the fruit and the dark chocolate was so delightful in her hungry state that it almost reached the level of Adacia's immaculate meals. The curious adventures in her father's store could keep her occupied for days on end.

Then ahead, the lantern light captured a long maple counter top that Emma was six inches taller than. Some sort of cash register folded into a locked portion of the counter. Emma, feeling playful, jammed her hands into three tin slides that fell into little bowls marked *Bank Credit, Silver Dollars, Boldger Coins* on the customer side of the register.

Beyond those, against the wall, Emma saw what looked like a several foot wide oval mirror. Water, filled with little flecks of golden minerals, seemed to sit along the surface, somehow not dripping onto the floor by the simple force of gravity. Emma set her chocolate bar aside and leapt onto the counter, throwing her legs over to the floor on the other side.

"Let's see what you can do."

With her right forefinger Emma touched the mirror. The water let out clear ripples each second from the point where Emma's skin graced the surface. The golden flakes formed into letters on the surface.

What communication do you desire?

"You're a ripple!" Emma said. Her smile widened when she turned around to view the store from the ripple's view, each table, item and far window still clear in her memory. "Exactly like in the shed cave."

A gaggle of voices roared past the avenue in front of the store window. All of these raucous belonged to twenty or so teenagers either skipping hand in hand or giving each other piggy back rides. Near the end of the group, Emma noticed a familiar face.

"Ciara!" Emma said. With a heave, she flung her body over the counter.

Emma ran a few steps towards the door, only to double back and take some more bites out of the chocolate, filling her mouth like a pig at a slop bin. She wiped away the cocoa that had melted onto her lips. Giggling like a fool, Emma bolted out of the door.

Emma shot under the arms of the long line of partiers, holding hands as they danced from side to side; their feet were never still. Dodging a few people as she ran, Emma never lost sight of Ciara, who looked so fixated with the sheer bliss of the festival and the frenetic folk song now pouring out from the stage, she didn't notice Emma run right up to her and snatch her body from the line.

"Watch it!" Ciara said as she tripped over Emma's feet. With a crash, Ciara bowled over Emma and they both landed on the cobblestone with a thud.

"Ciara! You'll never believe me," Emma said, bouncing back up like a coiled spring. "I just saw my brother!"

"Bo is here? Where?" Ciara pushed herself off of the ground and stood on her tip toes to look around. "Why do you have chocolate on your face?"

Emma wiped the corner of her mouth with her fingers, only to then lick off the chocolate. "He ran off to get my Grandpa. But look," Emma said, one arm positioning Ciara by her shoulder and the other pointing to J.W's shop. "That's my Dad's shop right there."

"Are you messing with me right now?"

"I'm not," Emma said, still surprised. "No prank is this planned out."

"Wow! Can we go inside the shop?"

Emma took Ciara's hand and the two attempted to mosey on by. Unfortunately for them the music shifted into an upbeat jig and more people, all decked out in the most elaborate Halloween costumes, started dancing. By moving left, right, or plowing straight through, Emma and Ciara had become glued to the moving crowd, carrying them down the block.

"The nimble Emma Adacia Grant moves left...she ducks right," Emma said, changing her voice to sound like an old time baseball commentator. She put Ciara into a laughing fit. "OOO, she ran into a chubby boy in a little girl's angel costume...that's gonna hurt her chances of escaping."

Seeing an opening between the hairy forearms of two broad-shouldered men, Emma tugged Ciara behind her. Right before they were out the dancing party, two men shouted an incomprehensible inebriated phrase and smashed their flagons together. A great deal of beer ebbed out of the glasses and fell onto the backs of Emma and Ciara.

"Ugh, gross!" Ciara said, touching the wet spot on the back of her hair.

"Thanks a lot, buddy," Emma said, flinging the malted beer from her fingers.

The taller of the two men turned to the girls, his embarrassed cheeks flush as soon as he caught Emma's eyes.

"Enjoy the beer shower, Emma?" Erik said, stepping out of the dancing line. He set down his flagon and handed Emma a clean handkerchief from his pocket.

"What are you doing here? Drinking?" Emma used the tailored cloth to dry out the moist spots on the back of her neck. "Why aren't you with Siobhan?"

Erik bent down to meet Ciara eyes; he cautiously avoided Emma's.

"You can look me in the eye, Erik. Why are people always afraid to do that?"

Ciara gestured to her eyes and whispered. "Maybe its cause…of that…you know, scary devil face you do?"

Erik cleared his throat and widened his eyes at Ciara in suspicion. "Well, girls. I was nervous, alright. I was going to…oh boy."

"Fine. But I know you like her," Emma said, seeing that Erik just wasn't ready as she fidgeted, showing his vulnerable side. "Where is she?"

"Siobhan? Eh, she had business to attend to. Vice-Governor and all. We're all busy tonight with things like this."

He pointed to one of the pumpkins that flew by. The spirited Jack-o-Lantern was being chased by a handful of young boys with outstretched hands and devious intentions.

"HELP! HELP!" the Spirit of Eugene Delacroix shouted. "These lads are trying to have their way with me!"

"That's a bit weird," Erik muttered to himself before he shouted, "Oi! Show some respect, boys!"

Hearing Erik's bellowing tone the boys pumped the brakes and stop giving chase.

"Yes, sir," the boys called, looking intimidated by Erik's brawny shoulders.

Erik took and sip from his mug and sighed. "Sit tight, girls. I will find Siobhan for you."

"At least tell her she looks pretty tonight," Ciara said, handing back Erik moist handkerchief.

"And that the perfume she's wearing is oh so lovely," Emma said, jokingly sniffing the air as she waved her fingers about her nose.

"She's wearing perfume?" Erik said, looking dazed.

Though no easy task, Emma and Ciara shoved Erik, easily more than their combined weight, in the direction of the government buildings.

"Fine! I can take a hint," Erik said, sauntering off.

"No, you can't," Ciara said under her breath as she shook her head. "Ghesh, some guys."

"Eh, he's an okay guy. Just a bit clueless. Don't like the way he talks about humans though." Emma ears began to notice that the sound that filtered in began to dim. She could feel her Alastar begin to warm on her skin.

"Emma? You okay?" Ciara said, her voice echoed at first.

Within a few moments, her friend's voice, along with the rest of the multiple layers of the festival, became silent, save for one distinct presence. Emma stopped Ciara from moving her mouth by placing her left forefinger to her friend's lips. Emma could hear the distinct sound of leather boot steps into the stone.

Ahead, there was a long train of festival patrons that began to dance past. Their elaborate costumes -one of a Champ/Lock Ness prehistoric water monster, and other of a cannibalistic ghost spirit, the Wendigo – showed to Emma that all of festival goers fascinated by the grim characters of legends.

The second to last figure in the wild dancing train caught Emma's attention. Every step this sallow man took, dressed as vampire with a long flowing cape, Emma happened to hear him and no one else. She could see that her Alastar began glow underneath her sweater.

The costumed vampire man made a spry movement out of the line. Out of the crowded space, Emma seemed to notice him duck into the doorway of B. Ross's weaver shop, next to Jonathan's trade goods store. She stepped forward to notice this man had the most unnatural pale and sallow skinned face in the shadows. From underneath his cloak his right hand, which was scarred with two old knife wounds, he produced a small pumpkin. With his long piano fingers, the joints bending in sickening ways, the man lowered a black oval grenade with sharp quills sticking out of it into a Jack-O-Lantern. Acting on instincts, Emma stepped up to him, her curiosity overpowering her concern. The sound of the festival came roaring back into Emma's ears and her concentration was thrown off.

Catching sight of Emma, the man hid the device under his black cloak. Though he was dressed as a vampire, Emma could have guessed by the deadness in the man's eyes that he perhaps was one.

"What are you doing?" Emma said. The man stared at her over his black cape, draped over his shoulder. "WHAT are you doing?"

The man, calm and collected, did not show an ounce of fear amidst Emma's confrontation; that is, until his eyes saw her Alastar.

"No!" the man said, his voice hoarse, drained of life. He dropped the Jack-O-Lantern in shock, the pumpkin shattering to pieces on the cold stone of the square. "It cannot be."

Still not understanding so many things about herself, Emma tried to appear confident as she straightened up her posture and took a firm step forward. Much to her disappointment, the man began to smile like a devil, aware that he had the upper hand. His lips parted to bare teeth that had been filed down into fangs.

"Emma, get over here," Ciara said, backing away, her lip beginning to quiver.

Emma caught a glint of the salvia glistening off of the man's teeth. She took Ciara's advice, only to trip over her own feet going backwards. She landed on her bottom with a thud at Ciara's feet. The man chuckled his raspy voice as he stepped forward, maliciousness at the edge of his fingers as they twittered about.

"You are my ticket back into the game! My my...to take one like you..."

"Sir! Get away from that girl!" Siobhan said.

Emma turned to see Bo marching down the edge of the square with Siobhan in the lead, followed by Grandpa Nicholas. Erik followed, his pistol ready to be drawn from a holster on his waist.

In the blink of an eye, the man tore away, running away with his cloak flapping behind him. He turned the corner next to Jonathan's shop, disappearing from the square.

"Erik. Go after him. I think he has a grenade," Emma said.

Erik's eyes caught the crumbled bits of pumpkin at Emma's feet. Drawing his firearm, he sprinted after the sallow faced man. The nearby crowd ended their revelry and stared at the situation at hand, some of them quite aware that things were not all well. One father took his little daughter, dressed as a blue faerie, into his arms and tore away from the danger.

Ciara and Emma ran up and hugged Siobhan, Nicholas and Bo, who were a bit short on affection for that harried moment.

"A possible terrorist attack and then the phantoms," Nicholas said to Siobhan.

"Too unsafe for my taste," Siobhan said, her concerned eyes scanning the crowd. "I know I am not supposed to be taking Marriagain's responsibilities…"

"Take them, already," Nicholas said, terse. "Remember, you are the elected Vice-Governor."

"Oh, you know that's just for sake of appearances," Siobhan scoffed.

"Not true," Nicholas said. Emma could see the apparent passion her Grandfather had for that government in his direct vocal cadence. "That post is so much more. And just because Marriagain is new on the job after the election is no excuse for her lack of organization when she's constantly kissing Eleanor's…"

"Nicholas, I am aware," Siobhan said, a repressed shudder of anger coming out. "Take the girls and go back to your house. I am closing down the festival."

Siobhan produced her mage orb from her side holster and held it up in the air. The glass began to glow like a streetlight.

"Siobhan, who are you calling?" Bo said.

"Take your sister and Ciara," Siobhan said. "Do this now, Bo. I will never forgive myself if you two are injured right before my eyes."

Erik came running back from around the corner. He holstered his weapon in frustration. "I could not find him. Slippery devil."

"All the more reason to close things down," Siobhan said.

"Come, girls," Nicholas said, giving Emma and Ciara a suggestive shove in the back. "Let us go to my house."

The flummoxed girls, swept up in the situation, followed Nicholas and Bo out from the edge of the square to a series of avenues forming to the north of the government buildings.

"What's happening, Bo?" Emma said as she tugged at her brother's brown cotton button down.

"Not sure. You might have accidently stopped a terrorist attack," Bo said, his pace quickening. "Let's just get out of here."

Emma looked behind her to the stage. Lady Eleanor set down her fiddle on a stand behind the band that continued to perform, unaware, like a great deal of the partiers, of any sort of peril.

"Emma! Stop stalling," Ciara called.

Glancing from Ciara back to the stage, Emma noticed that Lady Eleanor had disappeared.

"Where did she go?" Emma said, trying to find Eleanor's primary colored dress in the sea of autumn. As Bo came to tug Emma away be her left arm, she caught sight of Eleanor speaking to Siobhan hundreds of feet from the stage. "Whoa. How did she get there so quick?" Emma said.

"What are you talking about?" Bo said, letting go of his sister once she took the hint to walk on beside him.

Before Emma turned the corner she looked back to Burnham Square. Lady Eleanor was back on the stage in a matter of seconds, addressing the crowd. Emma heard the Lady's pristine, commanding voice echo off the walls of the mesh of folksy and neo-classical buildings that towered above her on her final walk to a stretch of two story houses that were imbedded into the western wall of Adoette.

"I regret to inform you my joyous partiers that we have to end our festivities for tonight…yes, I know. I know. Keep in mind this night, dear Adoette. We will all turn our hearts and minds to the ecstasy of the new season when the snow shall fall and the Gratitude Feast will bring us all together once again late next month. I bid you all a goodnight. Honor, wisdom, and fortitude to you all."

Emma tossed and turned in the spare bed of Grandpa Nicholas' house. The oak headboard was carved like the one Emma slept in at the Eastern Outpost, but with two differences – Adacia's name and a portrait of her face as a ten year old girl had been reproduced with stunning accuracy. Emma ran her fingers along the cheeks and chin of her mother. The engraved eyes looked into Emma's. For an instant, like when a baby discovers themselves in a mirror, Emma caught a glimpse of her own face in the thirty-plus year old wood carving.

Emma tip-toed out of the bed and to stretch her legs and lunge over the sleeping Ciara, who had fallen into an instant slumber once the snug wool and cotton sheets were pulled up to her neck. Emma so wished to continue her conversation about the splendor and mystery of the night with her friend. But as Emma looked at Ciara's hair falling over her fair, peaceful face, she decided to allow her friend to drift in an ocean of dreams.

The city was hushed. Emma couldn't see the entire square from the second story window of the bedroom for it was blocked by an inn, government buildings and what looked like a massive library just down the street. Guards moved about the avenues on alerted patrols, their firearms cupped by their nimble fingers. Once in a while, a driverless cart, made of metal and wood, would drift by without a sound, with tables and tents from the fair in their trunks, as if they were powered by remote control, not needing a man or horse to move the cargo along. Though Emma had already seen the dangers of this strange new world, she admired the seamlessness and the honor these Croatoans place into every hour of their lives. Those traits had been in Emma all along, though at that moment as she gazed out into the early November night, she dwelled upon herself being a girl of two worlds. For close to a half hour, she drifted around her mind at that windowsill, her fingers fidgeting with her Alastar.

With soft footsteps, Emma walked down the polished cedar stairs to the kitchen. She had hoped to find a cup of chamomile tea to tame her contracting mind.

"What are you doing up?" Bo said. He sat at the kitchen table in an old gray t-shirt and a pair of flannel sleeping pants, clutching a cup of steaming water. An opened container of herbal tea was next to him. He pulled out the chair next to him for Emma to take a seat.

"I couldn't sleep," Emma said, plopping herself down next to Bo.

"Me neither. Tea? Or I could make you some cocoa if you want without a burnt to a crisp marshmallow."

"Tea sounds awesome." She folded her arms upon to the table to lay her head down. Bo moved over to a tea kettle that hung from a moveable handle in the corner of the room over a small fireplace that Emma guessed was being heated by an odorless set of black rocks that rested beneath.

"Put some ice cubes in my water."

"I can't. Ice cubes don't exist here," Bo said, steeping some loose tea leaves into a small porcelain mug with no handle.

"Then what do Croatoans use to cool things down?"

"This." From a latched cabinet in the wall, Bo pulled out a small iron rod. By dipping the frigid iron into the scolding water, the temperature fell in a few seconds time, the steam even failing to rise from the no longer scalding surface.

After the tea was done steeping, Emma removed the loose leaves from the strainer, took the cup and sipped the lukewarm tea, taking a long, delighted gulp of the elderflower. Her nerves already began to relax.

Bo threw the cooling rod back into the sealed cabinet. He sat back down next to Emma, slurping his tea.

"Mom grew up here, didn't she?" Emma said.

"Yep. You don't remember this but we grew up in an apartment on the south side of the city."

"Seriously? How old was I when we left?"

"Almost four. I was ten when we left the forest to move into San Francisco to live as," Bo said, pausing to use air quotes. "Humans."

"I don't remember any of that."

"No. I never told you, I mean, we didn't."

"Bo, is this why you've been acting so strange the past few months? I mean, you were never around and even when you were home, I had to say things to you twice sometimes because you were like a thousand miles away."

Bo took a sip and sat up from the table. Walking over to the living room, Bo grabbed a small wooden coffer from a set of wooden shelves that were part of the wall. Emma recognized the unique box.

"That's the one that was sent to me!" Emma said. She took the coffer from Bo's arms and opened the lid to peer inside. The crystal vile with the red and silver gelatinous liquid along with the torn up letter was still inside. "Why do you have it?"

Bo wheeled his chair around to face Emma, eye to eye. "Mom told me to take it into Adoette and pretty much confront Grandpa about who sent these things."

"Did he send the coffer?"

"No. We still don't have a clue who did it. That's the problem. Someone could be looking for you. We had to keep things even quieter than usual."

Emma leaned in, her gaze and voice dead serious. "You know you I am, don't you?"

"My sister?"

"Really? What else?"

"Don't ask me, I was never told. But I know you can read minds..." Bo reached over and touched the Alastar, his right index finger gracing the metal prongs. "This star is indicative of Croatoans with magical powers."

"Ooo, careful," Emma said, backing away, surprised. Bo's skin wasn't harmed by the Alastar. "Wait, you didn't get cut. You're not bleeding."

"Nope. That wouldn't happen. I mean, I wore the thing for a few years when you were a baby."

"People other than me get cut when they touch it. How did you wear this for few years and not get cut to pieces?"

"Don't look so surprised. Someone had to take care of the jewel. I was told close blood lines don't feel any affects that the jewel will throw up in defense, unless the owner puts up defenses." Bo touched the Alastar again when Emma felt safe in moving closer to him.

Emma held up her Alastar. "So does this mean I can cast spells."

"From what I hear that's not even the tip of the iceberg of what that thing can do. Grandpa told me those jewels are made in labs and have a special connection to family bloodline and a child that will wear it once the kid is born."

Emma made a fist and tapped the flesh of her brothers left arm. "I can't believe you knew all of this. I mean I can kinda understand why you guys didn't say anything."

"Em, I wanted to but we should all be here at the same time to explain...explain why we had to lie to you all these years."

Emma plopped herself back into the chair, her eyes fixed on the small coffer resting next to her tea. The knowledge of being lied to all these years didn't do much to re-solidify her love and trust in the family.

"Why did you lie - you, not Mom or Dad - lie to me?"

"We were trying to protect you," Bo said. Bo coughed a few times. The words struggled to leave his throat. "Listen," Bo said, an odd, nervous laugh coming out. "I'm sorry. I'll never lie to you again."

Emma leaned up and looked her brother in the eye, beginning to grasp perhaps the pressure her Bo had been under.

"Never again?" Emma said, her voice sweet and sympathetic. "You know, you do this stupid little chuckle when you lie. I can tell if you will just so you know."

"Yeah. But I want to be forced to unless I have no other choice. I mean, hell, we used to tell each other everything about our day. You used to give me advice on girls, always making me smarter about how to handle things that I ever could by myself. What happened?"

"At least now there are no more secrets, right?"

Bo widened his eyes and nodded in acknowledgment before he took a careful sip from his hot mug. "Well, I'm not gonna share every secret about me. Look, I'll make you a deal."

Emma threw out her first educated guest, sensing out Bo's emotions in her mind.

"You're gonna introduce me to this Meira girl who's been writing you letters?"

"Yeah," Bo said, shooting her an odd look. "Did you read my mind?"

"I don't know," Emma said with a timid smile. "Just came to me!"

"Ha! Well, Croatoans with those jewels can. And I know you can because you do this little thing with your head when you know exactly what we're thinking," Bo said, tilting his head to the side with a dumb expression on his face, demonstrating for Emma.

"Totally wrong. It looks more like this." Emma didn't skip a beat as she turned her head to the side to stick out her tongue and fake poke herself in the eye.

"So much better," Bo said with a chuckle.

"So that explains why I knew what my teachers were going to say before they spoke up," Emma said, stopping herself, throwing up her arms in realization. "Wait…does that mean I was cheating all this time without even knowing it?"

"I hope so," Bo said, clasping his hands together in prayer. "Then I'd finally be the one Mom and Dad wait by the mailbox for the grades. I'd be smarter than you."

Emma flicked her fingers on Bo's nose, making him snort out his tea in laughter.

Bo re-filled his and Emma's cups with tea in those hours of darkness. They talked until the ticking second, minute and hour hands on the clock fell silent to their ears, the two of them getting back to the solace they had loved within one another for all the seasons that came before those first nights back in the Silver City.

Chapter Thirteen
A New Morning to a New Life

Emma was not disturbed by the soft glow of the sun rising, or the chirping of birds gathering on branches outside the second story window- her active mind wouldn't allow more than five hours of sleep. The revelation to this new life, both in her very essence and in the very land that she spent the past two night in brought out that puzzle in her mind, most of the pieces for once were logically fitting together.

Cracking open the window a smidge, Emma could smell the rising bread in Crescent's Bakery across the street. Families with parents and children stepped out from their houses and flats and into their favorite cafes and restaurants, their mouths watering for a plate of pancakes and eggs. Others dressed up in fancier clothing from fine linens to step outside the city and over bridges for a leisurely amble on the wooded trails.

Not wanting to be on the other side of the glass again, Emma tossed off the oversized sleeping shirt she borrowed from her brother and donned her sweater, jeans and winter coat. Realizing she had been wearing the same clothes for days, Emma darted over to the bathroom.

Once she figured out how to draw water from the deep saucer bowl on a stand where a sink would be, Emma used the washcloth to wipe away the collected oils on her skin. After throwing her hair back in a tie, Emma remembered to avoid the creeks she discovered in the wooden floor from the previous night and made silent steps all of the way out of the house.

Emma walked north, buttoning up her jacket in the late autumn cold that came in the night, frigid enough to almost bring snow. Her stomach knotted up when she passed the green awning of the *Ivy Café*, reminding her that although she could have eaten a shoelace at that point to curb her hunger, she still had no Croatoan silver dollars to use. Emma remembered a fifty-dollar bill she had placed deep within her inside jacket pocket. But before her hand reached in, she shook her head, knowing not a single currency exchange willing to take her American money after the anti-human receptions she was privy to in the past day.

Emma took in the changing facades of the houses and storefronts of the furthest northern East-West Avenue in Adoette before the northern wall. As she passed the due north gate, she witnessed those well-dressed folks she saw no more than a half-hour ago from her window coming back into the city, looking fulfilled and jovial, their faces and spirits cleansed by what Emma can guess was a worship ceremony. Though, Emma thought it odd that only the children seemed to carry the leather bound ecumenical worship documents, which had these words pressed into the binding in golden letters - *An Chéad Lá Solas agus Amharc – (The First Days of Light and Sight)*. The parents held square data tablets and books held tight to their sides, one of which became clear to Emma once one caretaker enthralled a child in a whimsical tale, gesturing with a science book entitled *A Concise Collection of Time*.

From the gate, the few city blocks that Emma walked along to the east fell away from massive government complexes, a community garden being converted into a winter greenhouse next the river that stemmed from the Burnham Square pond. Beyond that then the maple wood and limestone storefronts to houses on the road to dissolved into a two block area of ramshackle existences and industrial buildings, practically lifeless that morning in their sea of gray and white. The only lively soul that seemed to emanate from them was from a mural that was painted on the front of *Smithy's Ironworks*.

Emma walked up to touch the art history of civic achievements. She ran her fingers along the image of men constructing a rail line through the silver forest next to a series of frames showing the seasonal duties of a farmer and an apple orchard picker, providing crops for the Republic. Though this side of Adoette was sparsely populated at that time of day, Emma would bet that this wall fresco was a source of pride for the blue collar workers on a normal working day.

Then, without warning, the Alastar began to warm against Emma's skin. Holding the jewel close, she turned around, her eyes at attention.

On the corner, with an avenue alongside the one Emma was on, was a three story house, burnt and left to fall into disrepair for what Emma guessed was some many years. No ivy grew up its walls. No birds sat upon its caved in roof to sing a melody. The wooden trim and shingles that hadn't been licked by flames had filled with black mold. Even the air smelt acrid, poisonous. Death radiated out, sending an ominous chill down Emma's spine.

Then she developed a feeling in the back of her skull, like when one gets a slight headache – someone approached. Her instincts, like eyes in the back of her head, confirmed the familiar face.

"Morning, Bo," Emma said, turning to her brother. "What are you doing here?"

"Chasing after you as usual," Bo said, adjusting his black and white scarf over his green long sleeve shirt. Emma could see his eyes catch the sight of the burnt out house.

Bo crossed his arms as he shuddered, a sudden chill riding over his skin. "So you found the Timorale house, huh?"

"I guess. What is this place?"

"You know, I could explain but it's not gonna make any sense. Sorry."

"Oh, is it bad luck to go near the house or something?"

Bo snorted out a breath, shaking his head, confirming to Emma that she had no idea.

"Considering who grew up there, I don't know anyone who'd go in there unless they had a death wish," Bo said, looking hard at Emma. "And that means YOU! Don't go in there!"

Emma nodded, trusting her brother's words and the uneasy feeling the place brought.

"Let's get out of here. I don't know why the Timorale' house hasn't been condemned and demolished by this point. Nothing but bad memories if you ask me."

Emma set down her fork with a clang on the china plate. She laid back in her chair, her stomach feeling more stuffed than a turkey on Thanksgiving. Her mind rolled back on the recent delights of sweet rolls with pecans, patties of sausage and endless cups of cranberry juice so tart and fresh that she felt as if her body was being cleansed.

Having been so ravenous at the beginning of the meal, Emma and Ciara finished first. Crossing their legs, slouching in their low-back wicker chairs, they sipped their cups of chai tea. They listened to Bo and Grandpa Nicholas argue as they shared a slice of *The Ivy's* famous apple crumble.

"The alert has been lifted. It's not that big of a deal. I figure I'd be taking Emma and Ciara around town anyways. Give us at least until Mom and Dad got here," Bo said.

Nicholas wiped his mouth with his white cloth napkin, adjusting his glasses. "Emma deserves a bit of freedom, but not beyond the city limits."

"What's this about Mom and Dad?" Emma said, setting down her tea.

"They'll be here by nightfall or a little after." Nicholas waved over a frazzled young waitress.

"Are they mad?" Emma said.

Nicholas looked hard at Emma as he stabbed a loose apple slice on the plate. "Do you even need to ask that question?"

Emma nodded and returned to sipping her coffee. Her imagination painted what she could guess was a decibel shattering argument that Adacia and Nicholas had from one ripple communicator to another.

"In all honesty so should you. Either way we will clear all of this mess up by tonight, I promise," Nicholas said, offering his Granddaughter a reassuring nod.

The five-foot nothing late teenage waitress, Sarah, approached, her wrinkled brown shirt and white apron, with a pen and note sticking out of every pocket; probably her first day on the job Emma guessed.

"Ah, hello Sarah. Has the morning rush made you want to forget your duties and join us yet?" Bo said.

Though Emma could tell that she was a few years older than Bo, the bags under Sarah's eyes told a different story. As she regained her composure, Sarah flashed a brief but flirtatious smile at Bo, which Emma caught.

"Come and sit down with us, Sarah," Bo said, about to pull up a chair.

"Oh, thank you Bo but I cannot," Sarah said. "Maybe some other time, though."

"Yeah," Bo said, looking cool and flirtatious as well. "Maybe some other time?" Bo said. "Ouch!"

Emma drew her foot back over from a swift kick she gave to Bo to the shin. "Ahem, G-friend...G-friend," Emma said, coughing into her napkin.

Sarah handed over to Nicholas a wooden board the size of hardcover book, reinforced with metal trim, the front appearing to be transparent water. "Here is your news, Mr. E. I was able to program the NewsBook to the *Augustus Star News* and the *Silver Forest Gazette* this time. Is that alright?"

"Perfect," Nicholas said, taking the NewsBook. "I can guess you still remember me reading the *Star News* and the *Gazette* every morning at school."

"School? Grandpa, are you a teacher?" Emma said. Unconscious of her surroundings, blinded by more revelations, Emma fidgeted with her star.

"Yes," Nicholas said, with a nod, looking as if he felt a bit foolish. "I suppose we should talk about that too."

As Sarah looked over at Emma, her eyes moved down. They widened at the sight of the Alastar. Sarah drew her hands up to her mouth with a gasp.

"Oh my! This is your Granddaughter, Mr. Elywn?"

"Yes, Sarah. This is Emma." Nicholas widened his brow at Emma. She took the hint and placed her Alastar beneath her sweater.

Sarah pointed at Emma's star, which rested on the neck rim of her sweater. "You're a...Mr. E, is she a...oh my!"

"Calm down," Nicholas said, whispering. Heads from nearby tables started to turn around to catch the commotion in the packed house.

"Please, Emma…let me see if I can get you a free meal…" Sarah said, tearing off.

"You don't have to do that…okay, she's gone," Bo said. He sat up and gestured to Emma and Ciara. "We should go now!"

The girls looked over at the curtain that separated the entrance to the kitchen with the dining room. Right away, Sarah began to chat with the other waiters and waitresses, starting a frenzy of gossip and finger pointing in Emma's direction.

"Yeah, I agree with Bo," Ciara said, tapping Emma on the shoulder.

"Be back at the house by mid-afternoon," Nicholas said, pointing a stern finger. "Don't let the girls leave your side." Nicholas gestured to Bo's waist. "Do you have your…?

"I do. Fully charged," Bo said, taping a small bulge tucked into his belt, hidden by his shirt and jacket.

Ciara followed Bo out of *The Ivy* but Emma lingered behind, standing before her Grandfather, noticing the empty chairs.

"You want me to stay with you, Grandpa?"

Nicholas leaned over and kissed Emma on the forehead, his breath smelling like the strawberries he had eaten. "No, Blue Eyes. Trust me, I can handle the staff. Most of them used to be in my classes."

"Okay, Emma said as she wrapped her arms around her favorite storyteller. "Thanks for not getting mad at me for running away."

"No worries, my dear. Let's just say you're mother prepared me for this more than you know."

"Really? How so?"

217

Nicholas touched the screen of his NewsBook. A ripple of water appeared on the crystal surface, dissolving to newspaper print that filled the blank space with the front page from the *Augustus News Star*, apparently as Emma guessed was a respectable news source. The front headlines read...

-*Augustin Croatoan Family missing: family of five feared dead after boat drifted into human shipping lanes without cover of cloaking..."*

-*Human Famine Scatters Population: Croatoan's Concerned about Sealing Borders*

-***Opinion****: Though mostly innocent, humans will be forced flood our lifeboats.*

Looking at Emma over his glasses that hung on the lower bridge of his nose, the old man crumbled before Emma's sweet, blue-eyed gaze, transfixing him with her charm.

"Don't bother with those headlines now, Emma. In reguards to you mother, let's just say," Nicholas said, pondering, "That you and your mother are similar in many ways. Now go along before someone starts enough gossip to have you show up on the front page of the *Silver Forest Gazette*."

Outside on the street, Emma joined a patient Ciara and Bo. The revelation of Emma having more in common with Adacia, the woman that frustrated Emma to tears puzzled her. The issue distracted her enough to not hear her brother until he waved his hand in front of her face.

"Hello! Wake up!"

"Grandpa just said that Mom and I are a lot alike."

Bo nodded, looking off as he thought. "Huh. I guess you and Mom are pretty much the same."

Ciara, catching Emma's offended look, leaned into a punch that connected square with the joint of Bo's shoulder.

"Hey! What the heck?"

"Sorry," Ciara said. "But don't ever tell a girl she's exactly like her Mom."

"Right?" Emma said, crossing her arms. "How would you like it if I said you were exactly like Dad?"

"I am a lot like Dad. You are a lot like Mom. Deal with it."

"Fine, I will," Emma said, pouting. "So are you going to take us around town or what?"

"Easy there, Miss Sassy. Follow me," Bo said, almost laughing at the fact that he got to Emma.

The girls walked alongside Bo south through the city. As they passed through the Boldger Hall and the neighborhood of government offices named Capital Knoll, the street elevation played games with their feet, rising up and leveling out at random. Either because of the chaos or secrets of the previous night, Emma noticed in the daylight that the Capital complex and surrounding government buildings were almost on a very small hill within the city, looking down upon the citizens. Down the road, an employee of *Crescent's Bakery* in a white bakery smock was sliding a tray of soft, fresh baked biscuits and fruit pies before the front window. Emma's bottomless pit of a stomach felt like following a young mother and her children in the store to buy the fresh bakes of the day.

When they reached Nicholas' street, Emma turned to walk into her Grandfather's house. Bo whistled at Emma.

"Hey. We're not going back," Bo said, walking backwards as he spoke, his hands in his pockets.

"Where are we going to?" Emma said.

With a wave of his hand, Bo turned right around and continued on. "It's a surprise," Bo said over his shoulder. "Hurry up. We might be late."

Emma and Ciara exchanged an intrigued glance. Jumping back onto the road, Emma and Ciara jogged to catch up with Bo.

"This surprise better not mean I have to climb another hill and befriend a Sasquatch," Ciara said.

"Oh stop being such a scaredy cat," Emma said, "You know you liked Bigfoot. And I heard he came into the town."

"Really? Hmm, I haven't seen him. I wonder where he's hiding."

"Knew you guys made friends."

Near the southwest corner of Adoette was one continuous, massive building which stretched several city blocks. Emma had to crane her neck a bit to see up to the roof, past five floors of incongruous proportional windows, each one a different geometric shape. When they came up to a courtyard Emma thought it odd that there were no black iron gates to keep people out.

"What is this place?" Ciara said.

Emma and Ciara couldn't help but to notice all of the openness of the horseshoe shaped courtyard dotted with young ash trees and plenty of benches underneath their branches. Stuffed on these benches and around the courtyard were what Emma counted were about fifty teenagers of scattered ages, all of them with day packs at their feet, impatiently waiting around. Many resorted to playing card games, only the cards were floating images in the air, powered by a three inch long handheld device that shifted decks and organized hands no different than the creatures in Eleanor's story from the night before.

"This is Woodland Academy, the school for Adoette," Bo said. He gestured to his left to the double oak doors a few steps up a marble staircase with a stone balustrade on either side. "That door is to literature, writing and rhetoric classrooms." Bo then pointed to an identical set of stairs and a door on the opposite side of the courtyard. "That goes to the science and math classrooms. Believe me, they're awesome classes."

At the middle bend of the horseshoe square, smack in-between the other two doors were a dozen polished white marble stairs that led up to two massive double oak doors, wide enough to allow a truck to pass through.

"What's that? The main entrance?" Ciara said.

"Yep. That pretty much goes to everything else like History, Arts, assembly hall and dining halls, offices....whoa, watch out girls!" Bo said. He had to dodge a few girls, who looked around fourteen. They chased down a little boy with circular glasses and messy hair who hadn't hit his growth spurt yet.

"Good to know kids torture people anywhere," Emma said as she watched the boy get antagonized.

Bo shrugged. "It happens, especially to geeks," Bo said, sending an unappreciated smirk to Emma. "I think the whole set of classes are going on a day hike today."

Emma noticed near the middle of the square, sitting on a bench under a tree, was a rather striking mixed ethnic Native American/Caucasian girl with long brown hair that was styled into curls. This girl, about Bo's age, was sitting alone. Her eyes focused on a glass orb in her right palm, identical to the one Siobhan used to conjure magic.

"Bo," Emma said, pointing. "I think that girl over there is a Mage."

Bo smiled even before he turned to see the young woman. "Oh…that's who I wanted you to meet. She's the one who's been writing letters to me."

"That's Meira? You're dating a Mage?"

"For the last time, I'm not dating her," Bo said, elongating his words in frustration. "I'd LIKE TO, though. Follow me. And be cool!"

Emma couldn't help but to notice the dejected Ciara, who hung her head a bit low.

"I didn't know your brother had a girlfriend," Ciara said.

"Ohh, Ciara," Emma said, throwing her arm around her friends shoulder. "There's no way an almost eighteen year old would date a grade school kid like you. No offense."

"Yeah, you're right. Sorry." Ciara shook her head, as if her better nature overpowered her desires. "That would probably be weird."

"Probably?" Emma said, scrunching her eyebrows in a look towards Ciara.

"Will!" Meira sprang up from the bench and threw out her arms to give Bo a tremendous hug, which he heartily returned with a strong squeeze around her back from his right arm.

"Ummm, Will?" Emma said.

"That's not his name, right?" Ciara said.

"It's his first name, William. That's Dad's middle name. We just always called Bo, well…Bo. That's his middle name." Emma began to develop a devilish smile, thinking of all the ways she could torture her brother. "Oh, I have an idea."

"Who is this?" Meira said in the most pleasing way as she saw Emma saunter up. Meira's perfect white teeth and wide smile, making her radiant olive eyes disarm Emma in matter of minute.

"This is my sister. Emma and her friend Ciara," Bo said.

"You did not tell me you had a sister! You keep secrets!" Meira said, playfully pushing Bo aside.

Emma held out her hand, giggling at this. "Oh I like her, don't you, Willy?" Taking Meira's hand and shaking it, Emma noticed how smooth her skin was, a clear indication to Emma that she's never had to do manual labor in all her life.

"So they call you Willy at home?" Meira said.

Bo grit his teeth, his hands balling up in his pockets, holding back. "No. They SHOULD call me Bo. But..." Bo then developed a devilish grin of his own as he looked at Emma. "Mom and Emma get it confused. They're so alike sometimes. I mean, even Emma's middle name is even my Mom's. Weird, right?"

Emma narrowed her eyes at Bo, who winked back, looking satisfied.

"Same names. That is an honorable thing to do," Meira said, shaking Ciara's hand as well. "It is nice to meet you both. My, I have to say Emma that you have the brightest, bluest eyes I have ever seen, just like a Conjurer."

Emma was about to admit as such, touching the string on her necklace to remove the Alastar. She let her hand fall to her side when she saw Bo shake his head with extreme urgency. Meira looked between Bo and Emma, suspect of the secret at hand.

"Thanks for saying that, Meira. I get those comments a lot," Emma said, gesturing to the orb in Meira's hand. "You have an orb just like Siobhan."

Meira held the foggy orb out for them to see, beaming with pride. "Yes, I do. The Continental Council approved me three months ahead of my eighteenth birthday just a few days ago!"

"Congratulations," Bo said, teetering on his feet, looking to Emma as if he wanted to go in for a hug. "That's so great, Meira!"

"Thanks. I thought so too," Meira said, a tad haughty.

When Meira leaned over to show Ciara the orb, Emma spread her arms wide, closed her eyes and made puckered her lips at her brother, reveling in the mockery. Bo started to raise his hand with an inappropriate gesture before Meira popped back into view, forcing Bo to pocket his hand.

"Well thank you, Will…I mean Bo," Meira said, looking confused. "What should I call you?"

"Either one. You can call me whatever you want," Bo said, closing his eyes as soon as he spoke, almost as if he knew the line was lame.

Emma couldn't help but try to continue her streak of annoyance. "Awwwwwwww, so cute!"

Meira leaned over to whisper into Bo's ear, eyeing the girls as she did so. "She's trying to make you blush, isn't she?" Bo groaned in recognition, as if he was aware that Emma could hear them.

Emma stepped forward and changed her tune, satisfied in torturing her brother enough. "What does your orb do, Meira?"

"A whole gamut of things. Look at this."

Meira grabbed a fallen leaf from the cobblestones and held it in front of her outstretched orb. "I cannot do much yet. But Lady Eleanor said my conjurer tests I have taken over the years said I should be proficient in most of the three Mage schools of Fire, Frost, and Arcane."

"Are you serious? All three?" Bo said.

Meira pursed her lips in joy, supremely confident. "My father knew I would be."

"Is that rare?" Emma said.

Bo spoke ahead of Meira, cutting her off. "I'd say. Most Mages are proficient in one school, not all three."

"Wow. You must be in the top of your class at school," Emma said, her mind imagining Meira acing every test.

"Top two percent, Emma," Meira said, stressing the importance.

Holding the orb in the palm of her hand, Meira concentrated on the leaf. The mist inside the orb began to swirl like a torrential storm cloud. Without warning, the leaf went up in flames.

"Whoa! Blow it out," Ciara said, jumping back in fright.

"No problem," Meira said, concentrating on the smoldering leaf again. As her orb began to swirl once more, the leaf became filled with ice crystals, extinguishing the flames with a slow hiss.

Emma touched the iced over leaf with her right forefinger. It was sub-zero to the touch. "So can you do that third one…arcane?"

Meira dropped the leaf and placed her orb inside her one strap over the shoulder day pack, looking a bit sheepish.

"I'm sorry, Emma. I cannot yet do it," Meira said, patting her thigh. "I know. It's a bit embarrassing."

"Don't be so hard on yourself, Meira," Bo said. "You just got your orb. At least this won't impact your training."

Meira bit her lip, looking doubtful. "The Continental Council said that next year they would decide if Siobhan, Marrigain or Lady Eleanor would train me."

"Train you? Emma said, tilting her head to the side, concentrating on Meira's mind, which had this strange, wall-like aura to it akin to what Emma felt around Siobhan body. "Train you like a…what are those called?"

Meira laughed a bit at this honest question she took as a joke. "Of course not, silly. I would have been born with a conjurers jewel like Eleanor's comet necklace."

Emma faked a nod, acting as if she should know better. "Of course. You're right."

At the main entrance two older gentlemen and one excitable young instructor, looking about as thin as a string bean, propped open the door. "Students," the young student aide said, his voice cracking with every word. "The biology walk is leaving now." Needless to say, every boy and girl started laughing at this, cracking their voices on purpose as if they just hit puberty.

Meira threw her pack over her shoulder and moved close to Bo. Emma could feel the repressed romantic tension between them.

"I was thinking that we should start writing each other by Instantaneous Ink," Meira said.

"Then we wouldn't have to wait for the letters," Bo said, leaning his head against hers. They were inches away from kissing, both of their eyes eager.

"Ms. Rolfe! Would you care to join your classmates?"

Bo and Meira turned around to see one of the two older instructors with a crick in his back continue his barking at Meira from the front steps.

"Darn," Emma whispered to herself. "Thanks for ruining the moment, dude."

Meira, hearing what Emma had said, shared a tiny nervous laugh with her as she backed away from Bo. "I agree," Meira whispered to Emma. "I am sorry everyone but I do have to leave. Lady Eleanor is meeting us in the forest about a mile up for the walk."

As she crossed her arms, Emma kept the jealously of going on that walk as well and being in the presence of Lady Eleanor in a wish. "Oh, well, have fun!"

Bo leaned close to Meira. "So, I know you're busy and I don't want to get in the way of your schedule but…can I call on you tomorrow?" Bo said, his nervous hands back in his pockets.

"I'll call on you tomorrow night," Meira said, flashing another one of her sparkling white toothed smiles before she jogged away, her hair bouncing around as she joined her classmates filing inside Woodland Academy.

"Awwww, you're in wuv," Emma said, giggling.

"I like her. And I'm not in love," Bo said, shoving his sister. "You're such a brat, you know. I swear I'm going to tease the heck out of you when you get a boyfriend."

"Psh," Emma said, rolling her eyes. She wouldn't even know what to talk about with a boy she found cute. "Like that'll happen."

Ciara started laughing at this as if she expected Emma to as well. "Totally."

"What's so funny about that?" Emma said.

"Nothing. Oh you think..." Ciara said, her voice quick and nervous. It's just...hey! You know what? Let's have Bo show us around. Come on!" Ciara bounded away, looking determined to hide her head in the sand.

"Wow. She handled that well," Bo said. He turned to Emma and gestured towards the school. "What'ya think about Meira? She's pretty great, right. I mean, you didn't get a chance to see it but we have a ton in common and we can talk for hours. Pretty good sign, right?"

"Maybe. Well, Mom and Dad can still talk to each other without getting annoyed so I guess that says something."

"I think I'm going to start asking her out on dates. We've really only been friends, you know, writing each other back and forth."

"Go for it. Ask her out. If you're asking me, and I know you are, right?" Emma said, a smirk on her face, knowing the ins and outs of Bo. "I like her. She seems sweet."

Bo let out a long and breathy relieved sigh, which casted an amused spell over Emma's heart. "Thank God. Okay! So do you want to see the rest of the Silver City?"

"Sure! I wanna see everything," Emma said as she walked out of the Woodland Academy cobblestone courtyard with Bo, unable to repress her smile.

"Why are you smiling so much?" Bo said.

Emma shrugged and dug her hands into her coat pockets as she sauntered on, ready to give a good ear. "Long story. Alright, are you going to tell me more about this girl?"

Over the proceeding hours into the afternoon, Bo played tour guide to Emma and Ciara. The soles of their shoes touched every street corner in Adoette. When the girls pointed to ask about the line of houses on the south side of the city or about the five story, Empire Baroque style architectural exterior Aileworth Hospital on the city's east side, Bo was there to respond like a historian.

The city and the Croatoan's within went about their daily routines, never too much strife reaching their rosy cheeks in the near freezing temperatures of that day. Emma found it interesting how so many wore light jackets and sweaters in an air temperature near freezing, cold enough to make a thin skinned human run inside to thaw out. These Croatoan citizens, even in the crowded stone and building laden capital city of Adoette, seemed to love the feeling of the outside air on their pink cheeks, and a daily fair exposure of nature, be it wood, leaf or winter wheat in their gentle hands.

"That's Boldger Hall. The seat of our government," Bo said, "And that's Fraunces Tavern, that's the Sagan Science Academy, and that's the Mithra Temple of worship."

Emma and Ciara took in as much as they could of the Silver City, leaving little room for questions in their crowded, overwhelmed tourist minds. Bo was adamant in keeping the girls moving as casual spectators, not staying in one place too long to draw folks with long ears and divisive minds that might be lurking after the previous night. Some Croatoans, out for a philosophical talk or a bout of exercise, were beginning to stare at Emma and Ciara's clothing. Emma felt as if she was walking the streets of Rome and Paris once again, their American styles, the jeans and tennis shoes, sticking out like a sore thumb in a land that had no one wearing them.

At the bell tower of the Mithra Temple on Burnham Square, next to memorial and just a stone's throw from the banyan tree, a massive single bell struck a single resounding note that echoed through the city, resonating the strength and memory of the Republic.

"The Foundation Bell," Bo said, pointing to the tower close to eight stories up from the square.

"It chimed five times. Is it five o'clock?" Emma said.

"No. They don't go by twelve hours," Bo said, turning around to the girls. "Look up there."

Just beyond where they stood, just north of Boldger Hall, was a ten story clock tower which matched the design and size of another one at the southwest corner of the city. Emma and Ciara both titled their heads in confusion at the clock face.

"It's fifteen thirty-five," Bo said.

"In the morning?" Ciara said, "Oh, you mean at night."

"Morning starts at zero with the sunrise and the night ends at twenty-four hours."

"Okay," Emma said, trying to wrap her head around this. "But how can you tell what time of day it is?"

Bo looked at the girls, an odd squint in their direction, as if this was common knowledge. "You look outside?"

"But what if you're stuck inside?" Ciara said, still look a she looked from Emma to the clock as a haze of gray clouds rotated with the time.

Bo screwed his own head to the side as he looked at the dumbfounded faces of the girls with a perplexed, long stare. "You…get a watch?"

"I still don't get it," Emma said. "But I like the little cloud."

"Yeah, it's pretty cool. When it rains, little drops start falling on the weather ring," Bo said. "When there is a lightning storm, bolts of lightning show up on the clock."

"I gotta ask Dad for…a…Ciara? Where are you going?"

In a near trance, Ciara walked to a shop on the edge of Burnham Square, tucked into the end of the Marshall Building entitled *El Dorado*. The lettering on the front gleamed in what looked to be either 24 karat gold or polished brass. Without turning back to acknowledge Emma and Bo, Ciara removed her precious ring from her finger and palmed it to fling the door open.

"Oh, no," Emma said, slapping her brother on the elbow to follow.

"What's up?"

"Ciara is trying to find her Dad."

A sweet tune whistled in Emma and Bo's ears, like that of a flute from a distant land, as they entered *El Dorado*. An abnormally tall man with his bones almost protruding from his skin and with a brow ridge like a yeti, leaned into them.

"Don't touch anything unless you plan to buy the item," the guard said, his voice in the lowest bass note possible.

"We're just helping my friend, Ciara. She just came in."

With a long, bony finger, the guard pointed to a vault style door beyond them that was a foot ajar.

Emma opened the hefty cast iron door to find the room inside to be so overpowering with a golden light and shimmering crystals, that she and her brother were forced to squint. Next to the door was a sign that read "Glasses for Shoppers. Please put on. We are not liable for damaging your eyes." Emma and Bo were quick put on a pair of the sunglasses, softening the light, yet making each ruby and diamond set in silver and gold sparkle through the special lens. Emma slipped the glasses down on the bridge of her nose to see without the "Glasses for Shoppers" the jewels, though exotic and treasured, were simply high-end and nothing more.

Behind a low counter was a short, round faced man with a rather long, craggy beard that looked like cobwebs. He wore different dark shaded glasses than those issued to customers to balance out his sight. Ciara stood before him with glasses on as well. She handed over her precious ring. Emma and Bo cautiously hovered over Ciara's shoulders.

"What are you doing?" Emma said, tapping her friend. Ciara didn't respond. Her eyes were fixed on El Dorado's owner, a man named Francois, who spoke with a twinge of a French accent.

"Hmmm, yes the ring is unique," François said.

His fingers ran over every corner of the ring. He even raised his eyebrows for a moment at the design. Standing up, Francois bounced on his tiny, kid sized feet to grab a book on the highest shelf entitled Jewelry *Designs from The State of Chrysanthemum and the Kingdom of the Sugar Loaf Mountains*. As Francois flipped through the pages, Ciara's nervous fingers twitched all over the counter.

"Nope. I was wrong. I do not recognize the pattern, little miss."

"What?" Ciara said, a little too loud. "They said that you would know. The Watchers said you were the best!"

"Well, I appreciate the word of mouth but to be dead honest with you, I would pretty much recognize a jewel from any corner of the world."

"Really? Can you check again?"

"Miss, I have been at this for going on seventy years," Francois said, handing back Ciara's ring. "Jonathan Grant at J.W's might know. He's a good and persistent fellow for research. Don't listen to what those naysayers have spoken about him having the 'dirty human touch'…bunch of bigots."

"Are people racist to Daddie?" Emma whispered to Bo, her eyes remaining on Ciara.

"You don't know the half of it," Bo said, shaking his head. Bo stepped up and nudged Ciara's shoulder. "Hey, Ciara, you okay?"

Ciara took back the ring from Francois. "Thank you," Ciara said, her meek voice a whisper. Without a word she turned and stepped out of the glittered room, her head down, a hand clutching the ring to her chest.

"Did I say something to upset her?" Francois said.

"Her Dad gave her that ring," Emma said, pausing to look around. "She thought he worked here."

"No, sorry little miss. I know my two employees well. They are my sons, the jewel designers," Francois said, beaming with pride.

"Thanks for your help," Bo said.

"Of course. Mr?"

"William."

"Well, please do come again, William. We have a fabulous selection of bridal rings, young man. Any pretty girl in your life?"

Bo laughed, the crimson blush of his embarrassment sticking out from his cheeks in the golden glare of the room. "I'm not ready for that yet. Thank you."

Emma began to hum the 'Here Comes the Bride' theme on the way out of the door, much to the chagrin of Bo.

After Emma and Bo heard the El Dorado tune whistle in their ears once more they stepped outside to see a light dusting of snow beginning to fall from the low, packed gray clouds above. A few surrounding young children began to cheer as they danced around the snowflakes. The adults that accompanied them all let out either a sigh or a grown that autumn had unofficially ended.

"Where's Ciara? Ciara!" Emma said.

"Over here," Ciara whispered.

Sitting on the corner, Ciara sat with folded arms, tears streaming down the dry skin on her cheeks. Emma knelt before her and caressed her hand.

"I thought he'd be here. Where is he!" Ciara said, at a near shout. "I'm so stupid. So stupid!" With this, Ciara buried her head onto Emma's shoulder and allowed her defenses down enough to leak out a few tears. Like a good friend, Emma patted Ciara's hair, somehow not caring that her friend could be soaking her good wool coat. Once Emma recalled what Adacia use to do for her in these situations, Emma hummed a tune in Ciara's ear. Ciara backed away, almost laughing.

"You wanna rock me to sleep, too?" Ciara said, laughing through the crocodile tears.

"Well now," Emma said, her giggle trying to loosen Ciara up.

"Ciara," Bo said, kneeling down next to Emma. "We'll help you find out where that ring came from."

"Yeah," Emma said, holding Ciara back to get the attention of those hazel eyes. "We'll ask my Dad. And then he'll ask his business partners."

From the cold stone ground, Bo picked up Ciara's ring and slid the treasured band back onto her finger. Ciara shuddered after Bo did this, apparently snapping back to life with a new, hopeful emotion rising.

"Ohhh, she loved that," Emma said with a grin.

"Shut-up!" Ciara said, shoving Emma. The two friends couldn't help but to laugh as Ciara wiped away her tears.

"Thanks, Bo for that." Ciara said, waving at Bo to get his attention. "Hey Bo? What are you looking at?"

Bo stood up and stared at the clock tower. "It says it stopped snowing."

By all that Emma could see, the snow fell at an even steadier pace. "Maybe the clock is broken."

"No. The clocks have a reputation for perfection."

Standing up, Emma craned her neck to see. The weather wheel locked and remained still, left behind by the advancing seconds. Then, the wintery clouds were slowly replaced by a pattern of flat clouds on their bottom, black as night.

A tiny pricking sensation formed throughout Emma's skull. She could feel all of her senses awaken as her Alastar began to warm against her skin. The smell of the winter air, the flakes of snow melting on her face, the position of the people at that exact point in the stone square, their voices making a harmonious memory – the scene was all too familiar. When the puzzle within Emma's mind fit everything into place, she inhaled in shock.

"This was my vision! This was my vision, Bo!"

"Your vision? The one you said you had at school?" Bo said, his eyes widening.

"Look! What's that?" Ciara said, pointing to the eastern sky above the city.

A large, floating platform, half concealed by a choking black smoke appeared from the clouds above. It floated over Adoette and came to a halt in the northeast corner.

"Cloud Ships aren't supposed to touchdown within a mile of the city," Bo said. "This doesn't feel right at all."

The Foundation Bell began to chime in short, repeated intervals, carrying out across Burnham Square. The nearby Croatoans looked at the bell, almost in shock. From Boldger Hall, a set of four guards ran out of the building, two of them with guns drawn.

"Get inside!" one of the guards shouted at the top of his lungs. "Brace your doors. We have a security breach!"

The one guard, Sergeant Morales, communicated through her handheld device, which brought up a translucent image of the city. "Code: Matwau. Code: Matwau!"

The citizens let out the most terrible shriek of fear that Emma had ever heard. Mother's threw their palms to their cheeks. Little children starting crying. Older men and women suddenly became nimble and moved their creaky joints as fast as possible to safety. Guards began to pour out of The Department of Treasury and Department of Defense complex down the avenue, leading the panicked citizens to shelter.

"We can't stay here. Whoever that is, they're looking for me," Emma said. "This area was where I was at in my vision when the phantoms came."

"Then we shouldn't be here," Bo said, helping Ciara up and running ahead.

"Where are we going?" Ciara said, scared.

"There's a Watcher of the Wood office next to the Arboretum. We should be away from the main government buildings. They'll look for you there, Em. And if your vision is right…" Bo pointed to the street corner before the first bridge. Emma could feel her Alastar warm once again with the threat of a cold spirit, lingering, waiting to pounce. The hairs upon her forearms stood on end. "…they're already waiting for you around the corner," Bo said with a swallow.

The three ran north through the city as fast as their feet could fly. As Emma looked east, little shadowy figures were descending a long trail of vapor to the streets. The foundation bell continued to carry out the deafening pang.

Chapter Fourteen
Shadows of the New World

Their pace upon the cobblestones quickened. The wind blew at them, tossing their hair back, speckling the heads of Emma, Bo and Ciara with little snowflakes. Turning a corner, their hearts began to race at the sight of a small contingent of phantoms gliding in their direction down the long most northern east-west avenue of Adoette. The undead were being guided by three men dressed as Watchers of the Wood.

"Phantoms!" Ciara shrieked.

Taking the paralyzed Ciara by the hand, Bo turned left into a small street that led north, tucked between a few three story houses. A double wooden gate to the arboretum was the dead end to the avenue.

Emma lagged behind, watching the nearest phantoms terrorize. One fully formed, human-like phantom picked up an elderly man as he stepped into a doorway. The companion phantom plucked a teenage girl, a green apron around her waist, huddled behind a tree. Both of the innocent Croatoan's began to scream their lungs out as the phantoms shook them violently, copying their cries as they levitated into the air. Emma recognized the familiar face of the girl from the breakfast that morning

"Sarah! No!" Emma said, reaching out to them.

Her feet leapt forward where others ran away. Emma had not a thought on her mind other than to deliver the poor girl, sniveling in mental anguish, back down to the earth. From underneath her sweater, she took out what the demons sniffed the air for.

"Hey! Look what I've got!" Emma shouted, holding her Alastar out.

The bloodshot eyes of the phantom that carried Sarah became fixed upon Emma, never wavering. His hands, where rotten flesh and bone interweaved with a thin shroud of mist above like fog on a swamp, became loose. Sarah fell from the phantom's grasp and all of the power of her lungs screamed the ten foot fall onto the hydrangea bushes in front of The Ivy. Sarah rolled over clutching her left elbow, sobbing, tears flowing down her face.

"Emma! He said he would kill my Dad!" Sarah said.

"Don't listen to it. Get inside The Ivy," Emma said, her eyes staring down the phantom in this duel of fears. Sarah refused to move and the tears continued to roll. Holding tighter to her Alastar, Emma could hear her voice amplify. "Get inside. NOW!"

Sarah awoke from the spell of nightmares the phantom had cast upon her. Getting up with some difficulty, she took a few labored steps to force herself inside the front door of The Ivy, slamming the door shut behind her.

From behind Emma, Bo ran up and took a mighty hold on her hand like a vice.

"Bo! What about those poor people," Emma cried out, "I have to help them!"

"No!" Bo said, holding his sister even tighter, "I have to save you, Em. You're too important."

Before Bo could drag Emma to safety, three of the men dressed in Watcher clothing closed in on Emma.

"Oh thank God...wait!" Emma said, her mind flashing warning signs as the men, each with distinctive neck tattoos coming up from under their collars, best resembling protruding spider veins, held out their hands to her. "They're fakes."

Bo reached behind his back, ready to pounce.

"Grab the child!" the one said.

The eldest of these terrorists grabbed the collar of Emma's jacket. As he tugged Emma to him, Bo pulled out a ten-inch long metal rod that was tucked into his back belt and laid a vicious whack on the man's forearm, crushing bone. Not allowing the man to retaliate, Bo swiped the terrorist leader so hard across the face that two teeth flew out of the man's broken jaw.

"Bo, watch out!!!" Emma screamed.

One of the men, stocky and fully bearded, approached Bo from behind, the other terrorist, broad shouldered and built charged at Bo from the front. To Emma's surprise, Bo was well prepared. He pulled back on the rod, locking a mechanism into place. The sound of an electric charge filled the air. Turning around in a flash, Bo jumped at the stocky man and pressed the trigger on the rod. Out shot a blast of white heat and the searing sound of electricity, all pouring into the terrorist's chest. His feet left the ground and did not return to the cobblestone until Bo's weapon had flung him fifteen feet back, crumbling into a wooden fence.

Emma charged the unaware broad shouldered guard with the knife. Leading with her shoulder, leapt the full weight of her body into his knee, like a football linebacker on an illegal hit. The moment she collided with the man, his left knee ligaments and bone tore with a snapping sound. He fell to the pavement next to Emma. Bo charged up his device again and shocked the man, sending a wave of electricity through his body, knocking him out cold.

"What is that?" Emma said, picking herself up.

"Grandpa gave me this a while back. It's a government weapon that uses up to 10,000 volts of energy in three charges," Bo said, taking his sister's hand. "I call it my Don't Screw with Me stick."

Emma looked around at the battered terrorists. "I'd say they won't anymore."

In Emma and Bo's tussle with the guards, they had forgotten about what remained so close by. The phantom that had persisted so long now began to stare down Bo. The thin smile that was on the skeletal beast began to increase. His quick words squeaked their way out of his mouth rapid fire, as if he was not only speaking a hundred words a second but whispering so soft that Emma and Bo could not comprehend. The other phantoms on the avenue behind them ceased their torments. In unison, they dropped their prey and focused their bloodlust attention on the Alastar children.

"Okay, now it's time to go!" Emma said, taking off in the opposite direction with Bo at her side.

After rounding the corner, they witnessed Ciara pounding on the thick oak door to the Watcher of the Wood office. She pulled back on the rounded handle with the weight of her body, frantic. "Open up, please. Open up!"

"I think they locked it, Ciara," Bo said, letting go of Emma to try his hand at prying open the sealed door.

"Well, what are we going to do?"

"Here!" Bo took his weapon and began banging on the lock.

Before Bo could open the lock, Ciara and him leaped back in horror at a handful of phantoms gliding by at the intersection in which they just came. Ciara let out a little squeak. This poor girl and her irrepressible fears were enough to have the contingent of four phantoms with their wisps of smoke for half-formed bodies all stop in unison. They sniffed the air for the blood panic they craved, and turned to cast their cold, blood filled crimson eyes at Emma, Bo and Ciara.

"Oh, not good," Bo said, almost as frozen as Ciara.

Looking to the dead end, Emma noticed that one of the gates to the *S. Mather Research Arboretum* was ajar. She ran over to push the door open. The smell of dried autumn leaves and crisp tree bark filled her nose. Leaping over, Ciara and Bo went inside, dragging Emma along as they took cover. They had little to no time. Emma realized this when through the crack in the door that Bo was closing, the phantoms were flying at the door with all speed, their undead, horrible decayed hands outstretched.

"Help me brace the gate," Bo said, his back to the door.

Emma ran up to the gate and pressed against the wood with all of her strength, her toes digging into the ground behind her. The wind on the other end of the door blew hard, building in tenacity, accompanied by a sickening, wheezing laugh. Then, the door was hit with a resounding thud. The sheer impact threw Emma to the ground. Bo held his back strong to the door, almost doing an exercise squat as he used all his muscles to keep the phantoms out. Emma rejoined Bo, her palms flat to the door, pressing with all her might. Another thud hit the door. A sound of splintering wood filled their ears with each new battering ram of the phantoms bodies.

"Push the lock in, already," Emma said.

"There isn't any lock. It's a public park," Bo said. "They don't lock down public places."

A space of a few inches was wedged open between the two doors. A pale hand with veins of the deepest purple and blue reached around into the tiny space. The long, sickle nails of the phantom began to scratch at Bo's shoulder. With a free hand, he grabbed his electric rod and hit the beast in the hand. As his arm fell to hit a second time, the creature took the device from Bo and threw it where he could not reach.

"Here," Emma said, reaching into her pocket, producing her pocket knife.

Bo took the handle and opened the blunt end with his mouth to lock the blade into place. Taking the sharp knife into his nimble-fingered right hand, Bo stabbed the phantom's hand. The blade went clean through with a sickening squish, pinning the phantom to the wood. The creature howled not so much in pain, but in spitting anger as it unsuccessfully tried to free the hand from the door. His companions squealed in their thin voices, speaking so rapid fire to one another that Bo and Emma could not make out what they were saying.

"Wait. Where's Ciara?" Emma said.

Bo and Emma scanned the dim light under the shadows of the oak, elm, birch, maple, ash and silver trees over the two acre size tree sanctuary. "Ciara! Where are you?"

"I'm coming," Ciara said, repeating this a few seconds later, her voice coming closer each time. From the maze of the tree trunks, Ciara held the hand of a dazed and confused looking Sasquatch. He held a dangling scroll and leaf samples in his hands.

"Bigfoot! Thank God," Emma said, waving him over. "Get over here."

"I heard bells when I was working," Bigfoot said, looking at the struggling Emma and Bo. "Does that mean I'm done with work today?"

"Hey, dude!" Bo said, sharply, starting to huff and puff as he pushed back. "You wanna help brace the gate, buddy? There are phantoms trying to get in here."

The sheer mention of phantoms soured Bigfoot's face. Tossing his research aside, the growl emanated deep within his chest as he bore his teeth reminiscent of a grizzly bear. Ciara wisely let go of the sasquatch's hand as he stepped his nearly five-hundred pound body forward, pounding his fist into his right palm with a thwack only comparable to a fastball landing into a baseball mitt.

"Soul takers." Another slam of his fist, making an echo. "Get away from our land." The door took another resounding thud. Bigfoot responded with another pounding of his fist. "Leave Miss Emma alone!"

Emma and Bo couldn't hold back the pressure of the phantoms anymore. The impaled phantom forced his head around the gate. Finding Emma, he screamed at her, the grating sound severing Emma's eardrums with his too loose jaw and blood neon eyes that radiated intense heat onto Emma's face.

Bigfoot wasted no time. Drawing his right arm back across his body, Bigfoot swung his mighty fist around, connecting with the phantoms head, cleanly severing it from the neck with a fleshy tear.

"Whoa!" Bo shouted, letting go of the door for a second.

The phantoms body fell limp to the ground. Instead of remaining there, dead, the bones and skin dissolved into vapory clouds. The phantom's primitive existence drifted up into the air and into the canopy of trees with a long trail, beginning to reform. During this, the fierce pounding on the arboretum doors returned.

"Allow me, Emma." Bigfoot took one step forward and with his hairy arms, full of bits of leaves, and he pressed against the gate, closing the door. Emma and Bo stepped back a few paces, stretching their bodies with a great sigh of relief. "Run, Emma. Run to the steps. I will protect you."

Emma picked up the knife and Bo's electric rod that had fallen onto the white stones, covered in moss, next to the gate. "Stay safe, Bigfoot."

Bo led Emma and Ciara into the close woven network of trees. Not only was it dark and hard to find their way, but these trees in the late autumn by some miracle of science had shed very few of their leaves.

"Where's the stairs?" Bo said.

"I don't know…wait," Emma said, clutching her Alastar. Her skin began to feel a wave of electricity pour over her. "Do you feel that?"

"Oh, God. Look," Ciara said, pointing to where they had come from. "The door! The door is lighting up."

Turning around with Bo, Emma saw that about a hundred feet away the gate to the arboretum began to glow in a superheated mix of glowing blues and reds. In a blink of an eye, the gate exploded, sending Bigfoot flying off his feet along with a thousand splinters of jagged wood. Emma took Ciara and Bo and ducked behind a tree to avoid the shrapnel.

Out from the smoky air, with phantoms in tow, stepped the man Emma remembered from the last night. It was the man in the vampire costume whom Erik chased but never found – the man who's series of unhealed knife scars appeared deeper on that night. He held out a glowing orb, just like the one Siobhan and Meira had. Emma, Bo and Ciara crouched behind a tree, their eyes tuned to the dark mage speaking with someone out of their view just beyond the gate.

"They are inside the arboretum, I swear it. Kill her brother first," the muffled voice said. Emma tuned her ears, as Bo and Ciara looked to her for information.

"Great service as usual. Now return to your post, Agent Arnold. You will be called on soon," the dark mage said.

Emma turned to Bo and Ciara, her mouth agape. "Someone tipped us off! There's a traitor in the Adoette government!"

Chapter Fifteen
Tales Become Reality

Bo grabbed a hold of Emma's left forearm in shock. "There's a mole in the city? Who was the woman?"

"I have no idea if it's a guy or girl," Emma said.

"What do you mean you have no idea?" Ciara said, panic settling into her voice.

Emma waved her hands before their faces. "Listen, I don't know! Maybe it was the fact that there is a war on in here that I have trouble hearing, let alone don't know how to use..." Emma grabbed her Sorcerer's necklace... "any powers that I have with this!"

"Alastar. Alastar," the dark Mage said, his voice at a chilling nightmare whisper. "I can feel you quivering between the trees."

"Oh bad. Bad!" Bo whispered as he ran his hands through his thick hair.

Emma's mind sailed back to that fateful day in her classroom where her vision forecasted all that had occurred since the snow began to fall. From the memory of that book she read in her Woodland Academy classroom, Emma plucked out the mages name.

"Rakshasas? I thought those books were fairy tales."

"The books Grandpa gave you? No, they are history books," Bo said.

"Are you serious? They were all real? Why would he expose me to that?"

"Maybe he wanted you ready for all of this." Gunfire began to echo in the distance of the city. "The Watchers are at work....real ones this time I hope! God, what a security breach. This hasn't happened in decades!"

Bo had spoken too much. Rakshasas jerked his head to stare them down. "Alastar!"

Rakshasas aimed his orb at Emma from across the arboretum. A jet of red light shot from his orb and through the air like a bullet. Bo pushed Emma out of the way, just in time to have the arcane kinetic energy bolt avoid Emma but connect square with his chest.

Emma screamed as she watched her brother, in slow motion, get thrown back from the spell, his body sailing through the air. Bo's back collided with a low branch of an oak twenty feet away, sending his limp body to the ground with a crash.

"Bo! No. No. No," Emma said.

Emma ran to her brother's side. He lay prostrate on the grass, moaning, one more hit away from unconsciousness. As he raised his head, Emma could see the blood drip from a forehead gash. His eyes were dilated and hazy.

"Help me with him, Ciara."

Emma and Ciara lifted up Bo, throwing an arm over their shoulders to support his shaky legs.

"The stairs…they're over there…my head," Bo mumbled.

Ciara began to lead the mangled Bo away towards the stairs at the northern tip of the arboretum. Emma let go and allowed Ciara to carry the weight. These half-death, leaching souls were too close for her comfort to escape.

Emma drew out her knife with her thumb, the blade clicking into place. From under her sweater, she removed the Alastar and the jewel began to light up the darkness with an ethereal sapphire light.

"What are you doing?" Ciara said.

"Take my brother up the stairs," Emma said, gesturing with the knife.

"Not without…"

"Do it! Please, Ciara. I can hold them off."

"No you can't! Those were just books. This is real!"

Emma charged up Bo's rod and pointed it at Ciara. Shaking her head and moaning, halfway between scared and frustrated, Ciara hobbled away with a semi-conscious Bo to the stairs. If Emma was this unique magic maker, this conjurer, she knew she couldn't turn her back and watch her brother and best friend suffer in that arboretum. Emma knew deep down that despite her nervous, shaking hands, her heart was full of courage to test all that she hoped might be true.

Another jet of kinetic light came from Rakshasas' orb, whistling past Emma's forehead and severing the oak branch Bo collided with.

"Alright. Try and catch me, you demons!"

"Get her!!!"

Emma then took off, weaving in and out of the trees of the arboretum. When one phantom swooped down to take her as a prize, her nimble feet ran around a tree and dropped to the forest floor, dodging them in their deftness every time. When Rakshasas tried to pin her with a spell, Emma listened to her Alastar offer her nerves the nimble jolts she needed to stay alive. She so irritated Rakshasas and the three remaining phantoms that they took no time at all to reach the point of agitated screams.

"Take her for God's sake you witless zombies," Rakshasas said. "She's a baby. You've certainly killed those before! Just capture this one."

Emma meandered through the trees, crossing her tracks, dodging and mixing up the phantoms by having no ordered escape. Her heart was beating through her chest. One phantom approached in a dead glide. Another was in the back of her mind, ready to pounce as the demon's decayed, boney feet trampled the moss of the arboretum, bearing down. Emma had to drop to the dirt and allow two of them to collide with one another over her. Rolling out of the way as the two phantoms did a poor job of untangling themselves from one another like coiled snakes, she took long, spry footsteps away from the scene of collision.

Emma stopped to hide behind the trunk of one tree before then moving onto a new one, all the while aware of where her enemies stalked in the deep shade under the trees. Their screams, shrill enough to turn the blood in Emma's nervous veins to ice, confirmed their loss of patience.

Emma leapt over to hide behind a rather rotund trunk of an oak tree. She thought about climbing the branches and calling out to the guards in the snowy night for help. But then, a shot from Rakshasas' orb collided with the front of the tree. The shockwave threw Emma onto her back, her left ear ringing. Touching her fingertips to her neck, Emma felt a clean half inch cut and a slow trickle of warm blood.

Her eyes scanned left and right in the space leading back to the door. She could only catch a partially formed phantom glide between the trees in the distance, the blood red eyes searching left to right. She could hear the demon sniff the air for her presence.

"Where is he?" Emma whispered. Her hand still held tight to the knife. In the back of her mind, an ominous feeling clouded up her senses in the proceeding seconds. "Where are you?"

"Alastar," a voice whispered in her ear.

Emma could not move away quick enough for the mighty fingers of Rakshasas grabbed at her throat from behind, clenching Emma's youthful skin with his warm and leathery hide.

"Ah! Let me go."

Emma attempted to swing her knife around. Rakshasas used his other hand that cradled the swirling orb to use a spell and cast away the blade with one quick gesture. She reached for the electric rod. Panic came over Emma when she saw it on the ground where the two phantoms uncoiled each other.

Rakshasas began to laugh, giddy, as if he couldn't believe his luck. Emma tried to pry his hands from her throat, now closing off her windpipe. Rakshasas lifted Emma by her neck off of the ground to dangle before him.

"To kill or capture a young Sorcerer, especially one as important as you…my my," Rakshasas said. His eyes scanned Emma like she was a wounded deer from a glorious hunt. "Oh my Lord Orion, I wish you were alive to see your disappointment fade away. What joy!"

"This is no joy for me, creep! What do want with me?"

"I am not in the mood to indulge revisionists' views of sorcerers like you. Keep you alive, much to my dislike. I'd rather fall asleep to the pleasant thought that you were so helpless before your last breath left your body." Rakshasas shuddered, enjoying this gruesome act far too much.

"I'm liking the alive part…" Emma forced out, her neck aching with his grip.

Rakshasas tightened his grip, forcing Emma to struggle for air. He began to play with her body, shaking her like a dog with a chew toy. She could not stand to watch him torture her as the last bits of oxygen were leaving her lungs. Tightening her fist, she waited until his partially severed tongue slid out, as if he was to lick her.

"Damn fools thinking that you could be a Queen for…ahhh!"

Emma's fist connected clean with the underside of Rakshasas' jaw, causing his emaciated, filed down to points lower teeth to pin his tongue against the upper row of sharpened incisors like a nail into wood. He dropped Emma to the ground. She did her best to crawl to the nearest tree, gasping for her lungs to return to the damp air.

Rakshasas paced around, grabbing at his jaw in agony. He spit out a wad of congealed blood onto the bark of a white birch, staining its beautiful skin.

Against her chest, inside her jacket, Emma felt something. Reaching inside, she produced the vial from the coffer, still intact. A different note was attached to the bottle with a string.

Use this when you need to. Don't tell Mom I gave it to you.

Emma's heart almost melted as Bo's handwriting filled her with confidence. The red and silver flakes twisted in the water before her eyes, glowing along with her Alastar in a defensive harmony. Touching her fingers to her Alastar and then to the vial, the water inside began to gleam like a light bulb and swirl around like a storm transforming into a tornado.

"Argh! Little hellion!" Rakshasas said, wiping away a trail of blood from the corner of his mouth. "I'll skip the Silver Dollar bounty on your body! Come here!" He raised his orb and aimed the magic maker squarely at Emma.

Springing to her feet, Emma felt the top of her head warm as a fire spell shot over her and ignited a young ash tree in front of her in a torrent of flames.

Ahead, there was a silver tree. Emma ran and slid behind the wide trunk of the tree to protect her body from the dark mage. Like a soldier, pinned down, Emma could hear and feel the vibrations of his spells in blind anger against Emma's back. The branches on either side of her were tearing off in tiny explosions, some of them whizzing past and hitting Emma, making her crouch up to protect her head. Pinned down like a soldier in a foxhole, Emma touched her Alastar and breathed deep, focusing in on an escape. The spells were beginning to crowd out her hearing. Rakshasas was closing in for the kill. Tightly holding the vial that seemed ready to burst like a grenade, Emma peered out at the precise moment behind the tree to see a familiar face closing in on Rakshasas.

"Bigfoot. Get him!" Emma yelled.

The Sasquatch staggered on his feet. In place of his matted fur on his left shoulder was a bruised and bloody mess. Rakshasas' head turned right around to see Bigfoot crouch down and utter the most guttural roar of any beast in the Republic. Getting to her feet, Emma ran out from behind the tree with her right arm cocked back, the vial in hand.

In his vanity and arrogance, standing as if taking down Emma was an easy task, Rakshasas turned around too late to react. Emma felt her ethereal powers propel the vial out with all her might. The rounded bottom shot through the small distance between them with tremendous speed to collide with the bridge of Rakshasas' nose. The vial shattered, spewing the jagged glass and radiating flakey concoction all over his emaciated face. Rakshasas fell to his knees. His hands clawed at his skin that began to sizzle, bubble and blacken with massive second to third degree burns.

"My eyes! It's burning my eyes. Ahhhhhh!"

Emma kicked Rakshasas in the chest, knocking him flat onto his back. Right after her mighty kick, she received a hard shove on her shoulder blades from hands cold as ice. She fell flat to the ground. Looking up, she noticed the half formed, headless phantom gliding around and circling back, ready to strike again. Another phantom appeared behind Rakshasas, his scarlet eyes glowing in the faint light.

"Bigfoot. I have to get help," Emma said. "Keep him alive for the guards."

Rakshasas in his temporary blindness reached for his orb, soon wrapping his palms around the device. The gray smoke inside the supernatural device began to swirl, ready to send out another spell.

Bigfoot noticed this and picked up the writhing, severely wounded Rakshasas by the collar of his black, weather beaten leather jacket. He slammed Rakshasas's back into the nearest tree with a deafening thud, hard enough to shake a few leaves loose. He then held the demon man horizontally over his nine foot head. The Mage dropped his only line of defense at Emma's feet, which she was prudent enough to kick behind her into a thick juniper bush.

"Keep him alive…"

Bigfoot did not listen. With a battle cry, the Sasquatch brought the mage's spine down onto his knee. A loud snap of bone echoed off of the trees. Rakshasas fell to the ground, only his upper body able to move. Bigfoot growled yet again, keeping the phantoms at bay.

"I will watch the phantoms, Emma," Bigfoot said. "Don't worry. He can't run away anymore."

Emma hesitated, a cynical slice of her soul wanting for second to revel in Rakshasas' suffering but she had no time. The remaining contingent of phantoms began to chase her through the trees and up to the stairs that ran alongside and up the city wall to a series of wide ledge points in-between the ornate, domed silver guard towers.

With all the strength in her body, Emma pumped her arms and pounded her feet to the stone, tearing up the long staircase. When she reached the curved walkway on top of the wall, Emma felt a wave of relief reach her. On the opposite end, a mere hundred and fifty feet away, were two Watchers, their rifles at the ready. Bo and Ciara were being ushered into the observation house by Erik, who had his pistol in hand and his stocky body out in front to protect them.

"Come quick, little girl," the shorter of the two Watchers said, waving her over. "Captain Erik! Where have you been? Help us."

"I've been trying to save lives, all by myself, thank you very much!" Erik said, his adrenaline searing out in his voice.

Emma recognized the other guard as Ignatius. Aiming down into the arboretum, he fired a searing red bullet into the phantom. The creature tore the still early winter air in a defeated cry as its translucent form became paralyzed for a short time.

In this loss of focus for one moment by Emma and the guards, they did not see the headless phantom that Bigfoot had beheaded crawl up the wall with his rending claws chipping into the stone, hell bent on revenge.

"Miss Emma. WATCH OUT!" Ignatius shouted.

Emma turned her head to the right as she ran, somehow aware that danger was about to pounce. She gasped when in a flash the headless phantom crawled up next to her at an inconceivable speed, stretched out its pale, disgusting and rotting fleshy arms to shove Emma. So firm was the push that Emma could feel her fingertips glide over the edge of the stone of outer wall and connect with the open air.

Her body tumbled over the precipice in a free fall. The wind whistled in Emma's ears for over sixty feet before she fell into the icy river below.

Emma couldn't bring herself to leap into the salty sea. Adacia held her arms out, ready to catch her daughter while wading in the temperate waters of the Pacific right off of Maui's coast.

"Come on, Blue Eyes. You have nothing to be afraid of."

"But Mom, what if I die?" Emma said. Her little toes on her five-year-old body clutched the side of the boat. Bo and Jonathan uttered encouraging words behind her, anxious themselves to dive straight in. Emma phased their voices out, having recently learned to compartmentalize sounds and her mental thoughts, keeping only the sounds of the tiny waves lapping against the boat. Adacia never wavered, ready to receive the girl with the star jewel around her neck.

"Nothing will happen to you Emma as long as I protect you," Adacia said, continuing to tread water. "You can pretty much survive anything. I believe in you. Now…jump!"

Emma touched her star jewel and felt her heartbeat slow. Closing her eyes, she took a deep breath, closed her nose with a finger and a thumb, and sprung into the ocean. The submersion into the saltwater sea muffled her hearing, making her feel instantly engulfed.

When Emma opened her eyes underneath the surface, she could see beams of sunlight pouring down into the water from a cloudless sky. Adacia was in a silhouette above, waiting for Emma to resurface.

That random memory, once behind that vault of that amnesia of early youth, came back to Emma as she looked up from the river bed of the Rockland River, north of the Silver City. The air in her lungs held so little oxygen in the frigid waters and from a numbing pain in her right ribs.

Shadows of phantoms drifted above the water; the demons still on the hunt. When Emma thought that for an instant she might die there, alone, her soul ready to be leeched upon by those tempting undead, her Alastar began to glow. The crystal lit up the water like a lamp, full of silver and blue light as it drifted, weightless, in front of Emma's eyes, still attached to her neck by the black string. Her mother's voice echoed in her mind.

"You can pretty much survive anything…"

Taking her Alastar, Emma shoved it under her sweater. She pushed off of the muddy bottom, her legs brushing past healthy patches of kelpie river weeds. No matter how much her sides hurt, Emma swam up to the surface, drawing out those last vestiges of air, her chest burning. When her head broke the surface, she took a gasping breath before her body bobbed back down, her open mouth filling with bitterly cold water.

Emma screamed out. The shock of the water, the snow filled air, her aching ribs and the fresh breath of oxygen to her inflamed lungs all combined to make Emma beat her fists against the water in pain. "Help! Help!"

Erik called from the walkway above. "Emma, stay there."

No more than a second after Erik said this, a giant flash of yellowish light appeared above the city. Emma could see what looked like a thin force field forming above, encasing Adoette in a barely visible dome. The ominous cloud platform, the deliverer of the phantoms, was already gone from above, disappearing into the western horizon with the sun that had only just set.

"Damn!" Erik said, noticing the shield. "Get to Eleanor's house. There, up ahead in the tree homes." Erik pointed north of the city to a vast community of trees under a canopy where many ornate, nature conscious houses were tucked into a forested peninsula. "Emma! Move. The phantom is loose."

The headless phantom had eluded the dropping shield that trapped his comrades inside. He crawled down the stone wall neck first, like a crouching goblin. The demon's fingernails frenetically clicked on the stone as he descended upon Emma's position, shredding ivy as he went on by.

"Shoot the thing!" Emma said, treading water.

"We can't. We're on the other side of the dome." Ignatius said. He tapped his hand against the invisible dome and his handprint remained in mid-air before fading like warm breath on a cold glass window. "Run to Lady Eleanor's. Run!"

Taking the hint, seeing the phantom was ready to terrorize now that it had landed on the grass at the bottom of the wall, Emma knew only a few moments remained before he crossed the grass and snatched her from the water.

Without another thought, other than to survive, Emma swam to the riverbank. She ignored what had to be a broken rib. Reaching up a good few feet, Emma used her arms to pull herself up and flung her soaking wet body onto the mossy white stone landscaped along the edge of the river. She shed her black coat for all the water the wool had taken on. Standing up with a deep groan, her shoes excreted water as she ran into the forest.

The phantom screamed, precisely copying Emma's voice from her yelp in the river only a minute before. Then, the phantom suddenly fell silent.

Emma turned and stopped to notice the phantom wasn't crossing the water. To her horror, the headless being was forming a new skull in a cloud of vapor. The phantom scanned the water with the reforming head, eyes shifting from a lifeless black to a deep crimson. Looking up at Emma, the phantom's loose jaw cracked an evil grin, flashing crooked teeth, sharp as any mythical beast.

"Uh-oh," Emma said.

The phantom stepped down onto the water and took one step, then another, then another, the apparently solid form of the ghost now weightless.

"Go away!" Emma said. She moved the wet hair out of her eyes. "Go away right now."

The phantom continued to walk on the water, unfazed by Emma's anger. The demon would continue to haunt her until she made her stand. She knew how to prove her worth.

Emma drew out her Alastar and let the pristine ethereal device shine for the phantom to see. The demon, as it reached up to climb the bank, recoiled, advancing no further than the stony edge. The crimson eyes seemed to shrink before her.

In her heart of hearts, she felt the enchantment pulsing in her veins. "Back. Get back, phantom," Emma said. A faint, high pitched hum resonated from the Alastar as the light from the crystal increased, warding off the phantom like Frankenstein with a torch. "I know you're afraid of me now. You know you can't take me." The phantom began to lower itself back down into the water, afraid to make eye contact with Emma. The confidence was there. No fear remained. "Get back, demon! You know you're afraid of me!"

The phantom's eyes fell back into a color of black coal, losing all ferocity. The creature began to open its too wide mouth but clamped the jaw shut when Emma drew closer, holding out her Alastar. Gunfire erupted around the corner at the northwest entrance, the bullets ricocheting off of the nearby trees.

A contingent of troops, led by a running Siobhan, flew across the DuSable bridge, reloading their rifles. Then, from behind the wall of the city, Jonathan and Adacia, holding hands, followed the soldiers, sheer panic flushing their faces.

"Eleanor! Shoot," Jonathan called to the space behind Emma. "Shoot!"

Before Emma could turn around, a gunshot filled the echoed winter air a mere few feet behind. The bullet sliced through the air and connected square between the beady eyes of the phantom, paralyzing the beast into a stasis as it clutched the stony edge of the river bank.

"Stand, Emma. Hold out your hand to him!" Emma turned around to come face to face with Lady Eleanor. She holstered her smoking pistol as she walked to stand behind Emma, ready to instruct. "Touch your star and hold out your hand to him."

Smart enough not to argue in the crisis, Emma obeyed. She could begin to feel a connection building in strength between her open right palm and the phantom. "What do I do?"

Eleanor crouched down and spoke the calm directions to her over her left shoulder. "Feel the connection. Know you are the master of him now."

For a creature so bent on delivering horror, the fear then engulfed his face. Emma held tight, ignoring the burning pain of her muscles keeping the electromagnetic connection.

"The demon is only a man. Peel the layers and free him."

Concentrating, Emma could see in fact all of those guesses about voices being trapped inside were true. Her eyes, either through the Alastar or by her body adjusting to her powers, saw three thin veils encased over a body of a Croatoan man like a mummy in a soul sarcophagus.

"How do I remove them…I don't know what to do!" Emma said, realizing how though she might see, she could not understand.

"Allow me, child," Eleanor said. Touching her necklace of a comet, Eleanor held out her hand to the beast. With one flex of her left hand, the first layer flew off with a flash of light, dissolving into the air with a smoke. Another flex and the demon shed another layer. One more flex and the phantom's body congealed into a cloud that floated above the body in the form of a face and faded into the night air, terminated.

In the place of the creature was a body of a young man, a bullet wound in his chest. He looked to Emma and then Eleanor. "Thank you, my lady." His eyes closed and he ceased to draw another breath.

"Yes. I'd say that phantom was afraid of you, my dear."

Emma ran into the safety of Eleanor's arms, who led her off to the side, far enough away from the body. The Lady, dressed in a military uniform of Woodland colors similar to the Watchers, tightly embraced Emma, not letting go.

"I'm not sure what else I could have done to the phantom but shout even louder. Thank you."

"Of course. I am so thankful you are safe, Blue Eyes."

Emma released her arms from the waist of Eleanor and stared into the luminous green eyes of the Governor. "Blue Eyes? How did you know my nickname?"

Eleanor heaved a heavy sigh, her chest expanding. "I have know you all of your life, Emma," Eleanor said, her stern face in this conflict starting to soften. "I am your Grandmother."

Emma took a strong step back. She tripped over her own feet and landed on her bottom with a thud. "You're…no! Mom said that you were dead." That puzzle of histories was out in her head once more. Holding a finger to her lip, they all connected in a rush, almost too hard for Emma to comprehend. "Grandma Ellie…Eleanor…that's you?"

"The lies have hurt me as well, Emma," Eleanor said. Without turning her head, her eyes shot over to the approaching contingent of Emma's parents and the soldiers. "Try not to pass out from shock. Your mother is about to fight me."

Jonathan ran straight past Eleanor and swooped up Emma in his mighty arms, setting her down against the nearest tree. Adacia practically shoved Eleanor aside to get to Emma, barely moving the legendary Sorcerer. The words of Emma's parents ran together as they moved their hands over her, checking for wounds. Emma winced, inhaling sharply when her father pressed against her ribcage.

"I think I broke a rib."

"We need a doctor," Jonathan turned and shouted.

"Take her to the hospital, Jonathan," Eleanor said, approaching, cautious.

Adacia turned, her faced fixed into hysterical anger. "Why did you do this?" With one mighty push, Adacia attempted to knock over her own mother. More than able to defend herself, Eleanor took a simple, balanced step back to absorb the blow.

"Mom, stop," Emma said, tugging at her mother's arm. Jonathan had to come in and wrap his arms around Adacia, pulling back the wily woman.

"Adacia, she's your mother. Don't!"

"She brought all of this on Emma. She's doing to her what she did to me!"

"I am not, Adacia," Eleanor said, her voice fighting to remain calm. "I provided her with the tools she learned to defend herself with."

"You're a liar!"

Emma had never pondered the possibility of striking her mother. However, her fists clenched as the rage boiled in her heart.

"Shut-up! Just shut-up, Mom! You're the liar!" Emma screamed.

"Emma, mind your tongue," Adacia said. "That's, that's not nice." Adacia, along with Jonathan began to avoid eye contact with Emma. "Honey, calm down."

"How about you calm down, you psycho! Look what you did to me. I had to run away to find all of this. You made Bo lie to me. And now…" Emma sharply pointed to Eleanor, "I guess Grandma Ellie is alive. Thanks for keeping that one too, you liar!"

Adacia limply feel to the forest floor in Jonathan's arms. She covered her hands to her face and began to sob.

"I'm sorry, Blue Eyes. I'm so sorry!"

"At least look at me, please."

Eleanor placed a calm hand on Emma's shoulder, preventing her from jerking back violently. Eleanor handed her a knife, clear enough to see one's reflection. "They cannot look at your eyes, Emma. Look at yourself."

Emma gasped. In the reflection of the polished five-inch blade, Emma could see her eyes were no longer luminous and charming. The whites of her eyes had returned to that blood red stare in her rage, the awed blue of her irises had begun to swirl like fire. From her eyes, a white haze radiated out, intimidating even her. Once her heart and mind could feel the anger evaporate, the malice in her eyes dissolved back to the beautiful ones she was born with.

"I'm sorry..." Emma said, staring off into the woods. She handed Eleanor back her knife, remembering that day she last saw those predatory eyes on her front porch. "That's why people don't look at me when I'm mad."

"Yes. You're Sorcerer abilities have come alive," Eleanor said, sheathing the blade.

Two Watchers took the corpse's arms and legs and led him away to the cemetery. Siobhan crossed the bridge and ran with all speed over to Adacia.

"Start the cremation immediately," Siobhan called to her troops. "Adacia, please come with me." She took Adacia's shaking hand and lifted her up.

Regret was washing over Emma. "I'm sorry, Mom. I'm so sorry," Emma said, reaching out for her mother.

"Not now, Emma. Later," Siobhan said, leading Adacia away, rubbing her back. The horrific sound of Adacia's heart being torn asunder, her voice gasping for air in-between sobs, was awful for Emma to hear. Wanting to do more, Emma leaned in so that she could hear Siobhan whisper to Adacia on the way back into the city via the northwest DuSable bridge.

"She did…Emma was the one who stopped Rakshasas…I know. Not to upset you but I hope you realize that Emma is much like Eleanor. She is a Sorcerer."

Emma's ears picked up a rustling in the woods to her right.

"Go with your father, Emma," Eleanor said, her voice fading into the distance.

Turning, she saw Eleanor disappear into the air with a swirling wind. Those emerald eyes seemed to stay and hover in the wood for Emma, long after the Lady of the Beacon had flown away.

Chapter Sixteen
The Heart of a Secret

With her free left hand, Emma gripped the examination table in the emergency wing of Aileworth hospital on Adoette's east side. Emma had already changed from her drenched winter clothes into a pair of khaki pants and an aqua blue button up sweater that sat on the counter. There, feeling the doctor working behind her, Emma lifted up the back of her white under-shirt, exposing her ribcage and the blackened and bruised skin above. She was about to have the first experience of her life being healed.

"Hold your father's hand," Doctor Cornish said. The rather young physician, having grown a thin beard to age his baby face, was applying a greenish gel to a foot long strip of a white bandage. Without counting down the doctor slapped it onto Emma's right ribcage with a splattering sound. Emma winced at the searing pain of the gel permeating into her skin and bones.

"Squeeze my hand if you're hurting," Jonathan said.

"Oh I'm hurting! I'm hurting!"

"Ten more seconds, my Lady," Doctor Cornish said, his hands at the ready to take off the healing strip.

Emma could tell her Sorcerer strength and abilities were kicking in as she squeezed her father's muscular, working man's hands. Jonathan tried not to let Emma see his contorted face, more in pain than when Adacia was twice in labor with Bo and the little Blue Eyes. In those endless ten seconds, where Emma could feel her broken rib fuse together and the infection sterilized, making her grit her teeth. Some humor was brought to her by the sight of Jonathan balancing fatherly support and trying to keep his manhood intact and tears out of his eyes.

"Done. Relax, my Lady," Doctor Cornish said. "Very good. Most children cry their eyes out when I have to fuse their bones." He peeled off the bandage from one end to the other. He wiped away the excess gel with a towel before handing Emma her clothes. Though somewhat resilient to the natural elements with her harmonious Croatoan blood and her Sorcerer abilities, the new clothes Jonathan purchased for Emma did little to eliminate that faint chill in her bones from the icy river.

"Dad. You can let go," Emma said, her hand releasing with the lessening pain.

"Oh, of course," Jonathan said, stretching and flexing out his bruised hand. "I thought your ribs might still hurt."

Emma stretched her back and felt a mingling sore where the cracked ribs had been. "Not really."

Jonathan patted Emma on her shoulder a little too rough, as if he still saw Emma as that tomboy he had come to raise.

"Careful, Dad," Emma said, wincing.

"Sorry. Forgot about the ribs," Jonathan said, backing off. "Say Doc, any news on my boy, William Bo?"

The doctor was busy looking over a scroll that was handed to him by a freckle faced, giddy young nurse. Her clear inexperience showed as she held her hands behind her back and rocked on the heels of her toes, nervous. She couldn't help but to eye Emma and the Alastar jewel. Doctor Cornish looked between the nurse and Emma, his face forming into disappointment.

"Florence, give Lady Emma some peace for now."

"Sorry, Doctor Cornish," Florence said, giving a little curtsy to Emma, avoiding those luminous Sorcerer eyes, before she walked over to the nurse's station. Even from her exam table, Emma could see the white gowned nurses' gossip, doing little to hide their curious gestures in Emma's direction.

"She's the Sorcerer that Sarah at *The Ivy* spoke of…I heard she's half-human…I heard she's the Granddaughter of…"

Emma had to tune these girls out. The burning regret of those secrets and that bratty tirade were drowning out the rational observations.

"Does she need any pain pills, Doc?" Jonathan said.

"Probably not. For you and me, we would, but not her," Doctor Cornish said, writing on a scroll before closing the parchment. "I was going to prescribe her an antibiotic to fight off the infection. Though to be honest, Emma, I am sure your body already fought off any excess bacteria. Either way, drink some Flemming's Elixir with some tea. Do you like raspberry?"

"I do. Is this like a raspberry cough syrup?

"No syrup," Doctor Cornish said, laughing as he shook his head. "Syrup. By the Gods, humans can eat their sugar, can't they?"

A few minutes after the doctor left Jonathan to hold Emma's hand at the bedside table, Emma felt the need to touch her father's hand. His fingers sat on lips that seemed to quiver without speaking as his eyes stared out the window.

"Daddy? You okay?"

"That was stupid at times of us to lie to you," Jonathan said, shaking his head. "I'm sorry."

"Dad, it's okay," Emma said, holding her father's hand tight. "I understand."

Soft, yet direct, Jonathan pointed a stern finger at her. "You know as well as I that the forgiveness you just gave me won't be saved for your mother."

Emma huffed, looking away, wanting to be angry but knowing her father to be right. "Well, I still need my family. I don't really know anything about me or this Silver Forest, if that makes you feel better."

"Feels good that you still need us," Jonathan said, looking away, his hands clasped together once more.

An hour later, Siobhan sauntered into the room, looking irritated with her black hair a frizz, tied back and sticking out in places. When she and Emma met eye to eye, Siobhan hesitated, as if not sure of how to approach the Sorceress.

"You were most impressive in the arboretum," Siobhan said, holding her hand to her heart, looking quite proud.

"Stop! Stop with formalities," Emma said, throwing her hands up. "You can talk to me like a normal kid."

"You're not a normal kid," Jonathan injected.

"Seriously, Dad! Siobhan, what happened to Rakshasas? I didn't kill him, did I?"

Siobhan blinked as if surprised Emma had any pity. "No, he is alive. Lady Eleanor placed him in a defense cell below the city. You and Bigfoot did not let that scar faced cretin escape without further marks."

Jonathan looked from Siobhan to Emma, curious. "What did she do to him?"

"His tongue was lacerated, his vision is approximately two-tenths of what he once had, he has massive third degree burns on his face and will need skin grafts, and his back is broken in two places."

Jonathan looked at Emma in awe, as if the masculine side of his daughter was a dominating force. Though Emma knew Rakshasas was better off being subdued, she felt a humanistic pity for the demon of the Shaitan. She wondered why her heart even cared about a vision of Rakshasas being cared for by nurses and doctors for the rest of his days in a jail with assisted living.

"Emma," Siobhan said, bending down to her eye level. "He was not a man worthy of pity. God knows what he would have done to you."

"He's still a man. He probably has a family," Emma said, the guilt lingering.

Siobhan helped Emma off of the table and onto the floor. "Not all deserve clemency. Come now."

"Thank you for looking after her, Siobhan," Jonathan said, giving her an embrace. "And thank you for taking care of Adacia just now."

"Of course. Anything for you, Adacia and the children."

"I want to see Bo," Emma said. "Where is he? And where's Ciara?"

"Ciara is over at the Whitefoote Inn with her mother.

"Her Mom is here too?"

"She came with us," Jonathan said, placing a hand on Emma to calm her questions, knowing his daughter well. "Michelle and Ciara have a closer Croatoan tie that you might realize."

"And do not worry about your brother." Siobhan placed her hand on the back of Emma's soft, long hair. "He's sleeping right now. Jonathan, could you join Nicholas at Bo's bedside? Room 207. He's under guard so tell them the password is Willy."

Emma laughed as she made eye contact with Siobhan. "Too easy. Good one."

"I thought so," Siobhan beamed.

"That's not going to be good enough," Jonathan said, pointing to the security outside Emma's door. "At first the damn guards wouldn't let me in to see my own daughter."

Siobhan shook her head in shame, the familiar discrimination still in the air. "Guess I'll have to teach some people manners. Go. I'll see to your clearance."

"I'll head right over there," Jonathan said. He kissed Emma on the top of her still damp head, his breath smelling stale for that day. "I'll see you soon, sweetheart."

"Bye, Daddy," Emma said, watching her father jog off to tend to another sick child of his.

"Come along now," Siobhan said, gesturing for Emma to follow her out of the emergency room.

"Where are we going?"

"My apartment."

"Why there and not my Grandpa's house?" Emma said, sensing a reason, perhaps to keep her secret and safe.

"We're not waiting another night to tell you the truth. On this much we agreed."

"We?"

"Yes. Adacia is waiting for you."

By nightfall, Adoette had become a preverbal ghost town under the limited travel order enacted by the Defense Department. The winter wind echoed a hollowed whistle in the dry air as Emma and Siobhan's footsteps in the thin layer of snow made crunching impacts, every step leaving behind evidence of their presence.

Ahead, a warm, inviting light from Siobhan's fashionable apartment complex was the lone light reflecting off of the luminous reflective layers of snow. Though, most of the ornate metalwork around the windowsills of the buildings was hidden because of drawn shades, all hiding under the blackout.

Emma noticed straight away the two separate guards stood at ease in Siobhan's presence. One approached her, his eyes taking a quick look at the apartment building.

"Vice-Governor Hewens, you should not be trolling the streets without security."

"She's a mage, I thinks she's alright," Emma said, soon embarrassed of her loose tongue.

"Of course, my Lady Emma," the guard said, bowing to her.

Siobhan produced a key from the inside breast pocket of her jacket. "Emma, stop intimidating our Clandestine Service members. Walk in with me," Siobhan said, turning the key in the lock and opening the door to a wide stairwell.

"What should I say to her," Emma said. She dug her hands deep into her pockets. "What if she's mad at me?"

"Then she will be mad at you. Emma, you have every right to be just as angry. But please, avoid a tirade like before at the river."

Up five flights of stairs, Emma took particular notice of the murals of histories unknown to her painted on the walls. One that caught her eye was immigrants from the United Kingdom of Europe, hundreds of years ago, boarding cloud ships with what little ramshackle possessions they had to trek across the Atlantic to the new world Croatoan kingdoms, still in infancy. To her, these Croatoan buildings had no plain white walls or simple decorations of frames to brighten up a rather boring looking, conventional design she had seen again and again in the human world outside of the forest.

At the door of apartment 5A, Siobhan knocked three times, patted the door with her palm twice and pounded the door with her fist once.

"Is that Morse code or something?" Emma said.

"Morse code?"

"Never mind."

With a click of the door's latch, Emma was face-to-face with her mother. Adacia's face looked drained, her eyes surrounded by circles, still moist.

"Thanks, Siobhan," Adacia said.

Siobhan pressed her hand onto Emma's shoulder blades and gave her a slight shove. Emma stopped in her tracks with her heels, still afraid to enter.

"You're not coming in?" Emma said.

"Walk inside. Talk to her. I have some skulls to crack. You are sure Rakshasas spoke with a Government double agent?" Siobhan said.

"Bo, Ciara and I are pretty sure. There is someone in the city who isn't who he or she says they are," Emma whispered, aware that that people could be listening. "And they don't know we heard them either."

"At least we have the element of surprise for them," Siobhan said, pleased with the advantage. With this, Siobhan turned right round to gallop back down the stairwell, returning to her duties with haste.

Swallowing whatever reservations she had, Emma put one nervous foot in front of the other as she passed Adacia, feeling the pressure of those motherly eyes burning a hole through her. She couldn't bear to look at one inch of her mother.

The door then slammed shut, sending Emma's heart into her throat. She knew this was the feared time when the insubordination of any child would come crashing down with a verbal tongue lashing or a quick, stinging slap to the behind. Adacia had never abused Emma by fist, open hand or weapon. Emma and Bo both knew their parents wouldn't dream of it. However, in light of those circumstances, Emma felt in that moment as if her own breath shook in fear in the presence of her mother and that Adacia might return the previous favor to her young ears.

"We're not talking until you apologize to me," Adacia said, crossing her arms and leaning on one leg, defiant.

Emma opened her mouth to speak but only a hoarse whisper came out.

"Emma?" Adacia said, leaning in, her disappointed face turning concerned.

"I'm...Mom," Emma said, her voice still struck with fear.

"Are you sorry?"

Emma nodded her head in a burst of apology. "Yes!"

"Fine," Adacia said, pointing to the cushioned windowsill. "Sit down."

Emma situated herself on the feathered pillows next to the double latched windows. From her view she could see down a block, between two buildings was the vacant

Burnham Square and the city pond below. A cup of steaming hot chocolate, rested against the cold glass of the window. Emma couldn't help but to distract herself with the quiet square and the inspiring architecture, evoking a growing desire within her to remain. She hardly noticed Adacia sit across from her.

"How are your ribs? Do they still hurt, Blue Eyes?" Adacia said.

"Blue Eyes," Emma whispered to herself. Out there in that undiscovered country, Eleanor had to be hard at work, capturing and securing in all her majestic sorcery. Perhaps she was also aware as well that the lies would cease that night.

"Do you want me to grab you a pain…"

"Why did you tell me Grandma was dead?" Emma said, her sharp tone silencing Adacia's kind persistence.

Adacia fidgeted with her hands, placed in her lap. She took several deep breaths in and out through her nostrils, looking out the window as if she was composing herself. "Nothing I have to explain to you tonight will be easy for you to accept or understand."

"Can you at least start trying?"

Adacia nodded and looked Emma dead in the eyes. "Alright. I will. All of this reaches back to when I was your age. See…I was an only child. Everyone, especially Eleanor, expected me to be extraordinary."

"Did they think you should be a magic maker like me?"

"Yes, they did. I never was gifted by Mithra and the Ethereal Ones with any magical abilities like you and Eleanor. I could not even manifest those talents in the sciences to bridge the gap of ethereal powers to an earthly level. I was nothing special,"

Adacia said, pausing to shake her head in almost anger rather than regret. "I bet you're wondering why I haven't patted your behind for speaking to me that way."

Emma swallowed, once again nodding her head like a spring loaded doll.

"When I was fourteen, Eleanor and I were having an argument in my father's kitchen. I acted like a little you-know-what and decided to scream in her ear and push her over the edge of the table. Most people would have cracked their head open but Eleanor just stood up and looked at me with this face....my God! I started hyperventilating when I realized how I severed her soul in that tiny kitchen."

"Why did you do that?"

"No excuses from my current perspective. However, at that time I saw that Eleanor couldn't accept me being ordinary. No accomplishment came without what else I could have done better...job, school, boyfriends. She just tested me and placed me under more stress than a child should have to endure." Adacia scratched her head, sighing. "That was an awful thing for me to do."

"Was Grandma embarrassed of you or something?"

"Yes and no. More disappointed, which was stupid for such a brilliant woman. I was born this way, you know, nothing special," Adacia said, this time, her voice sounding sad.

Emma took a careful sip of the hot cocoa. She loved the familiar feeling of her mother's concoction of unique blended dairy milk, dark chocolate, a dash of cinnamon and a marshmallow in her belly. "It's good, Mom."

Adacia smiled, appreciative, as she used a pillow to lean against the windowsill, her right elbow embedded in the cotton, hand running through her hair. "I can imagine you've discovered that I'm not human by now."

"How are Croatoans different? How were they, I mean, we, created?"

"Confusing, I know. Well, there is the legend with half-truths and the history with more concrete evidence." Adacia rubbed her hands together, looking off into space for a moment. "Let's see. Well, we have gathered that about 12,000 years ago human beings started to see these offshoots in every one of their various races."

"Off-shoots?"

"Genetic off-shoots. Mutations of the gene into a different species, not that different from humans. We don't shoot lightening from out fingertips…well, Sorcerers can, but you get my idea. "

"Yeah, I've seen what you mean, Mom," Emma said, recalling all the fantastical elements beyond belief she had seen in the past three days.

Adacia shook her head. "In many ways we are equals with humans, despite what some Croatoans say to solidify foolish pride. Over many millennia Croatoans evolved to live longer than humans by an average of thirty-to-forty years, developed expanded mental capacities, faster adaptations to nature, and a higher resistance to diseases with persistently pliable anti-bodies. We are also adaptable to weather by literally having a thicker skin and a layer of very thin gel underneath. That keeps us warm in the winter and cool in the summer."

"Like a camel?" Emma said, her face twisted in confusion.

"Yes," Adacia said. "We all have giant humps in our backs."

"Alright, be cool. Just joking. So why do we have two last names? I mean, why did you tell me our last name was Grant when it is Alastar?"

Adacia nodded at this before she sat up and crossed the room to search a large duffel bag. Next to her mother Emma could see a toy chest with scratches in the cedar wood. A toy of what looked like a sleek, futuristic locomotive poked its head out. "Nice of Siobhan to fake that you and Ciara were some lowly orphans she took in off of the street." Adacia patted an oval baby crib that had been disassembled and placed alongside the wall with a government return label. Emma guessed that a child had lived in that apartment a mere few weeks ago under Siobhan's care.

"I can't believe how nice she is," Emma said. She wondered when the last time Siobhan had a blissful evening caring for desperate children that looked up to her the way that Emma and Ciara needed her in the recent days.

"That she is. Plus, a clever woman like herself realized how good of cover that was to hide you. I've got to find a way to make everything up to her. Ah! Found you!"

Out of her father's leather backpack, Adacia removed a thin picture frame. Crossing back over to Emma, Adaica flipped around the frame for her.

"This is your father and I on our wedding day." Adacia took her hand to the frame's base and opened up the image like a pop-up book to have the images of that joyful day many years back of a much younger Adacia and Jonathan appear in translucent images before Emma

To Emma, Adacia's shrugging laugh, much like her own fits of giggles, portrayed a simpler time. She ran her right forefinger over her mother's elegant wedding dress - a Croatoan display of marital unity in a charming blend of forest green and white silks.

Grandpa Nicholas, sans his nose-rimmed glasses, stood next to Adacia, beaming. Jonathan wore a tailored black three piece suit, sans tie. Next to Jonathan was Eleanor, who wore a unique design of a military/1940's- style, button-up suit and a skirt. Eleanor looked very much the same in age as when Emma saw her earlier that evening. The reserved smile that Eleanor bore, just on the edge of her mouth, looked ready to burst forth as her fingers touched Jonathan's shoulder. A small plaque in the shape of a European style family crest hung on the wall behind the newlyweds.

"Alastar. Our name. Why that and not Grant?"

"Grant is your father's last name. When a human like he and a Croatoan like myself get married, under international Croatoan law they have to start a new family line and choose and new name. Before we were married, we paid a visit to a Soothsayer and with an appointment with my Faerie to look into our future to best choose our name."

"I met one named Esylltora."

"Yes," Adacia said, looking at her daughter with wonder as she sat back down on the cushioned windowsill. "You met her so soon?"

"I met her in the forest the night I ran away."

"Yes...about running away..."

Emma handed back the wedding portrait to her mother, cutting her off. "No. I'm not saying that I'm sorry for that. Cause I'm not sorry."

"You realize that you had Bo, your father and me worried sick about you? We thought you were kidnapped by those terrorists."

Emma could still hear the echoed cries of the guards that evening, announcing the surprise attack. "Is that why you lied to me all of these years and changed our name and…" She removed her Alastar and held the jewel out for Adacia to see. "…tried to act as if I was nothing special."

Adacia threw her hands down, slapping her thighs. "Listen, you have to understand, you are the heir to the powers and leadership of Lady Eleanor Lumerious, the Lady of the Beacon, one of the most powerful and influential Sorcerers for over the past three hundred years. Those demons, like the ones you saw tonight, would love nothing better than to kill or capture you. Some aren't worth their weight in hay. You are worth the weight of some entire kingdoms. There are estimated to be only sixteen of your kind in the world today."

"Only sixteen," Emma said, knowing the oddness of her body began to sound justified. "So tell me how is Grandma Eleanor over three hundred years old but looks like she's in her early 40's, like you? Is she like those elves I read about who never age?"

"No. She's Croatoan. And to be more accurate, Eleanor is over 450 years old."

Emma's jaw dropped and nearly locked in place as she tried to fathom this.

"Eleanor," Adacia said, stopping herself when Emma shot her a look, still a little surprised at Adacia's distance. "My mother is like many near immortals on her side of the family. She was born in 1558 on the Christian Gregorian calendar and in 2006 on the New Croatoan Age calendar, almost four hundred and fifty years ago. She looks so young because near immortals, somewhat like elves in the ancient times before most of them died out and they passed into legend, physically age a year every decade or so."

Emma rubbed her forehead, eyes wide. "I can't even wrap my head around this. How come you, me and Bo aren't near immortals then?"

Adacia shrugged, looking unsure. "There are many theories. Doctors and such think that is because of your Grandfather's average Croatoan genes. With the illnesses he's had over the years," Adacia said, pursing her lips. "He'll probably only reach a hundred years old."

"Only one hundred? That's crazy long."

"For a human, that is. We Croatoans also have the fortune of our minds staying sharp and wise our whole lives unlike those poor human beings who have diseases eat away at their memories."

Emma downed the rest of her cocoa, holding her cup up-side-down to get all of the chocolate collected on the bottom. She didn't want to overwhelm her mind. Adacia edged forward and laid her gentle musician's hands upon Emma's. The surprising gesture made Emma shy away, a bit frightened considering the recent tirade. Adacia's hopeful expression turned fearful.

"I hope one day you will forgive me. I did all of this because I would rather die myself than have to bury my own children."

Emma set aside her mug and fought off her bitterness to do what she knew was necessary – she took hold of her mother's hands and then looked into those sad amber eyes.

"I'm not there yet, Mom. This is all so new for me."

"I know. I'm sorry."

Emma nodded, still not able to understand Adacia's motives. Holding tighter to her mother's hands, she knew to play the good daughter in these small, limited moments. "I just need time."

Adacia leaned forward and pulled Emma to her by the back of her head. Closing her eyes, Emma felt Adacia give her a kiss so soft and comforting that she felt five years old once more. Emma could almost imagine her heart back in the time when Adacia would kiss her before bed and fill her ears with a beautiful classical tune from the fiddle that Adacia was never bent out of shape to play for her beloved daughter.

Around what in the human world would be the midnight hour, Emma tossed and turned under the tartan wool bed sheets in Siobhan's queen size bed. The full moon had reared its celestial head after the light snow storm had cleared. The beams of moonlight poured through the cracks in the curtain, allowing Emma's keen eyes to see the room with infinite clarity. She wondered how many other Croatoans laid up that night, staring at the same moon as her, with all those hopes and fears for the future.

A rustling in the living room led Emma to slip out of bed. Careful, so as not to make a sound, Emma twisted the brass handle on the bedroom door, opening it ajar.

Rooted in the spot where Emma had been sitting on the windowsill pillow earlier was Adacia, tuning her fiddle, testing out the tuning with a scrape or two of her bow strings. Once satisfied, Adacia opened up the window.

From the first glide of the horsehair bow across the strings of the fiddle, Emma felt the hairs on her arm rise. Adacia played for the silent Silver City, each note the epitome of precision, echoing out into Emma's mind from that day forth that her mother was extraordinary in the way she could take a slow, enchanting melody from Mozart, Beethoven, Copland or Dvorak and pleasantly haunt all those who heard her fiddle sing.

All of the sudden, Adacia had stopped playing. Emma could tell in the thirty feet that separated the bedroom door from Adacia, the fiddle still resting under her chin, was that her mother's eyes were moving about from the room to the desolate square below. Adacia raised her bow and played. The notes to Aaron Copland's *Billy the Kid – Prairie Night* filled the room.

Emma could not hold herself back from whistling this meditative bedtime tune that Adacia played in forgotten nights many years before. Not being as musically gifted as her mother, Emma couldn't stay in harmony. Almost at once, as Emma's sharp whistling, like a sparrow on a tree branch, carried into the living room, Adacia stopped playing, lowered her fiddle and stared down her daughter.

"Get to bed, Emma!"

Chapter Seventeen
A Song for Lady Emma

The hours crept on by the next day, silence personifying the necessity of the city-wide lockdown. There were hunts and shakedowns, followed by bars and gates. A world in which a citizen seldom needed to lock their doors at night became riddled with barriers to keep out the shadows. Rumors spread from the checkpoints to the living rooms of Adoette, professing not simply the return of the terrorist group, the Chinday and their evil ways, but the discovery of the heir apparent to their beloved Lady Eleanor.

Emma spent a good deal of that day curled up under a blanket. She balanced the hours between reading the plethora of Croatoan history books on Siobhan's shelf and staring out the window for any sign that the limited travel ban would be lifted. The sight of the square filled with the spirit of the new season would be a relief to all. Adacia, like clockwork, made sure to cook a fulfilling breakfast, lunch and dinner, each one a hearty meal, every spoonful satisfying.

Emma tried her best to not break the peace and force a mea culpa between her and Adacia during those long waits for news on Bo's recovering condition or on how Ciara was getting on. There was only the adamant tone of her mother that Emma should stay put. The uneasiness Emma felt with the mingled glances they shot at each other from across the lonely room, unsure of what to say to break the tension, stretched the day out.

That very night, well after Emma had finally drifted off to sleep on Siobhan's down comforter, several whispering voices floated in from the kitchen. Half expecting her mother to be breaking out her fiddle once again, Emma ceased digging her knuckles into her eyes at the sight of Bo, Meira, Ciara and Siobhan huddled around the kitchen counter.

"Hey there, Emma," Siobhan said slowly, as if Emma was a little child once again.

"What's going on? Did they lift the travel ban?" Emma said, her mind still foggy with sleep.

Bo walked up to Emma to kneel down before her, looking eye to eye. "I heard about what you did after Rakshasas hit me with that spell. I kind of always thought you had it in your to kick some butt," Bo said, shaking his head in disbelief. He had three stitches sewn into the skin on his hairline.

"You knew I was a Sorcerer, right? So why are you so surprised?"

"I didn't know. I thought you might be but, damn. You threw them down!"

Emma bit her tongue, knowing the battle and then tumbling over sixty feet off a wall into a river so cold that her heart stop beating for a second was no easy task. "Yeah, I guess I can bring it!"

"Don't encourage her," Adacia said, appearing from the kitchen with a cup of tea on a saucer for both Meira and Siobhan. "Remember the time we went bike riding in San Francisco and you tempted her to ride down one of the hills?"

"Like that's my fault she flipped over the handles," Bo said.

"Yeah, I was only going twenty miles an hour. No broken bones. No problem," Emma said exchanging a smirk with Bo, both of them use to doing battle with their mother muddled sense of truth and emotion.

Ciara ambled over to Emma and gave her a half hug before backing away, looking afraid. "Oh. I'm sorry. Your ribs. Are you feeling better? I mean…" Ciara said, her face forming the terror she likely felt. "I saw you fall. It was terrible. Did you even hear me calling you?"

"No. I was underwater," Emma said. She patted at her right ribcage without a twinge of pain from her nerves. "They're fine. Already healed."

"Unbelievable," Meira and Siobhan both said, shaking their heads in disbelief at this level of strength that Emma had only just begun to harness.

"Thanks, I guess. So why are all of you here in the morning…its morning right?" Emma attempted to read the ornate clock in the shape of a four leaf clover above the stove. "Seriously, what time is it?"

"The twenty-third hour. The sun will be up in around forty-five minutes," Siobhan said, sipping and blowing on her mug of oolong tea to cool down the water. "Get dressed already. I am taking you all to see something quite special."

Emma immediately shot a hopeful look over to her mother, who stood a little removed from the group, arms cross in her typical uncomfortable stance.

"Fine. You can go. I trust Siobhan. But I do think a guard or two should come along," Adacia said.

Bo leaned in, careful to touch the cornered tiger that was Adacia. Emma could see by the frosted glass light hanging in the center of the kitchen, with no wires attached, that Bo wore a flesh colored bandage on the back of his neck, almost hidden by the raised collar of his cotton pullover.

"Really, Mom?" Bo said, gesturing to his present company. ""Out of five people, two are Mages and one is a Sorcerer. I think a soldier with a rifle is gonna feel pretty bored if someone decides to attack Emma."

Adacia mulled this over, softly and slightly nodding her head as she thought. Emma caught a gleam of appreciation from Meira that Bo surely caught, as he winked back at his date.

"The travel ban has been lifted, Adacia, as of sunrise anyways," Siobhan said, placing a hand on Adacia's shoulder, furthering the cause.

"Fine," Adacia said, pointing an index finger into Bo's chest. "Just have her back before breakfast. She needs to be somewhere."

So excited to get out, Emma's ears had glossed over Adacia's last statement. "So where are we going?"

"Go and get dressed," Siobhan said. "What would be the point of spoiling a good surprise?"

The pitter-patter of the groups' footsteps opened apartment shutters, lured terrified citizens out from behind peepholes. Like the shopkeepers and bakers already at work, the sounds of the city in a new day rang in with a cautiously optimistic tone, as if they were ready to dive back into their doorways at a given notice.

Siobhan led them out of the northwest gate, over the DuSable bridge that crossed over the Rockland River and into the woods that climbed into the hills and eventually grew to mountains in the miles west from the city high enough for a dusting of snow. Emma felt a chill run up her spine looking over to the spot where she fell into the Rockland. She had been thanking that extra epidermal protection from her Croatoan skin ever since.

Walking up a path, lit up by lanterns with an abundance of soft light, Emma loved feeling the cool breeze that carried the smell of various forms of timber like a visible trail now that she was back in the forest. The sky above the spare canopy of autumn leaves remained dark, not even showing a hint of the faint blue light of the morning. A few guards stopped in their march down to the city to bow to Emma. Unsure of the proper return, Emma waved back.

"Emma," Meira said, leaning in to whisper. "You should place your hand over your heart and slightly bow in return. Eleanor does this."

"Okay, thanks," Emma said, bowing to the guards. At once, they smiled back, as if an outside force set them at ease as they went on their way. "Is that what you have to do too?"

Meira laughed, her amusement sounding more annoyed than Emma expected. "No. I do not get bowed down to."

Ahead the path split in two. Siobhan led Emma and the company to the right lane, over fallen leaves sodden with the first winter snow, straight to a clearing ahead that was dominated by a tree trunk so massive that Emma guessed the tree had to be at least forty or so feet wide, several times what a redwood could ever be.

"Siobhan? Is that the tree you showed us on the hill?" Ciara said.

"Certainly. This is the Adoette tree," Siobhan said. Her fingers traced the winding staircase with a support railing all the way up. "This morning we are going to the top!"

Emma had to crane her neck and curve her back to see. "How high is the tree, again? Three hundred feet?"

"Try over five hundred, Em," Bo said, rubbing his sore neck after looking up. "Is the plan that we hike all the way up?"

Meira patted Bo on his belly and walked ahead, flirtatious looking back at him. "Out of figure, are you?"

"Not around you," Bo said, thereafter closing his eyes in embarrassment of his quick tongue.

"What does that even mean?" Emma said, wincing at Bo's poor attempt to flirt.

"Shut it," Bo said through his teeth.

He jogged past the girls to join with Meira at the first step. When Bo reached her, they let out a tiny, innocent chuckle at something Emma could not hear. Meira then shoved Bo, her laughter intensifying as she then bolted up the stairs. The nimble Bo didn't waste any time as she followed, giving chase to the young Mage through the square covered entrance made of silver tree fibers.

"Siobhan?"

Erik jogged to them from a wooden building with a burnt sienna triangular roof that looked like a temple or assembly hall akin to a Native American hut, complete with totem poles fashioned into the ground around the hall, carved with mythical creatures. Ciara nudged Emma, crossing her fingers.

"What are you hear for?" Siobhan said.

"I was told to await your arrival," Erik said, bowing slightly to the girls. "Emma. Ciara. Are you well?"

"Yes. Thanks for looking after my brother during the phantom attack."

"I tried to get to you as well," Erik said, hanging his head. "That will not happen again. I promise."

"It might," Emma said, shrugging. "But don't worry."

"Girls, why don't you run on up ahead and I'll follow you in a short minute," Siobhan said, pointing to the Adoette tree.

"Don't take too long, you two," Emma said, that devilish smirk back. Sauntering over to the tree, she could feel slightly agitated Siobhan's stare into the back of her head.

"Why did you do that?" Ciara said. She and Emma positioned themselves a few steps up, against the railing so they could stake out the brewing, awkward romance. Siobhan and Erik were inching close to one another with every sentence.

"Why? I don't know. It gives them the extra push they need."

"What are they saying?"

"Can't tell. I think Siobhan knows by this point that I can hear long distances."

Erik and Siobhan did their self-conscious waltz around one another for several minutes. Emma couldn't take the tension of what she felt were two people who seemed good for each other go on without a resolution.

"Kiss her, already!" Emma shouted.

Ciara, as if she had made a pact with Siobhan ahead of time, covered Emma's mouth and shushed her in the ear. Emma quickly retaliated by licking Ciara's hand, forcing her to withdraw in disgust.

Then, without warning, Erik grabbed Siobhan from around her waist and planted and long, wet one on her lips. She returned the favor, her hand brushing his cheek.

"See," Ciara said, holding her hand out to the new couple. "That was so cute, Em. You almost ruined the mojo."

"Do even you know what the means?" Emma said, her face contorted into an awkward stare.

"Hugging?" Ciara said with a confused shrug.

Emma shook her head, acknowledging how young and inexperienced she and her friend still were in the ways of passion.

Siobhan parted hands with Erik to attend to their early morning duties, but not before only final gentle kiss. Siobhan and Erik looked long at one another as they walked away. Emma couldn't wait to flash two big thumbs up when Siobhan finally turned her happy head around.

"You are a little brat, aren't you?" Siobhan said, biting her lip. "Lucky thing my abilities are only a forth of what you are."

"Sorry, I can't help that side of me."

"So I have noticed. Now come on you two, up the tree!"

Floating balls of light, no bigger than a marble, were encased in protective lamps along the railing. Their light made the exhaustive path up those winding stairs visible, the glow catching a glint of a fiber from a silver tree in the staircase, making the wood look as if a long silver vine was wrapping around the tree. Emma ran her hand along the bark of the Adoette tree, not at all surprised by the soft shell, ready to soak up moisture. Emma felt this ancient skin embedded with a thousand stories for all the years when Croatoans knew this reminder of the ancient world hung on for dear life in a tumulus new age.

At the twenty-second story, Emma and Siobhan took a few minutes to allow Ciara to catch her breath and consider using her inhaler. By that height, they were a good hundred feet above the tree line. The forty degree air cooled and expanded the lungs of the climbers as the jet stream evaded the curves of the mountains and chased the brightening horizon to the east.

Emma plopped down next to Ciara, curious. "What are you and your Mom going to do? Move away?"

Ciara's depressed the inhaler and took a long intake of the medicine and exhaled soothing relief. "Oh, I should have told you. We got a clearance from the government to stay for eight months."

"Wait, you did?" Siobhan butted in, surprised. "But your mother is human and you are a mere half Croatoan."

"A letter came in last night from Boldger Hall that said as long as we file proper documentation, we can stay six to eight months and then re-apply," Ciara said, shrugging. "Is that weird?"

"Certainly so," Siobhan said. "That never happens. Odd."

"I guess Mom and I are getting some good luck. About time too! Maybe we can find an apartment that's cheap," Ciara said, pocketing her inhaler, her breathing evening out. "Maybe your Mom and mine can look for places."

"I don't think my Mom…" Emma shook her head, troubled. "When I asked her yesterday about if we would live here, she said 'We'll see.'"

Emma, curious at this case of an immigration loophole, wondered how even the Vice-Governor in Siobhan was not aware of this. And yet, as Ciara spoke so frank about her future, Emma had roots to a land but no home; her family was a woven mystery without a promise of a return trip. Her open palm made a fist, which she tapped on her knee, staring down the spiraling staircase, her head and chest tugging at the notion she might fall straight down.

Ten minutes later, the lamps were of no use in the available light, merely minutes before the sunrise. Siobhan extinguished each lamp with a simple double tap on the glass.

Below the top branches of the Adoette tree, which covered the last hundred feet, was a wide platform which evenly wrapped around the tree for a 360 degree observation deck for views in every direction of the Republic of the Silver Forest. Even without the usual need for the keen, telescopic views from Emma's eyes, the party could see for miles from that height. The dew seemed to gleam on the branches of every tree. Fog in the miles of mountains to the west cut through the darkness and drifted over peaks and into valleys, some as close as a few miles away. She could see the rail line, like in the mural, cut through the forest from a nearby secluded station, past what looked like dozens of orchards and grazing fields for animals, and into the seemingly infinite western country of the Silver Forest. To the south, Emma saw the Shikakwa River run south and then west past more thick forest, rolling hills and valleys of carefully tended golden wheat. To the north, much of the same landscape, making Emma wish so dearly that Siobhan had brought a map to give a better tour of the Republic.

"Here," Siobhan said, reaching into her coat pockets. "Eat up. And don't tell your mother." She handed each one of them a chocolate bar. Emma traded her plain almond milk bar for Ciara's cherry and raspberry infused one, remembering the sweet elation she had in her father's store with that first sharp snap of a bite of cocoa.

Beyond the clouds of the storm that had passed in the night the first rays of the sun shot out from the horizon, amber colored heat illuminating the wind-hued faces of Emma, Bo, Ciara, Meira and Siobhan as they leaned on the railing, shoulder-to-shoulder, nibbling away at their chocolate. No one spoke for many minutes for fear of ruining a perfect sunrise from that crisp, majestic height.

A chorus of angelic voices in choral harmony below carried up to accompany the occasional gusts of slight wind making the girls tie their hair back. The chorus sang from the front steps of the temple more than four hundred feet below. Their voices, like with the artful liturgical choral pieces from the Baroque Era, weaved in and out of one another, the men and women taking their pitch perfect, elongated notes to highs and lows in English and what she guessed after much exposure was a dialect of the Croatoan language that Emma still could not decipher.

> Bless the Alastar
> Deontas a honor Soul óga, eagna agus fortitude
> The New Age has come
>
> Bless the Alastar
> Tá cailín ar dhá shaol
> She has returned to be the heir

"What are they singing?" Emma said.

"A prayer to the Ethereal Ones for the heir," Siobhan said. "And in light of the attack, we could all do to thank them."

"I'm the heir they're praying for, right?"

Siobhan nudged the little Blue Eyes. "Why of course you are, Emma."

Taken aback by this gratitude, Emma tuned her ears to the choir. With the blinding, fiery sun, emerging in the east, she squinted, wishing she had her goofy shamrock shaped sunglasses left on her dresser at home. Her heart was quite full in those small moments for all those who pledged their appreciation for her mere existence.

"Thanks for taking us up, Aunt Siobhan," Bo said. He allowed his fingers to wrap around Meira's, not afraid to hide his affections for her.

"Of course, Bo," Siobhan said, bashfully holding back a smile as her cheeks had become rosier, other than the pink burn from the high altitude winds. Siobhan nudged up to Emma and whispered in her ear, pointed to the west and stared with mere few blinks to the horizon. "Emma, have you ever read about the tale of Meriwether Clark in those history books of yours?"

"No. Who is he?"

"He was great explorer from the Appalachian Colony out east in the 2160's. On his year long journey to establish further ties with the Kingdom of the Bald Mountain..."

"Kingdom of the Bald Mountain?" Emma quickly shot in.

"That's a Croatoan kingdom in what is the American northern New Mexico. Mostly made up of Croatoan Native American tribes. Fabulous place and very gracious people. Anyways...Clark found his way up here, trying to find truth to the rumor of what Native American tribes called a 'God-like' land, full of trees that shone and creatures that flew with supernatural powers."

"Here. The Silver Forest, right?"

"That's right," Siobhan pointed to the eastern horizon once again, tracing her finger from far from visible forest edge, through the thick woods and to the Hetch-Hetchi valley. "Just think, Emma. Like Meriwether Clark, from the east, a mere few days ago, you crossed the wild and found us."

Chapter Eighteen
The Veiled Crest

Music was in their ears, the cacophony of rhythmic footsteps descending the Crann Mora tree playing along. At the last steps Emma came face-to-face with Adacia and Nicholas. Arms folded, they stood amongst workers who scooped up the falling leaves of the surrounding trees, making piles to keep the entrance clean. Emma had to repress the wave of immaturity that had crossed her mind in that instant, desiring to jump head long into the leaves and ruin a perfectly good pile.

"Follow me," Adacia said, ushering Emma away from the rest of the group.

"Where are we going?"

"Boldger Hall. Your Grandfather convinced me we should do this."

"Do what?"

Adacia and Nicholas fell into their old parental modes and tuned out Emma. As Adacia led Emma away, back into the Silver City, she turned back to see her friends and Bo, who were having a rather enclosed, secretive conversation with Grandpa Nicholas. Feeling left out once again reminded Emma of that bitter taste in her life before the forest, the coffer with the vial and the visions of the future. Adacia tried to small talk with Emma but she brushed off the timid connection with her mother with one word answers, curious and frustrated with her cunning ways.

After they had re-entered the city of Adoette, Emma followed her mother through the streets to the marble front steps of Boldger hall at the end of Burnham Square.

"What are we doing here?" Emma said, noticing that in-between the three flights of steps were quotations carved into the marble from individuals she couldn't recognize. One of the lines read as such...

> "Kindness and reasoning in the face of unmotivated wills and cold hearts is not weakness, but strength and patience to wait for the better angels in our souls to emerge."
> **~ Cornelius Benson**

Another line read...

> "Croatoans owe themselves to self-govern, and in leaders we seek the enlightened for we are not angels. Their presence assures we strive for Honor, Wisdom and Fortitude, as we assure them of not their dominance but their service."
> **~ Madison Adams**

"Eleanor invited you over for a light breakfast in her office," Adacia said.

"Just me."

"Just you," Adacia said, soon after quick to respond on cue to the round of questions Emma was prepared to fire out of her mouth. "I'm not ready either."

"To speak with Grandma?"

Adacia nodded before glancing at the northwest clock. The clock dial had a glowing sun face that smiled and closed its eyes as the celestial center of the solar system rotated around with the time. "Go on. You'll be late otherwise. Just promise me one thing."

"What?" Emma said, quite sure why she was suspicious of her mother.

"Come directly to your father's shop when you're done. We need to have a talk...all of us need to talk to you."

"About what?"

"I'm not playing twenty questions with you," Adacia said, throwing up her hands. "You'll see. Now get in there."

Emma turned and ran up the steps, taking two at a time. She had to use the weight of her whole body to open one of the two thick main doors made of wood from a silver tree and carved with panned silver and gold strips. Curving above the door, written on oak panels and in-laid with bronze was the phrase *'Honor, Wisdom, Fortitude.'*

Beyond the door was a wide entrance hall with stone tiles, oak and cherry wood paneling and the emerald Republic of the Silver Forest flag on either side of a round, vault style wooden and silver metal door, which at that time was sealed with a lock.

Congress Not in Session Today

The words, alight in the wood like soft red neon, connected to nothing, almost as if they floated there. A rather stoic looking young guard, stood at full attention before the door. His rifle was at the ready.

"Excuse me?" Emma said, waving at the unblinking guard. "Can you tell me how to get to Lady Eleanor's office?"

The guard continued to stare straight ahead, never wavering from his rooted spot.

"Sir?" The guard did not even blink for Emma. Taking a place next to the guard, Emma stood shoulder to shoulder to partially mimic him with her fists firmly dug into her hips, her head held high, holding back her giggles. The guard remained fixed to his duty. "Okay. Okay. Fine. Don't try too hard, Soldier."

Leaving the soldier behind with a salute, Emma walked down the hallway to admire the dozen or so hand chiseled life-size statues of white marble that were evenly placed into tiny coves in the wall. She stopped between the statues of Cornelius Benson, who held both hands firmly to his vest while looking to the distance, and Marie Brythonic, who was carved in an elegant gown, holding a quill to copies of diplomatic parchments in her arms. Above them, like with a good deal of the other statues, read *Members of the Founding Family of The Republic of the Silver Forest*.

"Lady Emma?" a voice called.

Emma turned to find Sergeant Morales approaching from a corridor off to the back left of the entrance. "Oh hey! I was just staring at people...no idea who there are."

"Fine history we have, eh? The Governor just sent me to find you. I will show you, Lady Emma."

"You can just call me Emma," she said, holding out a hand to try to calm the '*at attention*' Morales.

"Nonsense. You are a Sorcerer," Morales said. "Besides, that was wrong of me to speak to you in that way at the outpost. Let's just say many of us are skeptical of things these days. So when a young Sorceress appears one day, the Alastar of legends...well, let's say you were a surprise."

"I keep getting that," Emma said, still grasping with being treated as Croatoan royalty.

Morales smiled, and bowed to Emma. "I imagine. Follow me."

On the journey around the interiors of the building, Emma could catch a small peak into the hall, adored with scattered numbers of large formal desks in rows, wood tiled floor space, and two large chairs at the back of the hall that were elevated above the rest. Squinting in a space between these layered white Corinthian columns Emma could see these seats were reserved for the Vice-Governor, a Judicial Judge, Senate President.

There were a series of windowed offices in the back. All were abuzz with activity, contrary to the rest of Boldger Hall. At the end of the hall, Emma was led to a door placed into the wall at an angle, labeled *'Executive Office.'*

"Give two knocks and step inside," Morales said, pointing to the door that blended into the wall adorned with a watercolor mural with paintings of the abundant forests, hills and rivers of the Republic.

An older black gentleman stepped out of the nearest office, an open scroll dangling from his hand. His face was livid, the crevassed lines on his face showing his years in the political trenches.

"Morales! How am I supposed to keep the Gazette off of our backs if they keep talking to the Watchers and then start drumming up this damn editorial rhetoric that chastises the Department Secretaries? One of them even harshly criticized Lady Eleanor. Emma was kept a secret…sorry Emma…for a reason!! That's just wrong! Gregory Royal opens his mouth so much, I'm surprised that vomit he spews in the papers doesn't make him an anorexic! They knew better than to print those things about Lady Eleanor."

"I think the Governor can take the heat, Joseph," Morales said. Looking at Emma, Morales rolled her eyes, almost as if she was frustrated with herself for forgetting something. "My apologies, Lady Emma. This is Joseph Rainey, the Governor's Chief of Staff."

Joseph's traded the scroll with his other hand to place his open palm over his heart.

"Hard to believe it, Morales," Joseph said, giving a bow. "Lady Eleanor was right, Emma. You do look like your mother."

"You know my Mom?"

"Can't forget a face like that. I have been Lady Eleanor's Chief of Staff for twenty-two years now. My how have the years past." Joseph caught a glint of Morales about to deliver a clever retort but he pointed the scroll at her before she spoke. "You don't need to remind me again how many times I've been married in all those years."

Morales threw her hands behind her back at ease, laughing a little as she allowed Emma to have access to the door.

"Please, go inside," Morales said with a wave of her hand to Emma.

"Thank you. Nice to meet you, Joseph," Emma said.

For the first time, Joseph softened, his thick skin becoming loosened up by Emma's eyes and the glimmer from her Alastar. "And you, my Lady." He tapped Morales with the news scroll. "I need to speak with you, Sergeant. Excuse us."

Joseph and Morales stepped into the Chief of Staff office and shut the door behind them. The seal wasn't tight enough for Emma to miss their raised voices and flailing arms as they traded barbs.

Emma placed her left hand on the curved, tree branch-like door handle and knocked twice with her right. Without even pushing down, the handle moved, propelled by an invisible power inside. The door widened to several feet.

"Come in, my Emma."

Opening the door, Emma stopped in her tracks when she caught sight of the walls of Eleanor's office, about the size of Grandpa Nicholas' large sized living room. The walls were adorned with countless flags, portraits of Eleanor with famous political figures and Croatoan celebrities, honorary crests and diplomas, all of them looking aged, well-preserved relics in a museum. On the floor, blending in with the wood was a symbol of a

Thunderbird, surrounded by stars, the bird holding an olive leaf in one talon and an arrow in the other. At the fireplace, along the middle of the left wall, were portraits of the family set between Eleanor's sealed fiddle case.

Emma took a few steps closer with disbelief at one of the pictures in black and white. A rather adolescent Adacia, her nose and cheekbones a near match to Emma's, glanced over her shoulder with a scrunched up face, laughing without an ounce of knowledge of her complicated future.

"One minute, Emma," Eleanor said. She said behind a finely carved and lacquered desk that looked as if it was once made from timbers of a sailing ship. The desk had the Governor symbol on the front and read above the Thunderbird - *Honor, Wisdom and Fortitude*.

Emma blinked in surprise at the over six-foot tall and rather boney middle aged woman with a billowing flow of wavy red hair that stood before Eleanor's desk at attention, the lines and bloodshot eyes showing the physical drain on her body.

"My Lady Governor, I can assure you, I will not fail again. It was a foolish oversight to think I didn't need to confer with every department to watch the skies."

Eleanor's eyes flashed with an intensity that made the woman shrink. "Marrigain," Eleanor said, ice cold. "You were elected by the people as Senator to protect them and you failed miserably. Leadership in your first year of office should not mean cutting the very people who protect us, clothe us, feed us. I am so ashamed that this happened in my Republic. The Order of Erebys is clever but we have an edge…defense and resilience of the people to live in harmony. And now, we have my Granddaughter, Lady Emma. Can you at least show her the respect she deserves?"

Wanting to cut the tension of Eleanor's punishing blows Emma stepped up to Marrigain and cordially held out her hand.

"Hi. I heard you were a Mage, like Siobhan."

Marrigain took one look at Emma's hand and held a private scowl, which Emma caught as she drew back her hand.

"Pleasure, I am sure, Emma," Marrigain said, her eyes staring Emma down.

"Lady Emma," Eleanor snapped, instantly bringing Marrigain to attention. Eleanor proceeded to sign a document with her flowery calligraphy signature. "You are to appear before a Grand Jury…"

"My Lady Governor, that is…"

Eleanor snapped her fingers once again, silence washing over Marrigain. "You will appear before a Grand Jury either later this year or early next year to testify on gross mistakes in command. The Congressional Council approved this earlier, six to four, with the backing of the Judiciary."

Marrigain clenched her fist behind her back, so that only Emma saw her reign in her apparent anger. Her finely polished nails were digging into the whites of her skin. "Budgets do not balance themselves. I made those one hundred cuts in positions and security precautions because of the debts accrued since the war."

Eleanor listed and nodded, eyes still away from Marrigain. "If you wish to take some time away to sort out your life, please talk with me before you leave," Eleanor said, handing the leave order on parchment to Marrigain. "Now please, leave me with my Granddaughter. You are dismissed."

"You have made a bad choice, lady Governor," Marrigain said, nearly at a whisper as she placed her hand over her heart and bowed long to Eleanor. Turning on the heels of her shin high brown leather boots, Marrigain stepped out of Eleanor's office without so much of a look towards Emma. When Marrigain failed to close the door, Eleanor without looking up, casually gestured to the door with her right hand. The door gently closed from the spell Eleanor casted.

"I am so sorry, Emma," Eleanor said, signing off on another document. "Trust me, I did not vote for her as Senator. The people did. People are finally starting to see that she's a better celebrity politician than a leader." Eleanor set down her pen and placed a stack of prepared papers off to the side of the desk. "I do feel terrible but I have to leave on a Cirrus Flight to the Kingdom of the Bald Mountain and then to the Appalachia Republic to brief my fellow Governor's of the attack by the Order."

Emma had so many questions she hadn't a clue where to start. "Grandma, I really don't know what you just said."

"You shall soon know," Eleanor said, looking away to the fireplace portraits. "Well," she said with a deep, contemplative breath, "I have a few hours before I have to drag my defense secretary with me across the continent. Would you like to drink some tea and have a muffin with me out on the back terrace?"

Emma nodded as quickly as she could, desperate to know this long lost elder. "I like blueberry muffins."

"I like cherry," Eleanor said, leaning in with wide, squeaky clean white smile. "Come. I shall have the chef rustle that up for us."

On the back terrace there were a series of interconnected glass panels installed into the stone base, making an all-weather enclosure. Emma swore the room looked more like a solarium with all the scattered potted plants of exotic ferns and flowers that bloomed year round. A tiny weather vane opened a window on occasion, allowing the cool outside air in, preventing the guests from encountering a steam bath inside.

As Emma sat across from Eleanor on one of the many low back wicker chairs, her ears made notice of the winter wind screeching by, ready to creep in through the cracks and threaten their serenity.

"Were you aware that I negotiated two peace treaties from this room," Eleanor said, sipping from the teacup she held with grace.

"Really? Did they last long?" Emma said.

"Good catch! One of them did. You're already wiser than some politicians," Eleanor said, smiling before taking another sip of orange blossom green tea. "Do you like your treats?"

Emma had eaten the majority of her blueberry muffin in those minutes of small talk with Eleanor, each bite of fresh fruit and moist muffin passing the time. Eleanor set her tea cup down when Emma continued to chew, not answering for fear of being rude.

"I imagine that you likely have enough questions for me to fill a novel."

"I do," Emma said, swallowing a bite of strawberry from the tray of out of season fruits on a porcelain plate. "I suppose I'm most confused about being...a Sorcerer? I mean, I get the Silver Forest, I get Croatoans, but me. Let's be real. Am I really your heir?"

"By blood and ability, you are. What else would there be?"

"Then what does that mean for me? Am I going to be as strong as you?"

"That is another matter." Eleanor took out her own Sorcerer's jewel, the silver and white crystal comet, out from under her shirt. The jewel hung from an unbreakable black lace string, like with Emma's. "Take out your Alastar."

Emma pulled the necklace over his head and placed the star in the palm of her hand. Eleanor followed suit, her and Emma's sources of the incredible hybrid of engineered and supernatural abilities held out over the coffee table. Eleanor leaned forward and pointed back and forth like a college lecturer.

"This is the source of my magical abilities – the Celestalian. The energy core is developed from a strain from my father's."

"Your Dad was a sorcerer too?"

"Certainly. Once the energy was stable enough to transfer into your star..."

"How much energy does my Alastar have?" Emma said, imagining a surging power station in her hands.

"About enough to power the entire American state of California for a few years," Eleanor said, paying no mind to the jaw that dropped on Emma. "Now listen...the device was buried in the ground where it gestated all the months you were in your mother's womb. Around the time you were born, a star held above the canopy, deep in the Silver Forest. Venturing out alone, I was the one who found your Alastar, risen to the surface, in the same place I had placed it nine months before. And I am the only one who knows of your...." Eleanor fell silent, her hand to her chin, her eyes darting about.

Emma sat up and looked behind her. "Eleanor? Is everything alright?"

Eleanor held out her hands, palms down. "Take my hands."

"Where are we going?"

"A secret is not worth wasting. Take them now."

In the years leading up to those days, a change in air temperature, a malicious soul entering a peaceful room, a thought before one would speak it – Emma had anticipated all of them. When Emma took a hold of her Grandmother's hands, a foreign sensation, one of dizziness and the motion of being thrust forward while sitting still, was terrifying and exciting all at once. Wind circled about them in a torrent and their bodies evaporated into the air.

"Awake, my Emma! Awake!"

Eleanor shook the started Emma, surprised to find herself laying on the forest floor. Tilting her head left, thirty feet past the thick trees was a rock ledge, many hundreds of feet above the forest floor.

"Where are we?"

"Several miles into the Muir Mountains, west of the city," Eleanor said. "Hold firm to my hands next time or I will lose control of you in our ebbmersion."

Emma stood, her head swimming, throwing off her balance. She placed her hands on her knees, breathing deep. Even her stomach felt uneasy. "Is that what you did to me? What's ebbmersion?"

"The ability to appear and disappear through spaces," Eleanor said, waving Emma over. "Follow me, my child."

Not wanting to expel her muffin into the pure white snow and pine needles, Emma breathed deep, took courage and followed her Grandmother. In and out of trees they weaved for several minutes. Emma learned to pick up her feet after tripping on jutted rocks in the uneven terrain.

"Where are we going?"

"You are going to have to lead me."

Emma threw her hands out, puzzled by this game. "Is this some Buddhist saying? How can I lead you if I don't know where I'm going?"

"I understand. But look about you," Eleanor said, tugging at her own star. "Feel familiar?"

One touch of her Alastar and the jewel began to glow. Emma's eyes recognized each tree, each leaf as if they were her own hands. One particular silver tree, the roots pouring out of the surface, rested behind Eleanor. If the tree had a voice, she could feel choirs of ethereal voices pouring out. At the base of the trunk was a pattern of a star, a perfect copy of Emma's Sorcerer mark.

"Place your Alastar on the wood and you will see why I have taken you here."

Removing her necklace, Emma obeyed Lady Eleanor's command. The metal bottom flung out of Emma's hands and affixed itself to the tree.

"Hey! Get outta there!" She tugged, scraped and attempted to pry but to no avail, her jewel was rooted into the wood. Fear rushed over her heart, as if a loved one was dying before her eyes. "Help me get it out!"

Eleanor took a firm hold of Emma's shoulder. "Do not run wild with emotion. Hold your hand over the Alastar and repeat after me.

Emma did as told, feeling the ethereal pulse of her magical jewel through her skin. She repeated Eleanor after every line, closing her eyes to concentrate.

> I am the keeper of this water
>
> I am the owner of my heart
>
> Open the gates to my abilities
>
> A Sorcerer wishes to start

A hawk called from a branch in the distance. The trees swayed some in the wind of the higher altitude. Emma peaked out of one eye, seeing the forest as it was before.

"Nothing is happen...whoa!"

Emma released her hand from the tree. The Alastar, like a magnet, attached itself into the palm of her hand. Water poured out of any open crevice, the tree becoming a forest spring. The water had purpose and direction, filling the low space where Emma and Eleanor had stood.

"This is your Sorcerer Lake. This is the source of all of your powers, my Emma."

Emma kneeled down next to the tiny pond, forming several feet deep before her eyes. A translucent image, ten times larger than her star, floated at the center. A blue and silver light, the colors of Emma's Alastar, permeated throughout the water and lit up dim forest in no way that any human eye had ever seen. Emma's soul was staring through her transfixed eyes and the water back through her at an absolute beauty of a power beyond the realm of the known world. Angelic voices with no source echoed into the air and serenaded the sorcerers with music that tenderized their hearts into an enlightened state.

Eleanor fell to her knees beside Emma, holding her hand to her chest. "The beauty is unparalleled, and this is not even my Sorcerer lake."

Emma had to force out her words for every fiber of her being was fixed to what she knew was her second heart. "What does this do?"

"The water and the engineered fiber mechanics below hold your power here on earth."

Placing the necklace around her neck, Emma touched the Alastar, beginning to understand. "Like a backup of my memories and abilities?"

"In a way. It's function will be for you to reveal. When my Celestalian appeared, imbedded into a scotch pine in the Kingdom of Avenmore in Scotland, there were a series of images of myself carved into the trunk. I was only a newborn but the image was of my younger, twenty-eight year old face in appearance of the two hundred and eighty second year of my life, the year I came to the Silver Forest from my Governorship in the Republic of Glencar Aisling over in Ireland."

"Is that when you defeated the dragon?"

Eleanor oddly flinched at Emma. "I didn't sense you read my mind. How did you know that?"

"I overheard you telling the story on Halloween night."

Eleanor snapped her fingers, looking assured. "I knew I felt a familiar aura in that space. My my, you are sneaky."

Emma shrugged, confident even to evade a mighty sorcerer's eyes. Fidgeting, she rubbed the crystal between her thumb and forefinger. "Grandma, how strong does this make me?"

"Quite strong," Eleanor said, holding her comet jewel out. "If you harness your abilities and become harmonious, I have no doubt your Alastar will make you loved in the rights circles and feared by the shadows that creep into our lives, much like the other night when Rakshasas and his phantoms came to terrorize our people." Eleanor, her lips tightly held shut at the mention of those malevolent men, placed her Celestalian back over her neck.

"Are people afraid of you?"

"Yes," Eleanor said with a nod. "And they should be. I have not survived fire, heartache and the wounds of war to not send my enemies begging for clemency at the mere sight of me."

As imaginative as Emma could be about living out her Grandfather's books of tales that had become history, she could not see herself as a tyrant. "What am I supposed to do?"

"Start with questions like that and move forward, my dear," Eleanor said, holding Emma's hand. "Your childhood can no longer be after what you have seen and experienced. You are Emma Adacia Alastar, a Sorcerer and my heir."

As Emma let her heart sink at the idea of innocence having slipped away, Eleanor produced a small leather bound journal with a wave of her hand. The pages formed and were surrounded by the leather in front of Emma's eyes.

"For me?" Emma said, taking the journal and running her fingers over the etching of the Alastar in the brown leather.

"Yes. However this is no ordinary book. Here…" Eleanor said, producing a capped, quill tipped blue pen from her inside pocket. "Write your name on the first page and tap the line twice at the end."

Emma wrote her full name on the first white sheet. She keenly noticed Eleanor's signature – *Eleanor Lumerious* - was engraved into the side of the pen with a symbol of the Thunderbird. After tapping the edge of the line, the ink instantly dried and faded into the page.

"What happened?"

From inside her jacket, Eleanor produced a nearly identical brown leather journal, this one complete with an etching of the Celestelian comet on the front cover. Opening the first page, she held out the journal for Emma's to see.

The page lit up for a half-second, as if a light was turned on and off. On top, lettering began to take shape.

Incoming message from Lady Emma...

...Emma Adacia Grant

"You wrote Grant." Eleanor said, firmly, pointing to the writing.

"Sorry," Emma said, closing her journal to toss it on the table. "I mean, I just found out I have a new name."

Eleanor nodded, at least showing an ounce of understanding. "That is true. Well, this journal is for you. I had the Defense Department specially make one with security measures to keep our conversations between us. Whenever you wish to speak with me, write me a note and wherever I am in the world, I will write back to you."

"Thank you, Grandma." Without a thought of distance she might want to keep, Emma leaned in and kissed Eleanor on the cheek. When Emma returned to spot alongside the water, Eleanor gazed in Emma's brilliant blue eyes, simply taken aback by the gesture.

"That was unexpected," Eleanor said.

Emma fidgeted with her hands, doubting if she made the right move or a hasty, heart on her sleeve knee jerk. "I'm sorry."

Eleanor looked long at Emma, recomposing herself. "Emma, I fear for you, but not likely as much as your mother will. Do you know why I feel this way?"

Emma shook her head, ready to listen.

"The Order of Erebys and the various military arms of the Order, an underground organization that has gained political steam in the past decades - secretly want nothing more than to kill you, me, and your Cousin, Augustus IV, Governor of the Kingdom bearing his name. Of course they tout social reform to desperate people as they pour sweet honey words in their ears. And why they want death…because in the past year there is a movement believing that the Lord Orion Timorale's spirit is stirring once more. His minions hope to return him to Earth unchallenged…, which I dear say is impossible."

"Why's that? Did Orion die?"

"He did when I drove a knife into his heart."

Emma's jaw dropped, the image of her Grandmother killing this murderous man of legend in cold blood. "Why did you do that? Why not send him to prison."

"I wasn't about to make the split second choice between a fair trial and him plotting another attempt to kill my child and grandchildren. You must know that we are the guardians of our people, chosen by the spirit of Mithra and looked over by the Ethereal Ones to lead. You will see when you become the Governor of this Republic one day."

The thought of becoming Governor, the leader of this land which she was a legend in spooked Emma, removing her mind from the room. She had to fight her lungs from contracting in hyperventilation. Eleanor tapped her thigh, awakening her from the far off, pensive state.

"Do not let this vex your soul. You will find your abilities within your body and your Alastar in the coming years." Eleanor took Emma's right hand and ran the digits over the surface of the water. Each touch reverberated with a soft chime. "This will see to your mind. I will see to your growth. The trials you faced this week through the forest, in the arboretum and the Rockland River will seem trivial.

"I knew it was gonna get worse," Emma said, slumping down.

"Come now. You are quick in mind and skill. I must say I am certainly glad that placing Bigfoot back into the city was of good use…that and the fact that you used that vial of searing liquid I packed for you."

"Yeah, both really helped…wait, whoa! Hold on!" Emma slammed her palms down into the edge of the water, a large series of chimes following a splash of water onto her khakis. "You're the one who sent me the coffer in my mailbox."

Eleanor didn't even flinch. "Yes. I can see those materials came in handy."

"They did. I was lucky those weren't broken too."

Eleanor tilted her head, curious. "Broken?"

"Yeah. Mom saw your wax stamp with your comet and flipped out. She smashed the outer chest against the wall at home."

Eleanor sighed and closed her eyes, bringing her fingers to her forehead as if she suddenly developed a migraine headache. "Oh, dear. Oh, dear." After a good ten seconds of the great woman composing herself, Eleanor took a firm hold of Emma's tiny hands.

"I should be use to your mother by now. However, she had broken my heart too many times. Please do not try to be the peacemaker between us, Emma."

"You should still try," Emma said. Once glance at Eleanor's eyes and in a matter of seconds the air began to change, her vision hazy. Eleanor's outstretched fingers reached the smooth, youthful skin of Emma's cheek. A haze fell over Emma's eyes. She knew that Eleanor began the ebbmersion process.

"I will write you soon my little Blue Eyes," Eleanor said. Wind circulated about them, a hurricane tunnel in a blink of an eye. The forest fell away to a rushing sound of her body passing through space at an incredible rate. Eleanor's emerald eyes were the last sight Emma had that afternoon in the forest before darkness came.

Emma's ears woke her before her eyes readjusted to the light as she realized was alone, back in the solarium at Bolder Hall. The jolt of reawakening in the new space sent a shiver into Emma's leg, which kicked the table, knocking over a teacup.

Eleanor was gone, yet the air around her chair still holding the Plumeria flower scent of a perfume that would turn heads. Picking herself up, Emma sat down in Eleanor's chair to simulate Eleanor's proper posture and imagined the power of dictating orders that felt so foreign to her.

"Send in the army!" Emma said with an English accent, her poor version of a queen. "No, that's too mean," Emma said, slipping out of character. Her mind flashed with the memory of the poorer districts and she felt compelled to imagine trays of free food for a balanced population. "Make sure that everyone in Adoette has something to eat tonight. Everyone gets a bucket of fried chicken...that's it, fatten up the people. Have machines do the work instead!" Emma said, her head slumping into her hands. "...oh, gosh I'm such a dork."

Once the game faded, Emma slouched down, shoulders hunched in and held her journal to her chest. She wished Eleanor had ignored her adamant attentiveness to her duties for a few more minutes. The sudden departure confirmed a truth for Emma. She could then see what her mother was beginning to get at about Eleanor.

The bell did not ring on J.W's International Trade Shop when Emma gingerly pushed open the door she had broken a few nights before.

"I didn't want her getting the wrong idea in her head about the…" Adacia said, immediately falling silent as soon as Emma caught her eyes. "Where were you?"

"What's going on?" Emma said.

In a semi-circle, around a table cleared of every knick-knack were Bo, Siobhan, Jonathan, Adacia, Ciara and her mother, Michelle. There they waited, their previous conversations having become extinct. Each of their patient eyes never wavered from Emma.

"Emma, we have a surprise for you," Adacia said. She and Jonathan conspicuously stood in front of what Emma sensed was an open crate.

"What's in the box?"

Laughing to himself, looking a tad taken with his daughter's clairvoyance, Jonathan stepped aside. At his side, he pumped his fist, as if secretly proud of another victory Emma tallied up. Adacia remained, rooted to the spot as Emma came to stand before her.

"Bo? What's going on?"

Bo pointed to Adacia. "We've got something special in there. Mom? Let her see."

With some hesitation, Adacia stepped aside. On the table sat a dusty old crate that was covered with a thin white veil.

"This is our family, Emma," Adacia said. "This again will be our future."

Emma stepped up to the table and peeled back the shroud. In the crate was a metallic base that surrounded a small wooden shield. Together they formed a coat of arms. The name Alastar was etched above a star pattern at the center top. Below that a family tree had begun with the Silver Forest flag resting above *Adacia Eleanor Elwyn* and the flag of the United States of America resting above *Jonathan William Grant*. *Emma Adacia* and *William Bo* flowed out from the union of this human and Croatoan bodies.

"Alastar," Emma whispered, taking heart to her true name. The mere deep breaths the family and friends took in as Emma reached her hand out to let her fingertips grace her name cast in iron then confirmed, like in the multitude of adventures that would await her in the coming years, that the whole world was waiting for this blue eyed guardian.

THE END

Printed in Great Britain
by Amazon.co.uk, Ltd.,
Marston Gate.